The hijackers were trying to contact the satellite.

Kate hit autodial for Rooker.

He picked up immediately. "Yeah, Doc?" Caller ID, wonderful.

"We have a signal. Zed's making a first attempt to bring Heat Wave online."

Rooker began bellowing in her ear, demanding coordinates, then, "Give me a town, a county, anything to aim for!"

"You'll get it when we have it," she said, her voice cracking with tension. "Just hold on."

But Rooker seemed not to understand the concept of waiting for anything. "I'm at Andrews. I'll scramble my team and be in the air in fifteen minutes, twenty tops. You sort out your directions and call me back."

"No, wait! I'm going with—" But he'd already hung up. The bastard was going to make it impossible for her to accompany him. Or so he thought....

Dear Reader,

This month marks the first anniversary of Silhouette Bombshell. And just when you thought the bookshelves couldn't get any hotter, we're kicking off our second year with a killer lineup of innovative, compelling stories featuring heroines that will thrill you, inspire you and keep you turning pages! Sit back, relax and enjoy the read....

Once a thief, always a thief? The heroine of author Michele Hauf's *Once a Thief* says no way! But when her archenemy frames her for theft, she's got to beat him at his own game to keep her new life, a new love and the freedom she won at such great cost....

When hijackers steal her billion-dollar satellite and threaten to use it as a weapon, a NASA scientist must work with a know-it-all counterterrorist expert to save the day. The heat is on in Kathryn Jensen's exhilarating *Hot Pursuit!*

A Palm Beach socialite-turned-attorney gets into a killer's sights when she's called on to defend a friend for murder, in *Courting Danger* by Carol Stephenson. It'll take some fancy legal moves—and a major society shake-up—to see that justice is served.

And how far might someone go to win a million dollars? The heroine of *The Contestant,* by Stephanie Doyle, begins to suspect that one of her fellow reality TV show competitors might have resorted to murder—could it be the sexy ex-cop with the killer smile?

Enjoy all four, and when you're done, tell us what you think! Send your comments to me c/o Silhouette Books, 233 Broadway, Suite 1001, New York, NY 10279.

Sincerely,

Natashya Wilson
Associate Senior Editor, Silhouette Bombshell

Please address questions and book requests to:
Silhouette Reader Service
U.S.: 3010 Walden Ave., P.O. Box 1325, Buffalo, NY 14269
Canadian: P.O. Box 609, Fort Erie, Ont. L2A 5X3

HOT
PURSUIT

KATHRYN JENSEN

Published by Silhouette Books

America's Publisher of Contemporary Romance

SILHOUETTE BOOKS

ISBN 0-373-51364-X

HOT PURSUIT

Copyright © 2005 by Kathryn Johnson

This edition published by arrangement with Harlequin Books S.A.

www.SilhouetteBombshell.com

Printed in U.S.A.

KATHRYN JENSEN

has written more than forty novels for adults and children, under various names, and lived in many interesting places, including Texas, Connecticut and Italy. She currently resides in Maryland with her husband and two feline writing companions, Miranda and Tempest, who behave precisely as their names indicate—the first, sweetly…the second, mischievously. Their thirty-two-foot sailboat, *Purr,* promises to carry all four on many new adventures. Aboard *Purr* is where Kathryn does much of her summer writing.

Acknowledgments

I'm grateful to many organizations and individuals for the inspiration and technical assistance I received while writing this exciting novel. Among them are the National Aeronautics and Space Administration (NASA) and the Applied Physics Laboratories.

Roger Johnson gently and intelligently steered me through a minefield of information on satellites and the aerospace industry. Everything real about Heat Wave is due to his tireless efforts to educate this author. The fantasy is all mine, as are any errors.

My other experts include all the amazing folks at the Firearms & Fiction Conference, but particularly Peggy and Joseph Tartaro, Alan Gottlieb, C. J. Songer, Gila Hayes (a real-life Bombshell heroine) of Firearms Academy in Seattle, Keeva Segal for Taurus and Rossie firearms, Ken Jorgensen representing Ruger Firearms, Mark Tartaro/Retired Buffalo Police Officer and Defense Tactics Specialist.

Special thanks to Gary Mehalik, Director of Communications for the National Shooting Sports Foundation, who helped choreograph the climax scenes of this story. Gary, if I got anything wrong, it's not your fault. You did your job.

Bravo, everyone!

—KJ—

Chapter 1

Everything that night was going perfectly until the door that was supposed to be locked crashed open and the man with the gun stepped through.

Kate Foster turned in her seat at the NASA Command Center computer terminal and stared at him, her mind still caught up in the web of data she'd started entering to communicate with the HW-1 satellite. With only her core staff on duty, just seven of them were in the CC. Unusual for such a sophisticated project, but then, no one had expected anything but a routine telemetry adjustment.

Vernon, at the far end of the room, was the first to speak. "Sir, authorized personnel only in this area."

It took Kate a moment to realize that the cubicle partitions blocked her computer tech's view of the short-muzzled automatic weapon held hip level by the intruder.

Then Cambridge screamed, and Tommy, standing beside her, whispered, "Oh, shit." And Kate's brain snapped into gear.

Her left hand slipped beneath the desktop and found the smooth plastic panic button even as the fingertips of her other hand hit three keys in succession on the board in front of her. The monitor screen flashed once, then went black.

Her heart hammering in her chest, Kate stood up and turned to face the intruder as two other people, a man and a woman also in camouflage, also armed, stepped through the door behind him. Kate had seen the guns—she could only assume they were Uzis, or something similar—in movie after movie. Black with wood stocks, they were far more terrifying in real life.

"What do you want?" she asked, struggling to come up with a reason for their being in her laboratory.

"Which one of you is Dr. Foster?" the leader growled in a thick accent. His features and coloring could have been Middle Eastern or South American. His dark eyes rested on Kate before sliding around the room to her silent team members, searching their faces.

"I am Kate Foster." Somehow she kept her voice calm. "Listen, there's absolutely nothing here of value to you. No money. No drugs. If it's weapons you're after, we have access to nothing like that. This is a research laboratory."

"Shut up." The man waved the muzzle of his gun menacingly, inches from her face. "Go!" he barked at the woman who'd followed him into the room.

She stepped behind Kate, then started hitting keys on the keyboard. "Nothing. Goddammit, Zed, the bitch locked it down!"

"We're just running tests on a satellite," Kate tried to explain.

"It's a peacetime scientific experiment," Frank Hess added,

moving up to flank Kate from the opposite side as Tommy. "No onboard arms of any kind."

Hess, her senior scientist on Project Heat Wave, had worked with her on other NASA operations. A brilliant man, but he had a temper and sometimes acted irrationally when angered. When she glanced sideways at him, his face was flushed, as if he considered the intrusion a personal affront.

Not now, Frank, she prayed silently. *Keep your cool for once.*

But the man called Zed ignored the middle-aged, balding physicist. "Sit down, Dr. Kate," he growled, "and turn on your computer."

Before she could ask why or move, Hess stepped between her and the gun's barrel. "Leave Dr. Foster alone!"

"Frank!" Kate warned, but it was too late.

Zed swung his free arm wide, striking Hess a vicious blow across the side of his face, knocking him out of his way. Kate swallowed a scream as Frank crashed into a desk and slid to the floor.

"Dr. Foster? If you will?" Zed motioned toward her chair, his mock politeness contrasting with the violence of his attack seconds earlier. He gave her a tilted smile that made her stomach clench. "Let us now talk to your satellite."

She glanced quickly toward Hess, who had stood up and was now leaning against one of the terminals, a stunned look in his eyes, rubbing his jaw. Blood dripped from the corner of his mouth. Okay, she thought wildly as she took her seat, maybe industrial espionage? Is that what this is all about?

She knew that ASEC, Alternate Source Energy Corporation, the company that provided most of the funding behind the HW-1, had some tough competition from other groups hoping to expand into the field of renewable energy resources.

There were immense fortunes to be made. But an assault team and automatic weapons seemed a bit rash for the world of corporate crime.

Kate clicked on the power and entered her password. Without it, no one could access the satellite's onboard computer. The booting-up process started. Desperate now, she tried to think of ways to stall for time. How long had it been since she'd pushed the silent alarm? How many more minutes before Security responded?

Her palms itched, hot and damp with sweat. A wave of nausea flowed over her, like an oil slick over calm water, blurring her thoughts. What were they going to ask her to do? The initiation screen came up, a sky-blue background with the NASA logo. Kate hesitated, her fingertips hovering over the keyboard.

"Go on, contact the satellite." Zed's voice was low and dangerous.

Kate looked around the room at her team.

Cambridge Mackenzie stood stiffly between two cubicles, her dark skin glowing with perspiration. Their eyes met for an instant. Cam shook her head slowly: *Don't do it.*

She didn't have to look at Tommy, not even an arm's length away on her right, to know he was hyped. She could feel his energy pulsing through the air between them. Only twenty-three, he was the one she most feared doing something crazy. Trying to snatch a weapon away from one of the intruders. Attempting to wrestle one of them to the floor. She touched his arm, letting him know he had to hold back.

Frank—he'd just explode with no real purpose. The lab was his turf, and he'd defend it. But he wasn't a stupid man, and she didn't think he'd take on an Uzi, especially now, after Zed had landed a warning blow.

David—she didn't expect any interference from him. He

was a workaholic. Put him on task and he'd run forever, like the Energizer bunny. But he wasn't one to think outside of the box or take chances.

Vernon she didn't know well enough to say what he might be thinking at this moment. He'd transferred from the Applied Physics Lab in California only a month ago.

Last of all was Amanda, their Earth mother. A little on the plump side, with four kids and one grandchild. As the team's support tech she made sure they were on schedule, reserved time on the antenna and kept the project log. She looked pale now. Her lips quivered as if she were whispering her rosary.

Pray for us all, Amanda, Kate thought. Immediately, her own family came to mind. Last Christmas with her parents, brothers and sisters and their kids. All around the tree, laughing as they tore into gifts. Was that the last time she'd ever see them?

"I need to know what you intend to do with this equipment before I bring it online," Kate said, working at keeping her voice steady.

"Power this thing up now, or—" The woman swung her arm up, the butt of her weapon over Kate's head.

"No!" Zed roared. "She's too important." He glared at Kate. "I do not have time to play your games. Do as I say or there will be consequences."

The man beside Zed looked at his watch. A long, jagged scar ran from the outer corner of one eye and across his cheek to his chin. He wore a wool skullcap, and she couldn't tell the color of his hair, or if he had any at all. "Two minutes gone."

"She's stalling!" The woman slapped the side of her weapon with her palm, her impatience building. "Zed! Five minutes max, remember?"

So, Kate thought, they're racing Security's response. They know about the alarm.

But what did they want with Heat Wave? It made no sense.

Half a dozen very frightened, silent people—all looking to her for guidance.

Zed took a piece of ordinary-looking paper from his shirt pocket and handed it to her. "Here are your instructions."

Kate unfolded the sheet and scanned the sophisticated lines of script, the language programmers used to talk to their computers whether in the next room or launched in a space probe to circle the sun.

Frank was reading over her shoulder. "Oh, God," he breathed.

She looked up at Zed. "You're changing the FARM!" The Frame Acceptance Reporting Mechanism enabled scientists on the ground to communicate with and command the satellite. "You're hijacking my satellite. Why?"

"You cannot guess?" He laughed at her confusion.

"Three minutes," the man with the scar stated without emotion.

"Do it!" the woman screamed. "Now!"

Kate glanced at Frank. He was frowning, looking as confused as she was.

The HW-1, initially launched five years ago, was a prototype designed to test the use of microwave energy as a reliable alternate power source. If successful, their work would lead to a fleet of fifty or sixty similar satellites, massive structures assembled in space over a period of years, each with an array of solar panels and parabolic mirrors.

Positioned around Earth, these satellites would collect solar energy, convert it to microwaves and beam them to ground stations. The conversion to electricity would provide power that would light cities and run transportation systems and industry, replacing the need for fossil fuels—oil and gas—as they dried up or became too expensive.

No longer would America and Europe be dependent upon oil from other countries. *If* the theories of scientists such as Kate proved workable.

Zed lowered the muzzle of the Uzi to Kate's blouse and poked the cold steel circle into the valley between her breasts. "Now, Doctor."

She drew a shaky breath, felt the chill of death hover near, but slowly shook her head. "No. I won't do it."

Zed's dark eyes flared with rage. "I say to you, do it or I will kill you!"

"I don't know what you intend to do with the HW-1, but I have a feeling it won't be used for a humanitarian cause. And I won't help you do anything to hurt people." She kept her voice low, not taunting or challenging him. She wanted him to see reason, understand that his plan—whatever it might be—wouldn't work if she refused to cooperate.

"You don't value your own life?" he sneered. "What about the lives of your friends here?"

Her stomach clenched. She didn't dare look at any of the faces around her that she'd come to know so well.

"If you kill us all," Cambridge broke in, "there will be no one to carry out your demands."

Zed smiled. "Ah, but perhaps by the time a few of you have been sacrificed, those remaining will have a change of heart?" He turned to Frank Hess but kept the gun pressed against Kate's breastbone. "Or maybe someone else will be more reasonable without needing to see blood shed. What about you, sir?"

Hess dropped his hand away from his swollen jaw and narrowed his eyes at the man. "I wouldn't help you even if I could, you clown."

"You might." The muscles of Zed's gun hand and wrist tensed. "If I put a bullet through your boss."

"Wait, no!" Hess blurted out. "If you kill her, you'll never get in. She's the only one with the fail-safe code." He looked at Kate apologetically; such information was closely guarded. But she realized he might have just saved her life.

Zed's reaction was unexpected. He reached out and seized the physicist by the front of his shirt. "Is that right, Mr. Smart Man? Then maybe she needs a demonstration of the seriousness of the situation!"

Before Kate could react, Zed threw Hess back against the nearest cubicle partition and swung his weapon around. A look of horror flashed across Hess's face. "Oh, God, please no!"

Zed fired.

The deafening chatter of the gun cut off cries of protest from the HW-1 team. David Proctor lurched forward, and Kate was never sure if he was trying to make it out the door or rushing to help Frank. The woman fired two rounds into his back and he fell facedown on the floor.

For a moment after the shots stopped, there was only empty, shocked silence. Kate stared in horror as Frank Hess crumpled to the floor, gripping his bleeding shoulder, moaning in agony. David, she suspected, had died instantly.

"Now, Doctor," Zed sneered, "do I finish off this worm or choose another of your people for further exhibition?"

Chapter 2

Daniel Rooker pulled his black four-by-four into a parking space outside the main gate of the NASA-Weston research facility. It was a pain in the neck, picking up a temporary pass for each new consulting job. But since 9/11, security on all government and defense industry installations had been tight. Even a civilian terrorist consultant with top-secret clearance had to identify himself and wear a dated clip-on pass.

Two guards manned the glass-walled office, and he could see another pair at the nearby gate shack, behind bulletproof glass, waiting to screen personnel driving or walking onto the facility. At eleven o'clock at night few people came or went.

When he walked in the door of the main office Ed Green, the security officer in charge for the shift, gave him a mock salute. "Evening, Colonel."

"It's just Rooker these days," he reminded him. The marines had been another lifetime, back before his work as an operative for the CIA in Iraq. But somehow in this business, ranks were remembered and passed along with you. "I hear you guys have a ticket for me."

"Don't know why they keep making up new badges for you." Ed lifted a cardboard box from beneath the chest-high countertop and started flipping through badges. "They'll run out of plastic one of these days, all on account of you."

"Then they'll have to whittle them out of wood, right?"

Ed chuckled. "Something like that. Hey, why you here now, Rooker? Couldn't wait to pick it up in the morning?"

He shrugged. The Cove, his regular hangout, was just down the road. Live music and energetic women on weekends. But weeknights the bar was pretty well dead. Besides, when he wasn't on a job he preferred to be alone. He'd lost the last two men he could call real friends in Iraq. He'd grown up in a string of foster homes, so he had no family. Rooker supposed it was better that way, given his line of work.

"I was in the neighborhood. Besides, this place is a zoo mornings, everyone checking in. I have a nine o'clock with Davis Jessup."

"Chief of Operations, pretty impressive."

Rooker looked across the counter to the second guard, who was smacking the heel of one hand against a control panel that was buzzing loudly. "What's the problem?"

"Oh, this crappy alarm system is going nuts again."

"It's not supposed to buzz like that?"

Ed shook his head in disgust.

"Well, not for no reason," the other guard complained. "It's been doing this off and on for over a week now. Damn irritating. Even the electricians can't figure out why it's misfiring."

Rooker frowned. "Shouldn't someone check it out?"

"You mean drive over to Building Twenty-two? Waste of time."

"Yeah," the other man added. "If anything was wrong over there, the cameras would've picked it up and our guys on monitor duty would be in here raising hell. We're covered."

Rooker thought about this for a moment. "Where are your monitors?" He wasn't as familiar with the layout at Weston as he was with other installations.

"Back side of the building. Wanna take a peek? Be my guest. Take the shortcut down the hall."

Rooker nodded. Most likely there was no problem. But if someone wanted an alarm to be ignored, the best way to manage it was to give the thing plenty of playtime before the critical moment. Like the boy crying wolf. After a while, no one paid attention.

He reached a door, past the break room and lavatory, marked: No Admittance/Security Only. When he tried the knob it wouldn't turn.

"Rooker, WWS," he identified himself after knocking. "Everything kosher in there?"

"Hey, Rook!" a voice he recognized called from behind the door. Pete Genovicci opened it for him. "Haven't seen you in like, forever."

"Not since Baghdad," Rooker said, and they exchanged solemn looks.

Those were bad times. More than his lonely childhood, more than his troubled teen years or Marine training, those years in Iraq were what had set his course for the rest of his life. Since then he'd been obsessed with hunting down terrorists. By any means necessary—legal or not.

Rooker punched the other man in the shoulder and grinned. "Got yourself a cushy civilian gig, I see."

"Yeah." Genovicci laughed. "Never thought I'd see the day I was paid for watchin' the tube. Man, nothin' ever happens here. All we can do to stay awake. Want a cup of coffee?"

Rooker shook his head. "I just thought I'd check and see if anything looked funny in building two-two. Their panic alarm keeps going off."

"Yeah, it was doin' that last night, too. You'd think with all the engineers and computer geeks around this place someone could rig an electrical connection without shorting it out." He laughed, and so did the other man seated in front of the wall of monitors.

The closed-circuit TV screens spanned the width of the room, from desk level to ceiling, each numbered. Rooker found the one he was looking for. He watched the cameras cycle through and counted nine views, interior and exterior.

The picture show started from the beginning again—a shot of the main entrance, an empty hallway outside elevator doors, an unoccupied computer lab, an auditorium, another lab, a couple of offices with immense file cabinets, the power plant with AC units and emergency generator... nothing unusual. The building appeared to be completely unoccupied.

"Hold on a minute," Rooker said then jogged back down the hallway to Ed in the main office, his head buzzing in harmony with the rogue alarm. "Do you have a log showing who is actually in the compound now?"

"The gate does."

"Ask them if anyone has signed in tonight for twenty-two." Rooker's pulse sped up, making him feel as if he should be running without knowing where or why. Trouble, he thought instinctively. Maybe big trouble.

Ed sighed. "Man, you're like my old bulldog, Jo-Jo. Get hold of that shoe, and you just won't let go."

Rooker waited while Ed made the call. He could see the two men through the glass wall of the shack, checking a clipboard, one with the phone wedged between his shoulder and ear, talking to Ed.

Ed hung up and shrugged. "Just Dr. Foster and her crew. Seven in all. She told me they'd reserved antenna time for tonight—some project she's all excited about."

Rooker swore.

For the first time both guards looked nervous. "What?" Ed asked.

"Come back here with me." Seconds later, Rooker was staring at Screen 22 again, and so were Ed and Genovicci and his partner. The pictures cycled smoothly from camera to camera.

"I don't see anything," Genovicci said. "Everything looks normal."

"How many cameras are in that building?"

Genovicci looked at his partner and frowned. "I think it's ten...yeah, ten."

"Only nine are showing pictures." Rooker squinted, and there it was again—the blip. A brief, nearly imperceptible dead space between views, as if something had been there but was no longer. "One camera's been cut out of the cycle," he said. "Someone's tampered with the system."

"Aw hell," Ed muttered and rushed out of the room.

Within minutes, Rooker knew, the entire research base would be locked down—no one in, no one out. Every guard on duty scrambled.

Blood pounded in his head. *Go-go-go!* his body shouted. But he needed one more piece of information.

"Do you have a camera in Foster's laboratory?" he asked.

"Yes, sir." Genovicci, all business now, looking confused. "But I don't see it."

"That's where it's happening." Rooker bolted out of the room after Ed, hissing, "No sirens. We go in silent."

Chapter 3

Her hands trembling, Kate entered the scripts indicated on Zed's note. These strings of data would communicate through a powerful antenna to the satellite overhead.

The female intruder stood over Kate, watching every keystroke. "Don't even think about changing anything," she warned. "I'll know it if you do."

Kate glanced up quickly, really looking at the woman for the first time. The sleeves of her camouflage shirt had been torn off to reveal muscular bare arms that looked capable of lifting a small car. She had short, spiked white-blond hair. Black eyeliner thickly circled her pale lavender eyes. She looked like a throwback to a rocker. Benatar on steroids.

"You think I'd chance your gunning down another of my people?" Kate couldn't keep the revulsion out of her tone.

Hess moaned. Out of the corner of her eye, Kate could see him struggling to stay in a sitting position, his back supported by the blood-spattered partition. She dropped her hands from the keyboard and started up out of her seat.

"Sit!" the woman commanded.

"He's hurt! For God's sake, let me or one of my team help him." Obviously David was past help, but also past the pain of his fatal wounds.

"No!" Zed barked. "Everyone will stay away. If you did as I asked in the beginning, I wouldn't have had to shoot either of them."

"You bastard!" Cambridge sobbed. "How can you let the man suffer like this?"

"He won't suffer for long." The woman gave her a smug smile then glowered down at Kate. "Keep working."

What did that mean? That this insane trio intended to murder all of them before leaving the lab?

Kate risked a quick look to check on the rest of her team. Zed had herded them to the far end of the room. They were sitting with their backs to the wall beyond the last cubicle. Would any of them survive this night?

And where the hell is Security?

"Six minutes," their timekeeper announced. He gazed with a bored expression around the lab. The scar on his cheek looked blue in the fluorescent light.

"Hurry up, Doctor!" Zed barked.

"At least let me cover Dr. Hess with something," Amanda requested, her voice surprisingly strong. "He's bleeding and must be in shock. Show a little kindness, you're getting what you want."

"I'll be all right." Hess ground out the words between clenched teeth. "Don't give them an excuse to start shooting again."

Kate sensed the woman standing over her adjust her stance.

She glanced up cautiously. Her guard's attention had shifted to Zed, who was striding down the room toward Amanda and his other prisoners.

Kate's fingers flew, taking advantage of this moment of distraction. She hoped she remembered the encryption codes correctly. Within seconds she had scrolled down the screen and was back to inputting the last information from the page Zed had given her.

"Finished," she said.

"Move." The woman pushed Kate out of the chair and scanned the screen. "She's done it!"

Zed turned back to her, grinning. "Let's go!"

Kate could only stand by and watch as the woman slipped a memory stick the size of a flattened lipstick tube into the computer. She copied the data onto it, deleted it from the computer, then slipped the stick into her pocket.

"Come on," Zed snapped.

But instead of following him to the door, the blonde turned toward Kate with a malicious gleam in her eyes and lifted her gun. "First, we finish the job."

Kate planted her feet and faced her assailant, knowing there was nothing she could do to save herself. If her life ended this very moment, at least she'd done all she could to protect others from whatever this madman had in mind. Like a camera shutter her thoughts clicked to her family in Chicago. They'd always been close while she and her siblings were growing up, but somehow they'd gone their separate ways after college. Except for her parents and her brother Jeff, she didn't see nearly enough of her family. Modern life was like that. Now it was too late to change her priorities.

She watched as the woman's finger curled around the rifle's trigger. Her heart tripped, double time, then felt as if it stopped entirely. Swallowing, Kate said silent goodbyes to her parents, her sister, her little nieces.

Suddenly, the gun's muzzle jerked to the right by inches, then fired several rounds. Kate's computer exploded in a mass of sparks and metal shards, the noise deafening. The woman stepped back, leaving the computer reduced to a pile of rubble.

"Seven minutes," the man with the scar said, and Kate wondered, even as she was still absorbing the miracle that she was still alive, whether he was human or just a walking stopwatch. He turned to Zed. "We take him, right?"

"That's the plan—one hostage for insurance. Might as well be Mr. Big Mouth."

Kate's eyes flew wide as Scar and Spike moved toward Hess. "No, wait! What are you doing? You have what you came for."

"Stand back!" Zed warned. "He's coming with us."

Kate shuddered as the pair hoisted the wounded man to his feet. Hess's face was contorted with pain, and he shot her a frightened look as the three shoved him, staggering ahead of them, out of the room.

The door shut behind them.

For a moment no one in the room moved. Then Tommy leaped up from the floor and ran at Kate. "Why'd you let them take him! Jesus, you know he's dead meat now!"

Cambridge grabbed his arm and pulled him away. "Quit that! How do you think she was going to stop them? Cross that maniac one more time and they might have killed us all."

"But Frank…" Amanda whispered. "Poor man."

Yes, Kate thought, poor Frank. What did they intend to do with him? Use him as a shield if they had trouble getting past the guards?

"Where is Security!" She dove for the door.

"Wait!" Vernon shouted, his eyes wide with terror. "Don't go out there. What if they're still in the hall? What if they get cornered by the guards and have to double back? Better to barricade the door and wait for help."

Kate hesitated. He was right. She couldn't help Frank or recover the memory stick with the satellite's control data without help. The best she could do for the moment was protect the remaining members of her team.

But never in her life had she felt this heartsick, this angry or helpless.

While Vernon and Cam started shoving furniture in front of the door, Amanda ran to David and held her fingertips to his throat, as if she still wasn't convinced he was dead. She closed her eyes and whispered, "Dear God…"

Kate picked up the phone and punched in Security's extension.

Damned if the thing didn't ring busy.

Chapter 4

It seemed an eternity. But when Kate checked her watch, only four minutes had passed from the moment the three intruders left the lab to when she heard stealthy running steps outside the door. The knob jiggled. Someone shoved hard on the door, but it didn't give.

"They've come for us," Amanda breathed. "Thank goodness!" She started to weep, and Kate knew she was thinking of her children.

"Don't open the door yet," Tommy warned. "We don't know it's Security."

"Dr. Foster?" a man's voice called from the other side of the barricade. "Are you all right?"

The voice didn't belong to any of the intruders, she felt sure. "Who are you?" Kate asked.

"Daniel Rooker, Worldwide Security. I'm accompanied by NASA guards. If you're able, open the door."

Emotion filled her chest, tightened her throat, burned behind her eyelids. No, she thought, no tears yet. Not even tears of relief. There was still hope that the guards might stop the trio before they got off the installation with the stolen data. And there was Frank to think about.

"Move everything out of the way!" she shouted.

They'd only cleared away half of the mountain of desks and file cabinets before the men on the outside slammed the door up against the rest of the furniture, forcing open a passageway.

A dark-haired man in jeans and T-shirt climbed over the mess and into the room, his blue eyes darting left, right, always moving. He wasn't exceptionally tall, but filled the room with his presence. He held in his left hand a gray metal pistol. Kate thought she'd be happy to never see another gun.

"They've gone," she said. "You have to find them. They took valuable—"

"Into the hallway!" he ordered, as if he hadn't heard her. "All of you. Now!"

She stared at him. "I said, they're gone."

"Right. Out of here, lady."

A half-dozen security guards rushed in. Kate and her team were pushed unceremoniously out of the lab, into the hallway, where one of the guards asked each of them their name and checked their photo badges.

Kate leaned against the lime-green corridor wall and closed her eyes, exhausted, her head pounding, only vaguely aware of the sounds of the men knocking around inside cubicles. Checking, she supposed, to make sure the terrorists had indeed left.

Someone inside the room said, "Already called for an ambulance. Won't do him any good."

David, she thought, tears blurring her vision. She forced them back. There was no time for mourning now.

When Rooker came out, he was talking into his cell phone. He kept repeating one word in response to whatever was being said to him. "Right. Right. Right."

"Has Security caught them?" she asked when he flipped the phone closed.

He shook his head. "If we'd had more warning—"

"More warning!" she shouted, trembling with fury so long pent up that it now exploded from her. "I set off that alarm the moment they broke into my lab. A good fifteen minutes before you showed up. What the hell were you all doing— taking a freaking coffee break?"

He frowned at her. "This isn't helping, Dr. Foster."

"I demand to know why no one responded to my alarm. Or do you people always move like mimes on holiday?" She didn't care if she was being unfair. Not with one man dead and the life of another plus her life's work at stake.

Rooker seemed not at all fazed by her accusations. "The alarm had been acting up all week. The men on duty assumed it was another false signal."

"The cameras!" she shouted. "What about them?"

"Someone sabotaged the one in your lab." He started to turn as if to follow the guards, most of whom were rushing down the hall. "We've sealed off the compound. Who was injured in there besides the man we found dead? I saw a lot of blood across the room from him."

She filled him in on the scenario that ended with the intruders escaping with the memory stick. "They took Frank Hess, my lead physicist, with them. What will they do to—" But she didn't want to think about that yet.

Rooker looked away from her. "If they're still on base, we'll find them. If they've gotten away, I need to know what this stick thing looks like, what it can do and any details about the intruders' physical appearances or behavior that might help us identify them."

She stared at the man. How cold and totally devoid of compassion he sounded. He might be on the white-hat team, but his heart was full of darkness.

"My team and I were held at gunpoint," she said, making each word weigh as much as it should. "We were threatened with the loss of our lives. We watched two men being ruthlessly gunned down. *And you want me to file an incident report tonight?*"

"Right. And you'll do it or Security will hold you on base until you do." His tone was scalpel-sharp, not a sliver of sympathy.

Kate drew a steadying breath and locked him down with a glare. "Fine. Here are the first two points of my report—no techno-jargon, just plain English so even a thug like you can understand, Mr. Rooker."

A muscle twitched in his jaw—another sign of his irritation with her. She didn't care. She had nothing to lose.

"First—three armed intruders stole my satellite. Second—I don't know what they intend to do with it, but my guess is that we could be knee-deep in bodies before we get it back."

Chapter 5

By the time Kate was allowed to send her people home it was after three o'clock that morning. They'd given statements to the chief of security, and the FBI forensic team had arrived from D.C. and closed off the entire building. She waited breathlessly for word of the intruders, the memory stick and Frank Hess. All seemed to have disappeared without a trace.

On her way to her car, exhausted and barely able to fit the key into the lock because her hand was shaking so hard, Kate glimpsed something moving across the dark parking lot. She froze, held her breath and watched, as fascinated as she was afraid. The figure didn't walk so much as shift silently from one position to another, nearly invisible among the shadows of the old maples surrounding the building.

Then out of the gloom and into a pool of yellow light beneath an overhead lamp stepped Daniel Rooker.

She breathed again.

"Have they found anything?" she called out.

Turning, he came toward her. He didn't look particularly tired, even at this hour and with the stress of the search on his shoulders. His expression was unreadable. "We located where they got out. The perimeter fence behind a storage trailer has been cut."

She knew the place he was talking about. "But that's clear on the other side of the compound. How did they get way over there without being seen by the guards?"

"Tunnels."

"Tunnels?" She pressed her fingertips into her throbbing temples, feeling as if there wasn't enough sleep or aspirin in the world to release the pressure there. "You don't mean those abandoned underground passages from Cold War days." Back in the fifties people believed that bomb shelters dug a few feet below ground level really could protect them from the holocaust. Technology had fixed that.

He nodded. "The tunnels link a half dozen of the older buildings with each other and with subterranean shelters. One ends at a recently unsealed hatch within feet of the fence." He looked away for a moment. "Who knew about them?"

"Lots of people, I suppose. They aren't used anymore, of course." Kate frowned. "How do you know that's the way they escaped?"

Rooker turned back to face her, his gaze scrubbed clean of emotion. "Blood. Fresh."

She shut her eyes and shivered. Frank's, of course. And that's when she decided she couldn't take anymore. "I'm going home now." She desperately needed to shut herself away in welcoming surroundings—the cheery cocoon of her little condo. Swinging open the car door she dropped wearily into the driver's seat.

Rooker stepped into the space behind her, preventing her from closing the door. "If you'd held out for a few minutes longer—"

"Don't go there, Rooker." She stuck the key into the ignition and turned it. The engine rumbled.

"I'll damn well go where I want. And it seems to me you could have done more to—"

She shut out his words, anger and resentment surging through her. "If you feel compelled to blame someone other than those three crazies who broke into my lab," she said, "try pointing your finger at Security. I was just trying to keep my people alive. As important as HW-1 is to me, David, Frank… and all my team mean a hell of a lot more. And that's what I'll tell the chief of operations at the briefing tomorrow."

Kate grabbed the door handle and yanked hard, hoping she'd crush him. Unfortunately Rooker stepped to the side a fraction of an inch ahead of the door. "Neanderthal," she muttered under her breath. She hit the gas and sped away, oblivious to the 25 mph compound speed limit.

The D.C. traffic report blared from the radio alarm clock. WTOP's announcer reported the usual rush-hour hysteria on the Washington Beltway, with accidents on I-270 and massive delays along I-95 in Virginia. It was 7:00 a.m. and she'd had less than four hours of sleep.

As she tossed back the blanket Kate saw that the message light on her phone was blinking. The CoO's assistant had called a half hour earlier and she'd slept right through it.

Kate retrieved the voice mail and was rewarded with a sinking feeling in her stomach. She was now scheduled for a second briefing at NASA-Weston. Word of last night's incident had apparently reached Homeland Security and God knew who else. It would be an agonizing day crammed with explanations and, no doubt, accusations and buck-passing for the faulty security.

Fine. Let them point fingers and carry on all they liked. She'd defend her decisions and her staff's actions. They'd done the best they could with an impossible situation. Losing Dave Proctor and—she had to be honest with herself— probably Frank Hess as well, weighed heavily on her. But she tried to focus on the lives she'd saved last night and the steps she'd taken to protect the integrity of the HW-1 project.

By eight o'clock Kate had showered, rolled and pinned her still-damp blond hair into a dignified twist at the nape of her neck, dug her navy-blue power suit out of the back of the closet and dressed. But the nausea of the night before clung to her, and her head pounded with a relentless jackhammer rhythm. The only thing that gave her strength to face the day was the thought that Frank Hess, if he were still alive, would be having a worse one.

She left the coziness of her blue-and-white bedroom—bed piled high with white eyelet pillows that had soothed the aches of her weariest day. Kate moved into the condo's tiny kitchen. She had little time for cooking or entertaining, but it was just right for a nuked frozen dinner. Amanda teased her, saying it was like crawling through the Space Shuttle. On the wall beside the fridge was a bulletin board. Tacked to it were a dozen colorful mission patches—reminders of her earlier projects with NASA.

Before leaving her house she tried to call Dave Proctor's wife. Last night, the security chief had contacted the Proctors' minister and the two of them had broken the news to Gloria. But this morning a neighbor answered the family's phone. "She's not able to come to the phone," the woman said, her voice tight with grief. Kate asked that she pass along her condolences and promised to call back later to see how Gloria was doing.

Frank Hess was unmarried, and no one knew of close relations. There was nothing she could do but hold out hope that he'd survive the ordeal and be freed.

She then called each of the team members who'd been in the lab with her last night. She saved Cambridge Mackenzie for last, repeating the words of previous brief conversations: "Don't even think about coming to the compound today. The FBI won't let us into the lab until they're done anyway. Stay home and rest with whoever is there for you. Try not to think about last night."

"How are the others doing?" Cam's voice sounded distant, as if reaching out to her through a Chesapeake Bay fog. Kate had never known her to be anything but strong and sure of herself. Being confronted by mortality could change a person.

"Vernon was sleeping. His wife answered the phone. She said he was as upset as she's ever seen him. Tommy and Amanda are, I guess, managing as well as can be expected. Tommy's dad was with him. Amanda has her entire tribe around her."

"Good. So, what are you doing today?" Cam asked.

"I meet with Jessup at nine to prepare for a briefing of the top dogs in the afternoon."

"He won't be alone," Cam said. "You want me to come with you this morning?"

"No. You stay with your daughter. You need each other now. Give her lots of hugs for me."

"Uh-huh." Cam drew a labored breath, as if she were considering saying something more, something she had to think about. Whatever it was, she apparently decided against it. "You take care of yourself, hear? Don't let them dump this on you."

"One already tried." She pictured Rooker's arrogant expression. The nerve of the man! "I'll give it my best. Wish me luck."

"A truckload."

Kate's hand hovered over the receiver one last time after she'd said goodbye to Cam. She ached to call her father. Her mother would react emotionally to the incident, to how close her daughter had come to death. Her father was her rock. Just talking to him would clear her head. But she couldn't discuss classified information with him or anyone else. Standard procedure. She decided against calling them just yet.

Twenty minutes later, as Kate parked her little red VW Golf outside Building 5 at NASA-Westin, she considered the uselessness of her advice to her team.

Tell someone *not* to think about purple cats and they immediately picture purple cats. The brain works in perverse ways.

Her own advice had been less than successful even for her. The horror of the previous night stalked her like a wild animal, gnawing at her subconscious, interfering with her ability to focus on the critical tasks of the day. Regardless of the motive behind the hijacking of HW-1, it was up to her to arrive at possible strategies for reclaiming the satellite. But until she was given access to her lab there was little she could do. She didn't even know what options for contacting Heat Wave remained.

Walking from the parking lot toward Headquarters, Kate tried again to concentrate. But the terrifying sequence of events kept playing over and over in her mind, a nightmarish instant replay that always ended the same way: Zed casually turning his weapon on Frank Hess as he pleaded for his life. The woman callously slaughtering David Proctor as Kate stood helplessly by.

The ear-splitting cackle of their weapons.

The blood. So much blood.

Her stomach knotted and cramped, worse than the night before. Kate pressed a fist to her abdomen as she shoved her key card into the lock pad. She rushed through the sun-streaked marble lobby of HQ, eyes straight ahead, focusing on nothing.

Then it was there. Her nemesis. From the deepest recesses of her mind came an image of the rifle. That *other* rifle. The one that had changed her life.

She forced herself to keep on walking, moving blindly through the crowded lobby toward the elevators as she fought off the past. But she couldn't.

It was obscene, the damage a bullet was capable of doing to a human body. Suddenly, it wasn't just a weapon she saw; she was back in that other time, remembering every ghastly detail she'd struggled all of her adult life to suppress.

She heard the shot nearly at the same moment as Meghan's scream. At first she'd thought it was part of the game. Kate had still been laughing when she ran into the room and saw Meghan lying in a widening crimson pool in her parents' bedroom.

They'd said it was her fault. Kate's fault. Everyone had. For a time, she'd believed them. Now she lived day-to-day telling herself they were wrong and wanting it to be so.

Kate blinked away tears as she stepped onto the elevator. Thankfully, no one else joined her for the ride up. This isn't the time for guilt, she told herself. Remorse for the past would have to wait its turn. She had to deal with what was happening now.

The satellite—HW-1. Why had they taken it from her? What did they think they were going to do with it?

The corridor outside the chief of operations' office on the third floor was deserted. No one chatted outside the break room or swapped gossip around the water cooler. People stayed out of sight, in their offices.

As in an old Western movie, Main Street clearing before the big duel.

Kate took a deep breath for courage before letting herself into Davis Jessup's office. His administrative assistant didn't look up from the file drawer pulled out in front of her. Kate's lips automatically twitched up at the corners in greeting, but Sara Brown in her conservative pinstripe suit wasn't smiling.

"Go on in. They're waiting."

Kate swallowed. "Who's with him, Sara?"

"Max Archer." Still no eye contact. A bad sign.

"I don't recognize the name. Who is he?"

"Homeland Security. He replaced Evermont last week. Reports directly to the President."

"Oh, right." Kate's throat felt so raw she could hardly get the words out.

"And Special Agent Winston," the woman added, finally moving her attention from the files to glance uneasily at Kate. "FBI. I think someone said she was with the Terrorist Task Force."

Kate nodded. This had certainly gone high-profile fast.

"I heard about Drs. Hess and Proctor. I'm sorry."

"Thank you," Kate murmured.

She knocked then let herself into Jessup's office. The three people in the room looked up from where they sat around his desk. They all stood as she moved toward the only empty chair.

"Dr. Foster." Jessup's voice was cool but polite. "We're glad you're here." He was a man who'd disappear if made to stand against a beige wall—sandy-colored hair combed back from a moon face, a tan suit and shirt with matching tie that lay over a concave chest and well-rounded paunch. Diplomas covered the wall behind his desk, proof of his authority.

Kate recognized Special Agent Marissa Winston now. They'd run into each other at several government seminars, one at which Kate had spoken on the changing functions of Earth-orbiting satellites and the possible risk to national security from those that were armed, regardless of who owned them.

The FBI agent observed her with what appeared to be genuine sympathy. "I'm sure you'd rather spend the day at home. We're grateful you were able to come in and help us get a full picture of what occurred in your laboratory last night."

"I'm sure we'd all rather be elsewhere." Kate set her briefcase on the floor beside her. Her hand shook as she released the strap. She steadied it by gripping the chair arm.

Jessup spread his palms flat across the printed pages on his desk. "We've all read your report. It must have been a terrifying experience, Doctor."

"It was—" she swallowed once, then again, holding herself together "—for all of us."

"Yes, well…" Jessup murmured, then glanced at Archer.

The President's advisor had a bullish face with steel-gray eyebrows that looked so heavy Kate doubted there was anything in the world powerful enough to lift them in shock.

Archer said, "The President has been informed of the incident. He is, of course, most concerned."

"He should be," Kate stated, feeling her voice come to her stronger now. "To date, over eight hundred satellites orbit the Earth. Any one of them, in the wrong hands, could be potentially dangerous."

"Yes, Mr. Jessup has just been informing me of this." Archer folded his wide hands in his lap. "What I don't understand, and the President is having trouble grasping, is why such a dangerous mission was being pursued without proper safeguards and without informing the White House in advance."

Kate's mouth dropped open and, for a moment, she couldn't even form a response, she was so taken by surprise. Then she thought about all she and her team had been through the previous night. This interview—more accurately, this lynching—was, by comparison, a piece of cake.

She took a deep breath and described the Heat Wave Project as clearly and simply as she could.

"In summary," she said, "Mr. Jessup as CoO, I as chief project engineer and the dozens of scientists involved in Heat Wave have never doubted the safety of the mission. HW-1 is merely a prototype, designed to emit a safe level of microwave energy. In fact, to redirect or bump up the level of energy would be a very difficult thing to do. Heat Wave is designed to be used only for controlled experiments in energy disbursement. Solar power harnessed in orbit to provide virtually cost-free power, replacing our dependency upon fossil fuels. An amazing boon to humanity! Heat Wave was never intended to be used as a weapon or at a level of output that would be harmful in any way."

Jessup added solemnly, "Security was more than adequate for a civilian-funded experimental project of this kind."

Archer frowned down at his hands, then lifted an accusing gaze to Jessup. "What once was adequate is no longer enough, sir. The President's military advisors believe we now have a loose cannon poised above the Earth. Microwave energy turned up to ultrahigh levels can cause illness and even death. Germ warfare without the germs. Invisible. Odorless!" His voice rose until he was nearly shouting, pounding his fist on the desk to emphasize each word. "Undetectable until it's too late!"

"Now wait—" Kate interrupted Archer's tirade. "I think we're getting ahead of ourselves. First, whoever has control of the HW-1 needs advanced knowledge of how to increase the level of emissions and concentrate them to a lethal dose. They'd also need a means of pointing the energy at their intended target."

"But—" Archer tried to interrupt.

Kate rushed on. "This isn't like a video game or *Star Wars* where you just aim and fire lethal death rays. Even if they were able to do all of this, it would take time for the effects of the microwave pulses to be felt by people in whatever area is targeted. People could be safely evacuated."

Archer was shaking his head. "Unacceptable. You're assuming they don't have the technical know-how to use the satellite as a weapon. We can't take that risk."

Jessup nodded solemnly, taking Archer's lead. "That's true, we must assume the worst. Why snatch it if they don't know what to do with it?"

"And what if they change targets?" Archer glared accusingly at her. "One day we're evacuating Boston, the next we're moving all of Washington, D.C., into West Virginia. Mayhem!"

Kate swallowed, her heart tripping over beats. She looked toward Jessup for support, but he was avoiding her gaze. The man was an administrator, not a scientist. And it was cover-my-ass time.

Agent Winston had been silent throughout the emotional exchange. Now she said in a quiet voice, "All your fears, gentlemen, are based on the premise that this Zed is actually able to access the HW-1's guidance system."

Archer leaned toward Kate, fists clenched, putting himself as much in Kate's face as the furniture arrangement allowed. "I thought your report stated that they've stolen the encryption codes and blocked us out."

"They have, but they can't really do anything with what they have...yet."

The two men stared at her as if she were a talking wedge of cheese.

Marissa Winston's lips twitched but she controlled her urge to smile. Kate could almost hear her working out a tactful way of educating the two men. "Perhaps," the FBI agent suggested, "portions of that report were somewhat technically worded for the lay person. I believe the doctor included mention of a minor program change she made while the intruders were distracted."

Kate began to breathe a little easier. She had an ally. "I embedded an extra code to buy us time. It may give us a chance to reclaim HW-1 before they can bring it online."

Jessup sat up straighter in his chair, shot Archer a beige smile, then turned to Kate. "You jammed their program?"

"Yes, sir."

Smiles all around.

"Then we're sitting pretty," Archer said. The ripe-cherry flush of his face faded. "Why didn't you say so in the first place? They can't get in without knowing your code. Is anyone on your team aware of it? Is there anyone else you've told it to?"

"No, sir."

"Wonderful, then all we have to do is make sure they don't get to you, Doctor." He chuckled, enjoying his own humor. "Perhaps Jessup here will assign you a bodyguard?"

Marissa was shaking her head even before Kate could object to this overly optimistic analysis. "I don't think that's quite what Dr. Foster means. I've had experience with cases involving computer hackers. They can be elusive—some we've been tracking for years and still haven't nailed. A good hacker can break down almost any code and thwart it, given enough time. You can bet they'll have one on their side."

"Is that true, Doctor, of your code?" Archer, looking less pleased.

Kate wished it weren't. "I had literally seconds, no time for anything fancy. I did what I could."

No more smiles.

"How long do we have?" Archer asked grimly.

Kate's gaze tracked across the room to pure beams of sunlight cutting between the vertical blind slats. Light was power, and power could be used for good or for evil. The problem was, it was almost always easier to do harm than good.

"With luck, a week. Without it, we might have only a few days to locate the memory stick and whoever intends to use it."

"But we know who has it." Archer stabbed a finger at the papers on Jessup's desk. "The description of the intruders is in your team's report, along with the leader's name, Zed."

Winston made an impatient sound. "Those descriptions may mean nothing. The three intruders could have been disguised. Or they might merely be mercenaries, not terrorists at all. The plan could be to sell the stick to the highest bidder. We just don't know yet who we're dealing with—militant extremists, a hostile country?" She shrugged.

"You're saying we don't even know what these people are after? Who they're linked with?" Jessup looked confused.

"So far, no one is claiming responsibility for the action. And no demands have been made."

"What about my associate, Dr. Hess?" Kate asked. "Rooker, the security expert who arrived with our tardy guards—" she couldn't help getting in a small dig "—said he thought they'd ditch Frank after they'd gotten safely out of the compound."

Agent Winston shook her head. "State and local police are searching and questioning anyone who might have been in the area last night. The Bureau has also assigned agents as support. Nothing so far. I'm sorry." She hesitated. "How serious was his wound?"

"I'm not a medical expert. He lost a lot of blood, but it looked as if he was hit in the right shoulder. So maybe it wasn't that bad." A futile wish on her part?

"Our forensic people went over your lab, top to bottom. We didn't find the bullet, so it didn't go straight through. He'd be in better shape if it had. If he receives medical attention soon, he might make it." The agent shrugged in apology.

Might, Kate thought, or he could bleed to death in whatever ditch Zed had thrown him. Her heart ached at the thought.

Then it came to her—a thin thread of hope.

"There is a reason, other than escape insurance, they might want to keep Frank alive." All eyes were on her again. "I assume they have their own computer experts. Someone who knew what they were doing wrote those encrypted scripts. As I mentioned in my report, the first step was to clear the PSCIF, Power System Command Inhibit Flags. That cut us out of the loop immediately. HW-1 would then be vulnerable to com-

mands from any source, if properly entered. The next encrypted commands would capture the command database,
virtually handing Zed the satellite on a platinum platter. But
to reprogram the satellite's computer would require a scientist with specific knowledge of Heat Wave's systems."

Winston nodded. "It makes sense, then, that they'd grab
one of the senior scientists on the project."

"And now that I've interfered with their immediate access
to the system," Kate added, "they might decide to keep Hess
alive long enough to help them break my code and reprogram."

Winston gave her a gently reassuring smile. "That's good
news then. Buys us time." But her expression darkened. "Just
keep in mind that traveling with a wounded man won't be
easy. They'll have trouble hiding someone hurt that badly.
He'll attract attention, and they can't afford that."

Kate felt heartsick. There was no guarantee they hadn't
killed Frank before realizing they'd need him.

Chapter 6

It was to the credit of Marissa Winston that Kate was able to pull herself together over lunch and arrive halfway sane at the afternoon briefing. After the FBI agent informed Archer that she'd personally report any breakthroughs in the case to him, for the benefit of the White House, she whisked Kate off to the compound cafeteria for a cup of hot tea and a sandwich.

"I don't think they realize the gift you've given them," Marissa said after they were seated at a corner table, away from other diners. "You exhibited amazing presence of mind to be able to plant that code under such pressure and without anyone noticing."

"Thank you." Kate felt grateful for her support as she sipped the steaming Earl Grey, her favorite in times of stress. She kept a canister of the tea on hand at home, along with bakery fresh croissants, her favorite indulgence. But for lunch today she was having tuna salad on white bread, pure comfort food from her childhood. The chocolate layer cake served as a small reward for getting through the past few hours. "I'm glad you were there this morning. The briefing this afternoon will be bad."

"I have to leave, sorry."

"No, I wasn't asking you to—" Kate smiled. "Well, maybe I was hoping you'd be there. I can plot a satellite's launch trajectory, alter an orbit, chat with a computer on a space probe halfway to Jupiter, all while making peace between squabbling physicists." She wasn't bragging. These were just things she did, as natural to her as making a peanut-butter sandwich was to other people. "But *this*...this brutal violence..." She shook her head.

"It's not your job."

"No, it's yours." Kate observed Marissa over the rim of her cup. "How do you do it? How do you survive dealing with inhumanity and bloodshed every day?"

Marissa gave her a small smile. "Most days are paperwork and more paperwork. Or sitting at a computer, much as you do, in an office full of hyper people. For the rest of it—the really ugly stuff—you just do what you have to."

"You carry a gun." Kate gave an involuntary shudder.

"Yes."

"I couldn't."

"You could and would, if you had to."

"I—" Kate hesitated. Never, not once in her life had she talked to anyone about *this*. She still couldn't, not all of it. "Something happened once, a long time ago. An accident with a gun. I don't think I'll ever forget it." Her fingers curled tighter around her cup. It hurt. God, how it hurt to remember. "I swore I'd never touch a weapon of any kind."

"But you do," Marissa insisted.

Kate stared at her, uncomprehending.

"You work with sophisticated equipment that's launched into space and has the potential for causing unimaginable damage if misused. Your weapons aren't strapped under your jacket, they're in the sky."

"No!" Kate objected, trembling at the mere suggestion. "The HW-1 was designed for peaceful purposes, to help, not hurt people. If I'd thought it might be turned against—" Her throat closed up.

Marissa reached across the table and touched her arm. "Don't do this to yourself. My only point is that we live in a violent world. We can't foresee every new threat before it appears. You were amazing in that lab last night, looking out for your people and doing your sleight of hand trick with the computer. And, just now, with Jessup and Archer you held your own and—" She hesitated, her eyes skittering away across the room.

"What?" Kate asked, turning to see what had caught her attention. Nothing. Just a half-dozen worker bees moving down the food line.

Marissa continued. "I'm going to give you a tip that you'll promise to forget you heard from me."

Kate frowned. "That sounds rather espionage-y."

"It's what I do." Marissa smiled, a little wickedly, but still didn't meet her eyes. "Two things you should watch out for— the press and General Albert Kinsey."

"The press, because…?"

"Remember, not from me." Marissa drew a steady breath and lowered her voice. "Someone leaked word of the break-in to the *Washington Post.* Two of their best investigative reporters have started asking around and found someone who's talking to them. So now the word is out that a NASA satellite is no longer under NASA control."

Kate closed her eyes. "All they'll do is create panic."

"Eventually, yes, if they find out what we already know. But, so far, no one in the media has gotten hold of any real details. It's all very vague to them, like the Hubble Telescope snafu—confusing centimeters with inches in a calculation. That's as far as most of the public got with that story."

Kate nodded. "Yes, the technology has to be watered down for the average person to get a clue."

"Exactly. I've already made it clear to Jessup that absolutely no information about the HW-1 should be released without vetting it through the Bureau and Homeland Security."

Marissa went on, "The longer we keep this quiet the better. With any luck, we can round up your intruders before they do anything rash."

"And the general. Why is he a problem?"

The FBI agent leaned in closer to her and lowered her voice another notch. "Kinsey will sit in on the briefing this afternoon. He's pushing for an alternative to recovering control over the satellite."

Kate didn't have to ask what that was. There was only one option to recovery. Her mouth went dry. "He wants to destroy Heat Wave."

Marissa finished her tea and glanced casually at her watch as if she hadn't heard Kate. "I have to go, and you're due for that briefing. Keep your cool, you'll be fine."

But, Kate thought, would the HW-1 be fine? Would all of her hard work, five years out of her career and her life, be for nothing? If destroying the sat was the only means of keeping people safe, she'd have to accept the sacrifice, of course. But far more was at stake than an experiment.

Demolishing a satellite in orbit entailed dire risks. She'd

have to make sure that everyone involved, including Kinsey, understood what they were. And if they didn't get it, she'd have a fight on her hands.

Chapter 7

The second meeting of the day promised to be far less genteel than the first. Present were more than a dozen people, seated around a long mahogany conference table in a white-walled conference room, shades drawn, AC turned up to max. Kate was willing to bet that every person present would be looking out for their own best interests, determined to give no ground.

It was, she knew, a recipe for disaster.

Included were Jessup, Archer, General Albert Kinsey, ASEC rep Jerry Reingold, two computer geeks sent over from the FBI, a few other people she didn't recognize, and one she regrettably did.

Daniel Rooker.

When she walked in, set her attaché case on the table in front of her seat and snapped it open, everyone looked at her as if she had dropped the ball in the last inning of a tied Orioles game. Apparently she was the scapegoat du jour.

So you want to play politics, she thought, taking out her notes. Fine. She was ready for them.

Kate read her statement aloud, describing in detail the incident in her lab the previous night then filling everyone in on the current status of the HW-1, no longer controlled by NASA but not yet under the direction of its captors. While her lab was still closed down by the FBI investigation, some of the Bureau's computer fraud squad had taken over the task of trying to scan radio frequencies in a range used to contact the satellite. If they picked up a signal they might be able to trace it to Zed.

As Marissa had predicted, General Kinsey was quick to speak up. "The Pentagon appreciates your cooperation, Doctor. But we propose to make short work of this problem. Even as we speak, our people are looking into a long-range missile capable of taking out this rogue satellite—"

"Now wait a minute, sir!" Jerry Reingold exploded from his chair, his narrow face vivid with rage. "Alternate Source doesn't want to endanger innocent lives, but that satellite is worth seventeen billion dollars and represents technical advances that could someday save this country from being without vital energy."

"I'm afraid more is at stake than the satellite itself," Kate interrupted, her voice a good deal calmer than that of either man. "Even if our military possessed a fire-ready missile capable of reaching HW-1's orbit, which I doubt it has, you'd be risking untold lives."

Kinsey scowled at her. "What makes you say that, Doctor?"

At least now she had their attention. "To plot a trajectory for the missile and accurately intercept the Heat Wave would take time and planning. At least weeks, more likely months. And one hell of a powerful missile." She spoke slowly, choosing her words carefully. "This is a huge high-orbital sat bulked up with a lot of equipment—solar panels, huge parabolic mirrors. It's not a little communications job sitting just outside the atmosphere. The specifications are in my report." Even Kinsey was silent and listening now. "Then there's the wreckage to consider."

Jessup nodded, evidently seeing where she was headed. "Some of the debris that's knocked back into the atmosphere won't burn up on its way down to Earth. Huge chunks of metal may scatter across populated areas."

"It would be like playing Russian roulette with the wreckage, raining house-size shrapnel down on our cities," Kate explained, making eye contact with each person around the table, one by one.

The general turned to the man seated behind him, who whispered something in his ear. Kinsey faced the table again, his expression stormy. "Clearly that can't be Plan A. What do you propose as an alternative, Doctor?"

Kate gathered her thoughts quickly. "When I accessed the HW-1 last night during the invasion I was able to put the sat in what's called a Safe-Hold status. This is only temporary, until Zed's people hack through my block." She was trying to keep her explanations simple enough for all in the room to understand. "My team and I will scan for any ultra-high-frequency signals attempting to communicate with the HW-1. If we find any, we'll attempt to track them to their source. The FBI has already started working on this."

Rooker spoke up for the first time. "If Dr. Foster can give us Zed's coordinates, I can mount a team to make the physical apprehension."

"ASEC would certainly support that strategy," Reingold said quickly.

"You'll want military backup?" the general asked.

"I believe that's Homeland Security's call, sir. We coordinate through civilian law enforcement. Right, Mr. Archer?"

Archer gave a stiff nod.

Kate sat back in her chair and began to breathe again. Thank God she'd been able to reason with these people. She let the others at the table hammer out the details of a cooperative effort, relieved that her role could now return to familiar tasks.

An hour later, she walked out of the conference room, intending to head directly for her lab. Hopefully, the FBI would have released it by now.

Jerry Reingold intercepted her in the parking lot, flicking a lighter toward the end of his cigarette as he trotted to keep up with her. "You know what they'll do when it comes down to it?" he complained, puffing like crazy. "They'll go through the motions of trying to find our satellite-jackers, but in the end Kinsey will get his way. Those military types can't conceive of a solution that doesn't include firepower."

Kate winced. She feared he might be right. Which was worse, letting terrorists intimidate and wreak havoc in your country, or killing your own people while trying to stop them?

But it didn't help, Kate thought, to assume the worst...or to give up the hunt for Zed and the stolen data before they'd begun.

"Well, at least we've bought some time." She stopped walking and looked at Reingold sympathetically. There was a good chance he'd lose his job over this fiasco. When disaster struck, heads often rolled. ASEC and NASA would be looking for scapegoats to appease federal investigators, and Jerry was at the bottom of the food chain. "Jerry, do you know anything about this Rooker—the man in charge of catching Zed?"

"I've heard his name around. He's a free agent, terrorist consultant. One of our competitors hired him for an overseas security job. I've also heard he specializes in finding people who don't want to be found." He flicked ash, watched it float to the ground. "And disposing of some of them in ways you don't want to know."

"Then maybe he's the right man for the job," she said grimly. She still didn't like the man's attitude.

"You know," Reingold said, "it seems to me it would be a mistake to just send out a bunch of commando types like Rooker on a job like this."

"Why?" She dug her car keys out of her purse.

"What if they find the people who did this and they have the memory stick on them, along with twenty or thirty others? They'll all look alike to muscle like Rooker."

Kate frowned. He was right. Another complication that had flown right past her.

"Or, say by the time he arrives, the HW-1 has already been deployed, and there are only minutes to spare before it starts sending emissions. Do you think those Rambo wannabes are going to know what to do to stop it?"

"You mean one of my scientists ought to accompany them?" Just the thought of sending her own people out with Rooker's mercenaries to face unknown dangers sickened her.

"Not just *any* scientist." Reingold gave her a look.

Kate groaned. "Me? No thank you."

He laid a hand on her arm, his eyes leveling to hers. "You may not have a choice."

Chapter 8

The day seemed never to end.

After arguing most of the afternoon with Homeland Security, the U.S. military, ASEC and NASA over the fate of her satellite, Kate received a call from the facility's public relations officer.

"So far we've been contacted by the *Washington Post* and CNN," Morrie Pasturnak said, his tone urgent. "I've been fending them off for hours. But they have your name and want a statement." He was accustomed to announcing shuttle launches and discoveries from probes on Mars. Exciting stuff that the public loved. She could tell he wasn't as confident handling bad news as he was good.

So Marissa had been right about the leak. Kate had been driving back across the installation, wanting to check on her lab to see if the FBI had finished there and she could get into her office, when her cell phone had rung. She clipped it into the dash for hands-free operation and pulled into her reserved parking space.

"I'd like to take the heat off of you, Morrie, but you have to tell them, 'No comment' for now. Anything I say has to be cleared through Homeland Security and the White House. And they haven't yet decided how much to tell the public."

"That's what I thought." Pasturnak sighed. "We'll keep the wolves at bay as long as possible. But once word gets out to the rest of the press we're cooked. Just think what Rather and 60 Minutes could do to us!"

"I know. I'm hoping we'll retrieve Heat Wave before it gets that far. Just do the best you can."

"Right. One more thing."

"What?" she asked, looking down at her hands, still gripping the steering wheel. Her knuckles were white. She unclenched her fingers and told herself to remember to breathe.

"Security tells me a media van and a second vehicle are parked just outside of the main gate. The guards wouldn't allow them inside when they flashed press cards and claimed they had an appointment with you."

Damn. "That was a lie."

"Of course, but it's a pretty good bet they've staked out each of the gates, and if they know what you look like you'll be treated to company on your drive home."

She thanked him and rang off. So, Kate thought, maybe I just won't go home. A tactical retreat to her lab, if it was available, might be in order. She even had a small couch in her office across the hall where she could crash for a couple of nights if necessary, and emergency toiletries in her desk. Suddenly she longed for the cozy seclusion of her little condo. It might be a while before she could return to it. She'd have to find a way to at least return for a change of clothing.

When she reached her floor in Building 22, she could see from the end of the corridor that the crime-scene tape across the door was gone. She unlocked it, let herself in and felt the tension ease slightly out of her neck and shoulders as she surveyed the familiar banks of electronic equipment, monitors and cubicles. It was eerie. Usually people moved with purpose from station to station, screens flashed data or images. The click of keyboards, whir of hardware and hum of conversations filled the long room. Today, the place was utterly silent.

Someone had removed the blood-spattered panel Frank Hess had fallen against, cleaned the floor and removed remnants of her destroyed computer. But she couldn't forget the horror of witnessing the shooting of two men she'd worked closely with. Dave Proctor had only recently joined the project, but Frank Hess had been a familiar face around Weston for many years.

She tried to push aside the grim memory of the violence, but it didn't work.

Oh, Dave...Frank, I'm so very sorry.

Kate sat in the nearest chair, at Cambridge's console, dropped her head into her hands and, finally, the tears fell. Until this moment she'd been able to hold herself together. Now she allowed herself cleansing sobs as the madness of it all struck her full force. The worst part was how helpless she'd felt against the brutality of the intruders!

All of her life, her ability to create order out of the complexities of a modern world had given her satisfaction, made her feel safe. Science gave her power. The universe and everything in it operated according to a set of rules, and by studying these natural laws, she could make sense of life. She felt in control.

But when something like this happened... When life took a left turn and, suddenly, things happened against her will and in spite of all logic, then she felt powerless.

Guns. Violence. Guilt...always the guilt, then and now.

At last, she dried her tears and found the strength to stand up and walk around the lab, booting up computers until the room glowed amber and green from their monitors.

Each station in this lab interfaced with various functions in the HW-1, orbiting 36,000 kilometers above Earth. In similar control rooms, monitors linked with telescopes watched the skies thousands upon thousands of miles away. Still other NASA computers gathered data from probes on their way to Jupiter, circling the sun, or retrieved data from space millions of light years away.

This was her world. An exciting and beautiful place where she felt protected by her science.

She tried not to think about Dave and Frank.

In her heart she desperately wanted to hold on to the hope that Frank, at least, had survived. That he would be found. At one time they had started to date. Nothing serious, just friends who worked together, going out for a drink or a quick meal at the end of the day. She had wondered if more would come of their relationship, but then the position of chief project engineer had suddenly come open, and she and Frank were competing with others for the same job.

He had more years with NASA, but she had pursued the job as aggressively as he had. In the end, the powers that be had chosen her for her more recent degree in aerospace engineering from Purdue. After that, Frank seemed to lose any interest in a social relationship with her, but they'd continued to work well together.

Now she had to face the very real possibility that the physicist was already dead. Rooker was right, she reluctantly acknowledged. Frank was baggage Zed and his band couldn't afford to keep for long, regardless of his possible usefulness.

A hard rap on the door behind her snapped Kate out of her grim thoughts. "Yes?" She'd locked the door out of habit.

"Open up, Doc, or I'll huff and I'll puff, and I'll blow—"

"You have a sick sense of humor, Rooker." Kate's galloping heart took a while to slow down after recognizing the raspy baritone.

As she reached for the latch, a stray thought came to her then sped off at supersonic speed. She hesitated, trying to recapture whatever had bothered her. Something about Rooker? But it was gone. Probably she was just irritated that the man was intruding upon her privacy.

She opened the door.

Rooker stepped through, shut and locked the door again. Strangely, that didn't make her feel all that safe. Not that he frightened her, no. It was just that the man had a habit of rubbing her the wrong way. His ability to think through a problem seemed less cerebral, more a physical reflex. Some part of him was always in motion—his eyes, his hands, a foot tapping—never totally at rest.

He was wearing jeans and a black T-shirt under a leather jacket that seemed totally inappropriate for July. She suspected its purpose was to cover whatever hardware he carried beneath it. A plastic ID badge was alligator-clipped to the jacket's collar.

She moved away from the door, toward her desk. He followed.

"You all right?" he asked.

She dipped her chin in answer, then narrowed her eyes at him, feeling the dampness lingering in them. Hoping they weren't also red from crying and that he wouldn't notice if they were. "How did you know I was here?"

"The all-seeing eye." He motioned toward the security

camera high in the corner of the room. "We got it working again. A wire had frayed and tugged loose, or was cut. When you walked in here a few minutes ago, I was at the guard house talking to the electrician who's fixing the alarm."

"What did he say was wrong with it?"

"Not a thing." Rooker picked up the Waterford paperweight that was the only decorative touch on her desk. He tossed and caught the amethyst butterfly as casually as if it were a baseball. "Guy checked out the thing half a dozen times last week when Security reported it sounding off."

"I remember them showing up one day while I was working." Kate recaptured the crystal insect midflight and placed it on her desk, out of his reach. It had been a gift from a dear friend who had lost her long struggle with cancer. She took it with her whenever she traveled, as a good luck charm and a reminder of the fragility of life. Live for today, because time is fleeting. "They were going office to office, asking if everyone was all right. At the time I assumed Security was just being extra vigilant, making the rounds."

He grinned as if she were a little kid who'd just said something cute.

"What?" she asked.

"Nothing." He shrugged, making his shoulders look even more massive beneath the black leather.

Kate took a step toward him, irritated. "No, really. What were you thinking just then?"

Rooker shook his head but kept the grin. "I'll never understand you scientific types. You live in another dimension. Nothing outside of your work gets through to you." He laughed. "Hell, the building could burn down around you and you wouldn't even know it."

She crossed her arms over her chest. "The absentminded

professor is an old stereotype. I never lose touch with my surroundings." But, she recalled, it had taken her precious seconds to react to a man with a gun breaking into her lab. She winced at that thought. "Besides, I knew the alarms sometimes went off on their own. I saw no reason to be concerned."

His normal blank expression turned serious. "Who else knew?"

"What?"

"Who else was aware that the security alarms appeared to be malfunctioning?"

Kate frowned. "Everyone in the building, I suppose. I mean, when armed guards come charging down the hallway, you take notice. It's not as if sirens and bells go off in the offices, so unless you were the one who hit the panic alarm you wouldn't know why they'd shown up."

"Hence the reason it's called a *silent* alarm?"

"You've got it, sport." She winked at him and felt her annoyance fade. "After a while, we all assumed the guards were bored and looking for something to do. Checking badges at the gate, searching cars for explosives, which they never find, has to get old fast."

He nodded, as if satisfied for the moment, then looked around the lab again. "Your team is where?"

Kate leaned back against the burlap-and-metal partition behind her. Every muscle in her body ached, less from physical fatigue than from the emotional tension of the past twenty-four hours. She would have liked to sit down but didn't want to give Rooker the psychological advantage.

"I either personally called or had personnel contact each member of my team to tell them to stay at home at least until tomorrow morning. Then if they're okay with coming back—"

He scowled. "I thought you needed them here to scan for signals to the HW-1."

"The FBI has that covered for now, and I can work through the night on my own. The people who were here during the intrusion need some downtime, and I didn't want the rest of them showing up at the lab because I didn't know when the FBI would release the area." She paused. "You have no idea how traumatic it was, those monsters bursting in, waving around weapons, then gunning down those two men."

"But *you* are here," he pointed out.

Kate let her gaze drift back to Cambridge's monitor. Figures scrolled down a black screen. With a glance at the encrypted language, she could see that HW-1's systems were still at Safe-Hold, no changes since the readings of the night before. Good news for now. That meant Zed hadn't yet accessed the sat.

"It's unlikely Zed will try to contact the satellite this soon. I've thought about it. He's on the run, right? First he has to get somewhere he feels safe, or pass along the stick. Then he or whoever has it will try to contact Heat Wave."

He studied her. "But you still feel it's important for you to be here."

"Yes."

Rooker's eyes narrowed and darkened to blue-black. "Why?"

Because I feel responsible! Because maybe I could have handled this situation differently, like I should have done that other time. Then we wouldn't all be wondering what diabolical scheme these lunatics intend to hatch!

But she didn't say any of that. Someone like Rooker wouldn't understand. She doubted if he ever questioned his own motives or second-guessed himself.

"Have any demands been made yet?" she asked.

"You're changing the subject, Doc. Why are you here now? Tell me what's going on in that pretty head of yours."

She glared up at him, refusing to let him goad her. Or was he flirting? It was hard to tell with him.

"I need to know," she began carefully, "if Zed's people have communicated with Washington. Have you heard yet what they want in exchange for return of the satellite's control? Or what they intend to do with it if they keep it?"

Rooker hesitated. "There's been no communication." He turned away, apparently distracted by the rows of blinking monitors. "What are these for? They look as if they're just flashing random streams of numbers."

She almost smiled. The macho ex-soldier was out of his element and she was in hers. It felt good. "Not random at all. This is how we view stars, planets, satellites, moons…the universe around us and beyond."

He chuckled, hands on hips, swinging back on the heels of his boots. "Can't fool me. Those things don't look anything like telescopes."

"In a way, though, they are. I can *see* HW-1 by reading the data its computers send me. I know precisely where it is in its orbit and what onboard mechanisms are functioning."

"Just from numbers and codes? Dang!" He managed a scowl for her benefit but couldn't mask his interest. "And I have trouble programming my VCR."

"Oh, please." She didn't believe that for a minute.

Kate suspected Rooker had perfected his self-effacing, I'm-just-a-simple-country-boy routine for a reason. She didn't much care what it was. Much higher on her list of priorities was getting back to work and finding a way to retrieve her satellite. Only then would she feel at peace with herself.

"Tell me," she asked. "If I pick up Zed's signal to the HW-1 and can get a fix on his location, what's your next move?"

"We scramble like hell. A handpicked assault team travels with me. All you have to do is tell us where the perps are sending from and we'll nab them."

She pursed her lips and gave him a skeptical look. "Easy as that."

"Pretty much." His expression waxed from smug to concerned at her silence. "Look, if you're going to warn me that these people are ruthless and slippery and God knows what else, save it. I've dealt with worse."

"How do you know?"

"It's my business to know, Doctor," he growled, eyes in motion again, taking in the room as if still unconvinced only the two of them were there. "If they really were as dangerous as everyone's making out, no one in this fucking lab would have walked out alive!"

Had his intention been to shock her? He'd succeeded.

Kate swallowed, closing her eyes for a moment against the disturbing image of corpses sprawled across the floor of her lab. How close had she herself come to death? It was a question she hadn't chosen to face until now, forced to it by Rooker.

It took her a moment to catch her breath and mentally regroup.

"I wasn't going to warn you to be careful," she said at last. "Don't flatter yourself, Mr. Rooker."

"Oh?" The arrogance was gone; he looked amused.

"I was going to tell you that when we do discover where the memory stick is, you'll need me there with you."

Rooker laughed out loud. "In your dreams, lady!" She opened her mouth to object, but he plowed on. "You are staying right here, watching your fancy little TVs. End of story."

"Fine. And what happens when you walk into a roomful of look-alike memory sticks?" Reingold and ASEC could be a pain in the ass, but the man had been dead right on this point.

The security man stared at her, for a rare moment at a loss for words. "We haul them all back here to the experts."

"And what if you have minutes, or seconds, to shut down the already deployed satellite? What then?"

"The FBI has computer experts. We'll take one of them with us."

"Not trained to talk to *my* satellite, they don't!"

This time his laugh sounded forced. "Don't you think you're getting just a little possessive about a chunk of metal, Doc? Calm down. You just tell us where their signal is coming from and we'll take care of the rest."

She sighed and rolled her eyes.

"What now?" he groaned.

"First," she said very slowly, to make sure the big guy understood the importance of what she was about to say, "they can run their signal through a series of remote computers to mask their real position."

"I knew that." He blinked, shrugged. "Hackers do it all the time. So it takes a few extra hours to follow the trail. After all, how many computers can there possibly be with the sophistication and power to talk with your goddamn satellite?"

"That's just it. Whoever has the stick, the knowledge to use it, and access to the right kind of antenna—" she kept her voice quiet but forceful "—they can link with the satellite through any home PC or laptop computer with a modem."

Satisfied she'd repaid him in shock value, she let the words sink in and watched the tightness return to the sun-weathered skin around his mouth.

"You're telling me," he began slowly, "that Zed and his

crew have unlimited mobility. They can jump from computer to computer anywhere in the world?"

Finally, she allowed herself to sit down. "Hey, I think he's got it."

"Shit," he said.

Chapter 9

Rooker checked his watch as he dashed for his vehicle parked outside the highrise apartment house on M Street where he lived when he was in D.C. He had other places. One in L.A., another in Montana—that last was a cabin in remote mountains. And there were a half-dozen safe houses owned under different names where he could retreat if someone wanted to put a slug in him. No one else on the planet knew about those. They were spread out around the globe. Even so, he never felt completely safe.

He'd made all the necessary calls, lined up his people, would brief them at his Worldwide Security office in D.C. in an hour. The six men were now officially on red alert, ready to move out immediately from Andrews Air Force Base. A Black Hawk helicopter was fueled up and waiting.

He prayed, although he wasn't a praying sort of guy, that whatever voodoo Kate Foster performed last night on Heat

Wave's programming would give him enough time to find the data stick before it was put to disastrous use.

Rooker mentally checked off other arrangements already made. In case Zed was outside of the chopper's four-hundred-mile range, Kinsey had put on standby one of the corporate-style jets the government kept, painted in Presidential livery like Air Force One. They were often used as decoys when the President was in the air.

If Zed had made it out of the country? That would be more difficult. A military transport or commercial flight would be the only real options. Supersonic jets could beat a 747 on a short trip, but they couldn't carry enough fuel to cross the Atlantic if they traveled at their top speeds. Aside from that, diplomatic issues would complicate the situation. Without the necessary extradition agreements, he couldn't lay a hand on Zed or remove him from a foreign country sheltering him.

Not legally anyway.

Then again, it wouldn't be the first time he'd skirted international law.

"Hey, Rooker!"

At the sound of his name he spun around, one hand on the door handle of the four-by-four, the other beneath his jacket. FBI Agent Marissa Winston strode across the asphalt toward him.

"I thought you'd headed back to HQ hours ago," he said, letting his gun hand drop to his side.

"Did. Back again. Spare me five?"

A woman after his own heart. She didn't waste a word. And she was a brunette. He liked brunettes.

"Sure," he said. But if he had thought this was going to be a friendly chat, he soon found out different.

Winston took a spiral notepad from her shoulder bag. "Of

Dr. Foster's core team who were present during the intrusion, who do you know?"

"Not a one," he said.

"Foster herself?" She looked up nonchalantly, but her gaze penetrated.

"Nope. Never met the woman before last night. Why?"

"The NASA techs and Bureau agree that something funky was going on with the alarm and security cams."

"I know. I was over there with them. Funky? That a technical term?"

She gave him a dim smile and shook her head. "Not my forte, electronics. Let's just leave it that it's likely someone on the inside made sure Security wouldn't respond with undue haste to the alarm."

"Doesn't take an electrician to figure that one out. Someone with access to building two-two was paid off by or co-operating with Zed for reasons of his own. Possibly political."

"Right. So what have you done to follow up on that theory?"

"Me?" He put on an innocent face. "Not a damn thing, darlin'."

She tilted her head a fraction of an inch, slanting him the same look she might have given a pet cocker spaniel after it peed on her Kasmir rug.

"Not a damn thing, Special Agent Winston, ma'am," he corrected his previous response. Although he'd originally been contracted to handle security on a new solar probe project, NASA had pulled him from that job to take charge of the recovery of Heat Wave. "My priority one is to recover the missing data. Priority two, capture Zed. Base Security will handle the internal investigation. Your job is—"

"I know *my* job, Rooker," she said coolly. "One small part

of it is finding out what happened here last night, who is responsible, and making certain it doesn't happen again. I just want to be sure we understand our roles and aren't working at cross-purposes."

"Right." He could see evidence of strain in the tight lines around her eyes. She was an attractive woman, but the job was weighing on her, and she wasn't about to take crap from anyone. He decided he'd best ease off. "So, do you have any theories about who helped Zed?"

She thought for a moment, closing her notebook. "A lot of people have access to that building."

"True. What about someone in that lab?"

"I haven't dismissed that possibility. That's why I'll be in there tomorrow. I just got off the phone with Dr. Foster. She expects her entire team in tomorrow morning. I'll be interviewing each of them. But—" she added, giving Rooker a look "—I want you to know I respect Kate Foster."

"And you're telling me this why?"

"You have a history of being—" her eyes flashed "—a smidge hard on suspects, even on witnesses. I heard you and she have swapped words, not always the most pleasant."

He stuck his hands in his pockets and smiled. "You do get around, don't you?" He suspected the Bureau had a file a foot thick on him already. He'd gone straight from high school into the Marines, then into the CIA, and finally to his most recent missions as a corporate warrior. Might be interesting reading someday, if he could get his hands on it. "It's a tough business. You said yourself, someone in that room might have been in collusion with Zed."

"But Foster has too much to lose to have sabotaged her own project. I'm telling you, ease up on her. Let her do her job."

He shrugged noncommittally. He didn't see why the

woman should get special treatment. Hell, she was already trying to weasel her way into tagging along with his team!

"I'm serious, Rooker. You offend that woman and she's going to be thinking about wringing your neck instead of scanning for Zed's signal. We need her cooperation."

"So you want me to play nice, is that it?"

"Say it any way you like."

He hesitated, feeling as though he'd been pushed into a corner. Feeling like he wanted to push back. He wasn't used to taking orders once he'd accepted a job.

"What are you thinking now?" she asked, looking suspicious.

"Nothing," he lied and reached again to open the truck's door. "You'll let me know the results of your interviews tomorrow, right?"

"If they pertain to this incident. Otherwise, don't hold your breath," she snapped. "You do your job. I'll do mine." She turned and walked away.

"Yeah, right," he muttered. If anyone thought he was going to babysit some Ph.D. princess while he and his team were on a mission, they were out of their minds.

Chapter 10

Kate studied the monitor in front of her, too aware of the tension in the lab to be able to concentrate. She'd slept in her office last night, washed up in the ladies' room and grabbed a breakfast of vending-machine coffee and toaster pastries from the break room. By 8:00 a.m. her entire team of twenty-six had arrived. They hugged and told each other it would all be okay, but she heard the doubt shadowing their words of encouragement.

Everyone expressed shock and regret over the loss of David Proctor and the kidnapping of Frank Hess. No one said out loud what they all knew. Terrorists didn't simply give back hostages, not unless it served their purpose.

The only good news was that Zed hadn't yet broken through Kate's hastily configured firewall. HW-1's Safe-Hold status hadn't changed. FBI geeks had monitored the satellite overnight and the day before. They'd continue searching for any attempt to contact HW-1, but now Kate's own people, who knew the satellite best, would be on the job, too. She held out hope.

Kate's phone rang. She picked up immediately. It was Security, letting her know that Marissa Winston was on her way to the lab.

"I thought the Bureau was done here," Kate said after she'd buzzed her in.

"This has nothing to do with physical evidence. I need to speak to each person on your team, whether or not they were working the night of the intrusion."

Kate frowned. "I don't understand. Those who were here already gave statements. Those who weren't—"

"—might have seen or heard something in the days prior to that night. An innocuous detail, but something we could use."

Kate shook her head at the woman she'd counted as a friend, and now wasn't sure she should trust. "No, that's not it. You think one of us had something to do with what happened here. And that's just not so. Everyone on my staff is absolutely loyal to this country."

"I hope so. I really do. Listen, it's not just your people. We're questioning everyone with access to this building. If that doesn't turn up something, we'll look at anyone who has set foot even once on the Weston facility in the past six months." Marissa drew Kate toward the back of the room, lowering her voice. "Someone is responsible for Zed's knowing which building on this installation housed your Command Center. And that same person might have been the one who messed with the alarm and camera."

It suddenly came to Kate, what had bothered her the day before when Rooker had to knock to be let in. "The door wasn't locked," she blurted out.

Marissa looked at her. "Maybe, or the bolt was electronically triggered from the outside. Our lock expert determined that the mechanism wasn't forced or broken. But it's nearly impossible to tell whether the source of the signal to open the door came from the inside or the outside. Since it's card-operated, Zed could have gotten hold of an employee's entry card either with or without their knowledge. We're checking with Human Resources to see if anyone with access to Building 22 has been recently out sick or on vacation. They might not realize their card is missing."

Kate sighed. "You're doing your job. I understand." She massaged her throbbing forehead. She hadn't slept any better last night on her office couch than she had the night before in her own bed.

"I've already picked up personnel records for everyone in this building, for maintenance, too," Marissa continued. "I'll use your office for the interviews, if that's all right with you."

Kate nodded. She supposed this was necessary, even though it felt wrong to her. Was she supposed to trust no one now? "Starting with me?" she asked.

"Not unless you have something you want to add to your report."

"No, not really."

"Then let's start with your support tech." Marissa flipped open the notebook she seemed to carry with her everywhere. "That would be Amanda Becker. Point her out to me and I'll take her with me."

As soon as the door closed behind a very nervous-looking Amanda and the FBI agent, laughter broke out on the other side of the partition from where Kate stood. She peered around the edge.

Thomas Best, the youngest member of the HW team, stood holding his sides and wiping tears from his eyes. "Leave it to the Freakin' Bureau of Idiots to waste their time investigating the people least likely to have anything to do with Zed!"

Kate shook her head in mild reproof. "The agent is just doing her job, Tommy."

"Yeah, but—" He flipped his hands, palms up, as if to say, *Who can figure?* He wore blue jeans and a T-shirt that looked like a relic from the sixties—a peace sign on the front, something faded that might either have been a bouquet of flowers or an atomic bomb mushroom cloud on the back—the customary workday clothes for many computer geeks at Weston.

Cambridge stood up and looked out over the top of her cubicle. "I gather we're all under suspicion?"

Kate shrugged. "It doesn't matter what the FBI or anyone else thinks. The truth is, if Zed or whoever planned this wanted to find the CC for the HW-1, he probably could have done it just by monitoring our transmissions."

"Right," Tommy agreed. "There's no reason why any experienced hacker couldn't have latched on to our signals. Hell, drive around Capitol Hill with a mobile antenna in your car and you can pick up a dozen government wireless networks within four or five blocks!"

"And you know this from personal experience?" Cambridge asked. She wasn't smiling.

Tommy's face colored. He looked away from her. "I quit black-hat hacking a long time ago. You all know that."

Cambridge didn't respond.

"Agent Winston is just covering all bases," Kate said, hoping to soothe frayed nerves. "It's important that we cooperate."

Amanda returned to the lab, her eyes brimming with tears,

her hands trembling at her sides. She tapped one of the physicists on the shoulder and he left for his turn. Amanda headed straight across the room at Kate.

"She wouldn't tell me anything about Frank!" she wailed. "Did she say anything to you? They must know something by now."

"No." Kate patted her plump shoulder. "We'll just keep hoping, right?"

"Yeah," Tommy scoffed, "like that's gonna do the old guy any good."

"Old?" Amanda exploded. "Frank's a young man, barely forty, with his life ahead of him! A brilliant scientist."

"I didn't mean anything by it," Tommy complained. "It's just—he didn't have to get himself shot. If it were me, I'd have made my move way before that creep squeezed off a round. Zed wouldn't have known what hit h—"

"Can it, Tommy," Cambridge said tightly. "Any one of us could've got that bullet. The monster just picked on Frank because Frank irritated him."

"Do you think that was it?" Amanda asked Kate. "That simple? Because Frank stood up to him?" Tears trickled down her cheeks.

"I don't know. How can any of us be sure what goes on in a mind that warped? I'm just glad all of you came through." Kate sighed, taking in Amanda's distraught face, Tommy's wounded expression, Cam's anger. Her troops. Somehow she'd have to rally them and keep them on task.

She looked down the room toward Vernon's area. He alone, of those who had been here that night, hadn't come out of his cubicle all morning.

"Back to work, everyone," Kate gently prodded. "I want to know the second any attempt is made to contact HW-1."

She walked through the lab, watching Vernon. He was hunched over his keyboard, earphones clipped over black curly hair. He and Tommy were supposed to be scanning ultra-high-frequency radio transmissions, hoping to pick up signals between an antenna selected by Zed and the satellite. Right now, though, Vernon was staring at the blank wall beside him. She couldn't tell if he was totally focused on his task or worlds away.

She tapped him on the shoulder. "You okay, Vern?"

His spine went rigid, as if he hadn't known she was standing there. He unclipped the phones and turned to look up at her. "Yeah. Fine." But his expression seemed artificial, his eyes red-rimmed, the lids puffy, as if he hadn't slept in a week.

"It's hard on all of us," she murmured.

"I didn't even know them," he said.

A warning alarm went off at the tension in his voice. "Know who?" she asked.

Vernon Hernandez was the newest of the group, transferred from Silicon Valley. He kept to himself. She'd thought he was just shy, but something about the way he was acting this morning made her wary.

His voice shook when he spoke. "Frank and Dave. I worked with them and now they're dead and—"

"We don't know about Frank." She laid a hand on his shoulder.

"Right. They dragged the man out of here bleeding like a stuck pig, and all the FBI can do is accuse *us* of—"

"Now wait a minute. No one has even implied that a member of this team has done anything wrong." But how could she be sure of what Marissa Winston was saying in private conversations to Archer, Kinsey or her bosses?

"I'm sending Tommy back here to work with you. The two of you together are more likely to find Zed before all of the FBI." In reality, she hoped that by partnering the two up she'd fend off two problems—Vernon's depression and Tommy's impulsiveness. "Is that okay with you?"

He nodded. "I guess."

She waited another minute to see if he'd say anything more, but he didn't.

At the end of the workday, Tommy and Vernon were still tag-teaming the UHF bands but had come up with nothing, and Kate and Cambridge had detected no change in HW-1's status. The soft hum of voices in the lab as other scientists or support crew came and went was periodically broken by Tommy's shouts of, "C'mon, you creeps, show yourselves! I dare ya!"

Two people would be on watch throughout the night—one monitoring the satellite, the other scanning for transmissions. Cambridge and Tommy volunteered to stay on until midnight, then Vernon and Kate would take a shift from midnight to 4:00 a.m.

The rotating four-hour shifts would continue around the clock, for as long as necessary. They'd use Kate's office as a place to sleep. She'd have a cot brought in so that the two off-duty members could sleep close by, in case something happened. Amanda, who didn't have the scientific training to do either of the most critical jobs, suggested she pick up Cam's five-year-old daughter after school and take her to her house so that her mother could remain at the facility.

Dave's funeral was planned for the following morning. Several of the team who hadn't been working the night he'd been killed volunteered to cover the lab so others could go. It was one of the saddest times of Kate's life. The flowers in the church were beautiful. So were the organ music and the sermon. But they couldn't replace a lost life.

Afterwards, back at the compound, they all pulled together, no one complaining about the extra hours. But Kate saw silent prayers in their eyes. For their still-missing cohort, Frank. For their families, who might soon be in jeopardy.

Kate McKenzie

Amanda dropped by several times a day. There was a change in her body language. She wore a kind of smirk...

And truth is... or its equivalent has an underlying...

Mixing or converging areas do exist...

Her eyes... the... Kate will include report...

Kate... conditions...

Chapter 11

By that second day, everyone was hyped on coffee and sugar. Amanda delivered a generous fresh batch of donuts every time she came into the lab. Kate had to ask her to stop or bring something a bit more nourishing.

Amanda switched to egg-and-sausage sandwiches for breakfast, fried chicken or pizza for other meals—a marginal improvement for their diet.

It was during a change of shifts on the third day of their round-the-clock watch that Tommy shouted, "Bingo! I got you, sucker!"

Kate ran to his cubicle. "What?"

"It's them. Has to be. I've got a strong signal coming from a source west of D.C. Are you picking up anything from Heat Wave's end?"

Kate ran back to Vernon's monitor, ignoring the worried stares of others in the room.

The young Latino had gone back to working on his own and was frowning at a stream of data dancing across his screen. "Most of this is garbage," he muttered. "No, wait. There! Looks like an entry code."

"It can't be coincidental," Kate agreed, her mouth suddenly parched as she peered over his shoulder, her heart thumping in her chest.

Zed was trying to contact the satellite. If he broke through her virtual barrier, they were lost.

Kate reached for her cell phone and hit the auto-dial for Rooker.

He picked up immediately. "Yeah, Doc?" Caller ID, wonderful.

"We have a signal. Zed's making a first attempt to bring Heat Wave online."

"Damn. Where is he?"

"We're not sure yet. Tommy? Anyone?" she shouted down the room. "Do we have an originating position?"

"The antenna's somewhere in West Virginia!" Cambridge called out.

Kate relayed that information to Rooker and added, "But that's just the general location. There's no telling where Zed's computer—"

"I know, I know," Rooker growled, sounding as if he were running while talking. "But the Appalachians would be a smart place to hide out. Those mountains can keep secrets forever."

"Vernon, what do you think?" Kate shouted. "Can we come up with exact coordinates for the antenna and the location of the computer driving it?"

He glared with a pained expression at his screen, typed information, then shook his head. "Too soon."

"Tell him to head for Wheeling!" Tommy called out.

"No way," Vernon grumbled.

Rooker was bellowing in her ear, demanding coordinates, then, "Give me a town, a county, anything to aim for!"

"You'll get it when we have it," she informed him, her voice cracking with tension. "Just hold on."

But Rooker seemed not to understand the concept of waiting for anything. "I'm at Andrews now. I'll scramble my team and be in the air in fifteen minutes, twenty tops. You sort out your directions and call me back."

"No, wait! I'm going with y—" But he'd already hung up.

Kate clicked off her phone, breathless and furious. The bastard was going to make it impossible for her to accompany him. "Do we have coordinates yet?" she shouted.

Silence.

"Answer me, someone!"

"Sweet Mary, he's right!" Vernon jabbed a finger excitedly at his screen. "Look at this—antenna's in West Virginia."

"And I've got a signal between it and a computer. It's a freakin' dial-up Internet service!" Tommy laughed, sounding manic from lack of sleep. "You believe this shit?"

Within an hour, with the help of the local phone company, they'd verified that the exchange was right there in Wheeling.

Tommy and Vernon were high-fiving over the tops of their partitions while Kate forwarded the information to Rooker, already in an Air Force chopper with his team. But she didn't feel as elated as the rest of her people. Something felt wrong. Very wrong. She just couldn't say what.

"You're a worrywart," her mother always used to tell her. "You worry even when there's nothing to worry about."

Kate sat down in Vernon's vacated chair, exhausted. She'd slept very little on her breaks between shifts, mostly just catnaps on her office couch. Her eyes burned, her butt ached from sitting too long and the muscles of her neck and shoulders felt as tight as piano strings from the strain of the past days. But she forced herself to watch the monitor. They'd need to give Rooker even more detailed information if he was to trap Zed.

Cambridge came and stood over her. "I'll keep in touch with the phone company in Wheeling. They're back-tracing the signal as we speak. We should have an address within the hour." Kate felt the other woman studying her. "You should take a break."

"Can't." Kate shook her head. It swam.

"Why the hell not?"

"Because I don't trust Zed," Kate said. If only her head were clear. Her brain had slowed to a muddy crawl. "After a few failed attempts to connect with the satellite, he'll realize he can't bring it online because I've blocked him."

"So? We all knew that would happen."

"But we found him right away. West Virginia. It's too close, too easy." Too something. Frustrated that she couldn't make sense of it all, Kate shoved herself up out of the chair and dove around the partition into Tommy's station.

Vernon had pulled up a chair beside him. The two of them were taking turns at the keyboard, looking more like two little boys sharing a video game than computer scientists tracking a terrorist.

"Is there any chance that's a bogus signal?" she asked. "Or routed from somewhere else?"

"Finding that out will take a while." Tommy looked up at her apprehensively. "And it's not exactly in my job description, ya know?"

She knew.

There was a time when Tommy had been on the other side—a black-hat Internet saboteur. He'd made the FBI's list of most-wanted hackers. The arresting agents had been shocked to discover a sixteen-year-old kid had broken into the Pentagon's war-room database on a lark, in addition to stealing over three hundred credit cards in one of the most aggressive identity theft schemes by an individual. He'd used other people's credit to buy expensive computer hardware, pay for airfare, college tuition, books, a car and a mountain of CDs and gaming software.

Only the threat of jail time and an unusual proposition, to let the young man use his skills on the good guys' side, had persuaded him to change his ways. For four years Tommy out-hacked the best, helping the FBI's elite squad of white-hat geeks hunt down and trap scores of scam artists. His record cleared and loyalty proven, NASA had hired him at the ripe old age of twenty-one, and he'd been a godsend as far as Kate was concerned.

But hacking was like any addiction. Tough to beat. Some said impossible. Kate still wasn't convinced that Tommy didn't dabble in weekend Internet hacking. It was a question she hadn't wanted to ask since he'd come on board. One she wouldn't ask now either, because she didn't want to know.

He was looking up at her now, a glint of excitement in his clear gray eyes. "But, you know, if my boss orders me to hack a bad guy…" He shrugged.

"Do it!" Kate snapped. "And don't stop at the first jump. If you find more computers, follow the string and keep on going until you hit the end." She'd warned Rooker that this might happen, but had he listened to her? And now, because of his obsession for being in charge, he might have jeopardized their chances of capturing Zed.

She punched his number again. It rang for a long time before he picked up.

"Got an address yet, Doc?"

"The phone company is helping us track down the computer that's connected with the antenna. So far, we know it's from a Wheeling, West Virginia, exchange."

"Good."

"But I told you we can't be sure they haven't run the signal through other computers. I don't think you should—"

"This is my game now," he growled. "Just give me your contact at Ma Bell and let me take it from here."

The man was maddening. No, he was insane. Absolutely demented and past reasoning with.

She had Cambridge read the number of the phone company's rep to him. Then, "He wants to talk to you again," Cam said, holding the phone out to her.

Kate was ready to blast him but she didn't get a word out. "Until we find Zed I'm shutting down communications," Rooker shouted over the roar of what she assumed were the helicopter's turbo engines. "He might have the ability to listen in on our calls. I don't want to tip him off that the cavalry's on the way."

She groaned, every brain cell screaming at her that this was a recipe for disaster.

She tried one final time. "At least stay in touch with us until we're sure Zed's actually in West Virginia."

He laughed. "You just don't give up, do you, Foster. Signing off. We'll let you know when we have him!"

Chapter 12

Kate let most of the HW team leave by eight o'clock that night. Only Cambridge, Tommy and Vernon stayed with her, back to their four-hour rotations. With the FBI also scanning for suspicious signals, it was useless to keep more people in the lab until they'd reclaimed the satellite. Then she'd need everyone on deck and well rested.

The four of them drank coffee by the quart and grumbled over Amanda's most recent delivery. The pizza had congealed to a cheesy, greasy mess. And the microwave in the break room had died. Kate could feel sleep and nutrient deprivation taking its toll. She felt restless and drained at the same time.

Move...move...move! her brain shouted. *Do something!*

But all she could do now was wait for Zed to take the next step, to reveal where he and the memory stick were hiding.

The hard-wired phone beside Kate rang at 9:05 p.m. She picked up, praying it was Rooker or the FBI with good news.

"I feel as if I should be there." Amanda again. She had been calling every other hour to check on them. "But the kids are all asleep and I don't think Elvis is old enough to watch out for all of them. Do you?"

Elvis was her eldest boy. To his mother's disappointment, he had shown absolutely no talent or interest in music.

"No," Kate agreed, "twelve isn't old enough to be responsible for the little ones. You just sit tight. We're fine. How's Kristi doing?" She felt guilty for asking Cam to stay at the lab and leave her daughter for so long.

"Oh, don't you worry about that one. She's having a ball. The older children fuss over her, treat her like a little doll. She's so tiny for a kindergartener."

No matter how delighted the little girl was to have the attention, Kate knew she'd be glad to see her mom again. But now that Frank had gone MIA, Cam was her chief physicist. She might need her at a moment's notice.

"I'm hopeful everything will be resolved before too much longer." Kate meant what she said about the hoping part but feared any positive resolution would take more time than they had. "After the kids are all in school in the morning, you can make a breakfast run for us. How about fruit, yogurt and bagels?"

"If that's what everyone wants," Amanda said doubtfully. Breakfast wasn't breakfast to her without eggs, hash browns and a pile of crisp bacon strips.

"It is."

"You need to get some sleep, too."

"I will," Kate promised, "soon."

She hung up but found she was having trouble focusing. Time for more coffee.

* * *

Sometime after three o'clock in the morning, the watch schedule broke down. Vernon crashed on the cot in Kate's office, and no one was able to wake him up. Cambridge alternately nodded off or carried on serious philosophical conversations with her computer. Tommy was acting as though he never needed sleep at all.

He had warped into hyper-drive. Chattering or humming to himself as he scanned UHF waves. Snare-drumming pencils on his desktop. Doing jumping jacks at his station, only the earphones keeping him attached to his cubicle, as though he might spin off into orbit himself if someone cut the wire.

The kid's constant motion reminded her of Rooker—obstinate, bossy jerk that he was—only without the security man's intense focus. She wondered if Tommy was doing more than coffee. Perhaps riding an amphetamine wave? She didn't dare ask.

Trying to ignore the bizarre antics of her two still-conscious team members, Kate studied the monitor of the new computer Central Services had set up at her station to replace the destroyed one. She'd been at it for about ten minutes when she realized the room had gone deadly quiet.

"Oh God," she murmured, launching herself out of her chair, tearing off toward Tommy's station.

She was prepared to find him passed out on the floor. But when she whipped around the corner, he was sitting bolt upright. He was scribbling on a yellow legal tablet, an expression of sheer joy on his unshaven baby face.

"What have you got?" she asked breathlessly.

He held up his pencil-free hand: Wait! Kept on writing, intent on whatever he was picking up over his earphones.

At last he tossed aside his pencil and punched keys. Coordinates flashed across his screen, then a map.

"What is that?" she gasped.

He unclipped the phones and gave her a smug look, eyes bright. "They funneled their signal to the antenna in West Virginia through eight different computers. *Eight!* This is the last one. This is where the fuckers are."

Kate stared at the map. "That's not mountains. That's ocean...Long Island?"

"Close. The coast of Connecticut, nearly to the Rhode Island border." He pointed at the display. "Right here on Long Island Sound. A small navy town, Groton. Got the address and everything. Rooker will be thrilled."

"No." Cambridge stepped up beside Kate. "Rooker will be pissed as hell."

Kate nodded, already in motion, darting back to her workstation. "He's broken contact. God knows where in Appalachia the man is now."

"What are you going to do?"

Kate grabbed her cell phone. "I'm calling General Kinsey to see what kind of transportation and backup he can rustle up for us. I hate to ask you this, Cam, but are you up for a trip to lovely New England?"

"We're going up there without Rooker?"

"Yes, without Rooker."

"He'll kill you, Kate, if you go without him."

"I'm more worried about what Zed will do if we don't go." And if Rooker came gunning for her, she'd be ready.

Chapter 13

The petite jet, in Presidential livery, took off moments after Kate and Cambridge were on board. Under new rules governing Homeland Security, the military couldn't be involved in searching for Zed unless their assistance was requested by local law enforcement, so the state police would carry out the raid. But nothing could beat the U.S. Air Force for the fastest transportation with the least hassle over tickets or air clearance.

Kate barely had time to buckle herself in before they were airborne. Andrews AFB dropped away beneath her, a mere pattern of lights in the blackness below as the plane banked and headed north.

She thought about the last time she'd flown. Home for Christmas, coming in over Lake Michigan with a load of presents. A much happier time.

Cambridge's molasses-hued skin turned a milky tan on

takeoff. It didn't regain its natural color until the plane landed ninety minutes later on a small commercial field in Groton, Connecticut. It hadn't occurred to Kate to ask if her friend was nervous about flying. But then Cam's loyalty would have barred any such admission.

"For some reason I thought I'd be able to catch a nap during the flight." Kate stood up and slung the strap of her laptop computer case over one shoulder.

Cambridge laughed. "Yeah, right." She stooped to look out a window as they taxied the last few feet toward the edge of the runway. "There's our welcoming committee." She pointed toward a Connecticut State Police car, headlights on.

Military ground crew helped them down from the plane.

A police officer in SWAT-team black met them on the tarmac beside the plane's steps. "Lieutenant Jefferson Smith!" he shouted over the still whining jet engines. "Homeland Security requested we stake out several buildings on the UConn campus at Groton Point, but we don't have orders beyond holding anyone who tries to leave." He looked irritated to have been kept in the dark, and Kate didn't blame him.

But Archer, press-shy to the point of obsession, had insisted on keeping everything hush-hush until Kate arrived. She had strongly disagreed, wanting the police fully informed as soon as possible. But he'd refused to give her permission to send ahead any information on Zed or the hijacking, Archer's reasoning being that the more people who were in the know, the more opportunities there would be for people to run to reporters.

"I'll fill you in while we drive, Lieutenant," Kate said.

She couldn't help thinking how much she hated all of this. Yes, armed force was sometimes necessary to protect the innocent. But a metallic taste filled her mouth and her pulse echoed in her ears whenever she thought about the confrontation that was to come.

She'd bet money that Zed and his people wouldn't allow themselves to be taken without a fight. There would be guns, a firefight...and it looked as if there was no way she could avoid being in the middle of it.

Kate and Cambridge climbed into the rear seat of the police cruiser, the lieutenant into the front passenger seat. His driver floored it.

They raced off through the gate of a barbed-wire-topped fence that separated the runways from what looked like a Little League field, then down a narrow road bordered by tall marsh grass. She could feel the heat of August still radiating off the asphalt. The briny smell of sun-warmed water rose from the marsh on either side of the road. It would be an hour or more before full daylight, but the sky already had begun to feather a faint pink glow along the eastern horizon.

"How much do you know or have you guessed?" Kate asked.

Smith turned in his seat to look back at her. "All we've been told is that this is a possible terrorist situation. Keep it low profile, no press. Come to the party armed and ready for action." He frowned. "What have we got here, Doctor? Sounds like war to me."

"Cyberwar, at least." Kate quickly described the assault on the NASA compound and the theft of the satellite.

The man's expression shifted from serious to incredulous as she spoke. "And they sent two female scientists to deal with this maniac Zed?"

"That wasn't the initial plan. Our muscle went off on a wild-goose chase." There was no sense getting into the details of her confrontation with Rooker. "We only learned the true location of the originating computer after the capture squad was out of touch."

"Time is of the essence and you had to move." He nodded his understanding. "Hence, our involvement."

She didn't point out that she was supposed to have been with Rooker—the arrogant prick—when his team moved out. She supposed now she should be glad that he'd ditched her. If he'd let her go with him, they might not have discovered where Zed really was.

"Right," Kate said. "Whoever now possesses the memory stick might break my Safe-Hold code at any time. When they do they'll have the ability to power-up the satellite and choose a target. We don't yet know how they intend to aim the energy stream or use it. But it's my guess that's been worked out already."

"So they're a couple jumps ahead of you," he commented.

"Unfortunately, yes."

"All right, so our job is to retrieve your stolen information and, with luck, capture the enemy?"

"Exactly." Kate described each of the three intruders.

While the lieutenant radioed descriptions to his men staked out on the campus and made other arrangements, Kate looked out the window as the swamp gave way to a residential area.

"Tell me about the place we're headed," Kate said when he was done.

Cambridge turned from the window to listen in. Her complexion looked a good deal healthier now that they were on the ground.

"The area you're interested in is an old private estate, turned over to the U.S. Coast Guard in the early twentieth century, used for training purposes for several decades before becoming an extension campus for the state university. Classrooms, dorms, power plant, an old stone mansion made into administrative offices. This time of year, the place is pretty much deserted. Campus security doesn't expect students back for another month."

Good, Kate thought with relief. If there was one thing she didn't want, it was a hostage situation. Or more chances of innocent people being hurt or killed.

"We've erected roadblocks across all land exits and I just now requested assistance from the Coast Guard. They'll position two boats off the point, in case anyone tries to slip away by water."

"Fine." Kate pulled her laptop out of its case and onto her knees. She booted up. Cambridge was already on her cell, talking with someone back at NASA.

They sped through cozy streets lined with graceful old maples and chestnut trees. Manicured lawns, summer flowers exploding from generously mulched flower beds, New England clapboard cottages stained driftwood gray or painted scrubbed-clean white or barn red. How soon would the early-morning peace be shattered?

"What are you doing?" Smith asked, watching Kate's fingers fly across the keys.

"Downloading information from our database back at NASA-Weston. I need to check my satellite's status." She remembered Rooker's teasing, and mentally changed her "my" to "the."

Cambridge said, sounding breathless. "Vern's functioning again. Says whoever has the stick is still trying to contact Heat Wave. Signal's been pinned down by the phone company to one building on the campus. He's sending us a map right now."

Kate dared to hope. "We may be in time then. Tell him to

keep on trying to reach the WWS team. Rooker must have figured out by now that all he's going to find is an antenna. We have to let him know what's going on."

Smith studied her with a frown. "Can't your people just destroy the antenna?"

Kate shook her head without looking up from her keyboard. "That wouldn't solve the problem. Zed can skip to another one. Destroying the one he's using will slow him down but it won't stop him. Any antenna from 5.4 to 10 meters will work, as long as it can be pointed at Heat Wave."

"Then it would have to keep moving to coordinate with the satellite's orbit over the U.S.?"

"Not necessary," Cambridge said. "HW-1 is in a geosynchronous, high-altitude orbit."

Kate explained. "That means it's traveling at exactly the same speed that Earth is rotating. So it's in a stable position in relation to, say, Washington, D.C."

"Bloody hell," Smith muttered, looking shaken. "I thought my worst nightmare would be losing one of our nuclear subs from the navy base upriver."

At least now, Kate thought, he's taking this seriously. She didn't want his SWAT team going in after Zed with half an effort. Underestimating the man would be a fatal mistake.

By the time they arrived at the deserted campus, Kate had received an updated map from Tommy. She showed it to the police officer.

"Looks like that's the building." Cambridge pointed out a red-brick dormitory as the car rolled silently to a stop, headlights off, beside three other police vehicles. All were parked well short of the two-story building marked Whitney Hall.

Kate held her breath as Smith stepped out to talk to a group of six men in black uniforms. Two of them took off with rifles in hand, and she instinctively shuddered at the sight. Were these sharpshooters taking positions on nearby buildings? She worried about the light. If they didn't act soon, morning would arrive, and catching Zed by surprise would be far more difficult. Was the lieutenant aware of this? Of course, he must be.

But she couldn't stop her mind from racing. Kate started to open the cruiser's rear door to get out.

"Better wait here, ma'am," the young driver said.

She forced herself to sit back in the seat, feeling as though the sides of the car were closing in on her. Needing air. Wanting to get this over with. Wanting just as urgently to not be there at all.

Two more men armed with automatic weapons disappeared into the dark at their commander's orders. She assumed he was placing people in strategic positions.

"Can you see anything?" Kate asked Cam.

"No. Let's hope Zed can't either."

Not a sound came from outside the vehicle now. Only Smith and a final pair of men in black jumpsuits and skullcaps remained in sight. Kate held her breath. Slowly her ears adjusted to the silence. She heard the soft splash of the ocean on the rocks beyond the edge of the campus. The call of a gull. A foghorn in the distance. Early morning sounds. Peace, soon to be—

Suddenly, Smith's face filled the window beside her. He spoke through it in a whisper. "You two will wait in the vehicle until we've secured the building and taken whoever is inside."

"No!" Kate shook her head emphatically, pushing open the door. "I have to go in with you," she insisted. "We can't chance anything happening to that data stick. If they've managed to connect with the sat I may need to intercept a signal."

"I can't let you do that, Doctor. Sounds to me as if you're pretty important to this mission. My head will roll if anything happens to—"

"Then give me the same protective gear your men are wearing."

Shaking his head in dismissal, Smith stepped away from the car.

Kate rushed after the police officer. "Ms. Cambridge is your witness. I'm refusing to follow orders. You're no longer responsible."

"Kate!" Cam appeared behind her. "What are you doing?"

"My job!" She turned back to Smith. "Until I put my hands on that computer and data stick, we won't know the status of the program. If your men rush in there while Heat Wave is being deployed, they won't know how to stop it. I have to be there when they go through the door into that room. This isn't negotiable, Lieutenant!"

He swung around, staring at her incredulously. "I expect you have the authority to insist on this," he said, solemnly. "But please reconsider."

Kate stood firm. "Neither of us have a choice." She drew a deep breath. "Are you going to loan me some protection, Lieutenant, or do I walk in like this?" A rayon business suit stood up just fine in a job interview but wouldn't do a lot to stop a bullet.

Smith peeled off his flak jacket and handed it to her. "I have another in my trunk." He didn't look happy.

"Kate, no," Cam pleaded. "I can do it. I'll go instead of you."

Kate tugged the bulky, too-large vest over her suit jacket. She cinched up the waist strap and accepted a helmet held out to her. Blood roared in her ears. Every movement she made felt supercharged. Adrenaline, she thought. She was swimming in it. Drowning in it.

"Kate?" Cambridge asked again.

"Absolutely not. You have a little girl at home waiting for you. I'm not going back there without her mother!"

Cambridge looked to the cop for support. "She can't go in there unarmed."

"Take this, too," he added, holding out what looked to her like a standard military sidearm.

She waved off the gun, remembering Tommy's comment about job descriptions. "Wouldn't have a clue how to use it. I'd end up accidentally shooting myself or one of your people."

"Have it your way," he whisper-growled, "but I'm assigning two men to cover you." Smith waved over the two remaining officers and gave hasty orders for her protection. "Get her in fast…in one piece."

Kate glanced at the two young men flanking her. They looked just as young as Tommy. They were putting their lives on the line for her.

Not just for her, she reminded herself. For their country. Maybe for the world.

Chapter 14

The phone company had supplied directions to the cabin. Because of the heavily forested mountains where they were headed, the chopper had to set down in an open field. Rooker had arranged for three all-terrain vehicles to meet them there. They left the delivery drivers behind with the helicopter pilot.

"Sit tight," Rooker told them. "We'll be back with a few guests."

He turned off his cell phone to avoid signal interference and his team of six boarded the vehicles and took off. He estimated the distance to Zed's hideout was about six miles.

Peterson was sitting beside him in the Jeep as they climbed higher into the remote mountains of West Virginia. "Maybe you should call one last time, sir?" the younger man shouted above the grinding of the engine. "In case they have new information."

"Naw, the doc would give me hell. She'll be pissed because

we didn't wait for her," Rooker said, looking out at the lights in the valley below. No moon tonight. That was good. The air was clear and sharp and almost like fall up here it was so cool. A nice change from D.C.'s heat and humidity. If he hadn't been on a job, he would have enjoyed himself.

The young former marine beside him grinned. "Hey, sometimes even girls want to play soldier. My sister's like that. A tomboy from the time she could walk. With five brothers, guess she didn't stand a chance with Barbie dolls."

"Sounds like she needed to be able to defend herself." Rooker smiled. "Foster isn't like that. She's just a control freak." It sounded funny, saying it like that. Wasn't that what she'd accused him of being?

Donnelly looked back at them from the driver's seat. "Know what I think?"

"No, Don, what do you think?" Peterson asked, a smile in his voice.

"I think the woman wants the chief real bad." He nodded sagely. "That's the first sign. They want to be around you all hours of the day and night."

"Do they?" Rooker mumbled.

"Sure. Hey, Peterson, don't you know, the chief's a babe magnet?"

They both laughed. Rooker didn't object. The men needed to blow off some of the tension they'd carried with them from D.C. He could handle a little ribbing.

But the thought that the little blond scientist might find him appealing nudged at his libido. If nothing else, she'd be an interesting challenge. Why not? Why shouldn't she be attracted to him?

Yet he remembered how pissed she always looked when he was around. And he hadn't exactly done anything to make her day since they'd met. Practically accused her of incompetence the night of the raid on her laboratory. He winced at the thought. Maybe he'd been too hard on her. It wasn't as if she was used to standing up to armed intruders.

"The doc's got the hots for Rooker," Peterson chanted.

Enough, Rooker thought. "Won't do her any good. That's one woman this man is not going to tangle with."

Peterson frowned. "Why not? I saw her in the compound the other day. She's a good-looking specimen. Got all the necessary parts."

"Nice ones, too," Donnelly added.

Rooker shook his head, grinning. "You ever try to get friendly with a dog that's got too much wolf in her? Beautiful fur, eyes that just pull you in and shine with intelligence. Gorgeous animals. But you move the wrong way, or even smell funny to them, and they'll take your hand off."

He thought about Kate's eyes. They scared the hell out of him. She knew things he'd never begin to understand. He hated that—feeling inferior because he didn't have her level of education. He'd always felt intimidated by intelligent people. Maybe something about having been kicked out of school three times—but that was for fighting. Every time it had been to defend some puny kid from bullies. But did the jerk principal understand?

"You come between her and her cub," he added, "and you're dead."

"She's got a kid?" Donnelly steered around a sharp right, and the road angled upward even higher.

"No, you idiot," Peterson groaned. "He's talking metaphorically."

"Meta-who?"

"The chief means her satellite. She's, like, protective of it."

"That hunk of metal?" Donnelly laughed. "Strange thing to get attached to, if you ask me."

For some reason Rooker felt the need to defend Kate. "I guess it's sort of like us, you know, the team. What we'd do for each other. That thing is her life. You should have seen her up against the bigwigs at the briefing after this went down. She stood her ground against all of them."

"Cool," Peterson mumbled.

"I still think she's a looker," Donnelly of the one-track mind persisted.

"Not worth the trouble." Rooker sighed, shut his eyes and leaned back into the seat for the rest of the ride.

They made good time and arrived at a clearing where a few cabins clustered near a stream. They looked like summer places. But the one where the dial-up connection had been made with the satellite appeared to have year-round residents. Firewood stacked behind it. An Explorer utility vehicle parked beside it. Garden to the other side, full of vegetables. An outside floodlight had been rigged up, maybe to catch varmints from the woods raiding the garden.

If this was where Zed or one of his people lived, they'd put down some serious roots. If it wasn't...

If it wasn't...

A warning bell went off in Rooker's brain. Could they be walking into a home invasion situation? He'd need to move his men in cautiously. Go in hard and fast from all sides of the building at once, but no firing until fired on. Quickly assess possible danger to innocent civilians.

He gave his orders, and they all spread out.

"Lights on inside," Peterson whispered into his body mike from somewhere in the trees. "Good sign."

"Maybe." Rooker still felt funny about this setup. "Remember, everyone, if we find anyone transmitting over a computer, he's mine. We don't damage the equipment. First priority, that data stick. Second priority, Zed and whoever is with him."

Rooker waited until they were all in position. He pushed aside doubts and concentrated on the satisfaction of walking up to Kate Foster and dropping her precious memory stick into her hand. How could she not thank him then? It would be a nice change to see a look of admiration in those cool green eyes instead of that critical glare she always shot his way.

"Ready on the north," Donnelly reported over the radio.

"Ready on east." From Sanchez.

"Ready on…" When they'd all checked in, he gave them the go. With perfect precision, they stormed the place and took it with no resistance from the occupying force.

Thirty minutes later things had calmed down enough for Rooker to figure out what the hell had gone wrong.

"I can't tell you how sorry we are, ma'am," he said for the third time, as he sat at Sarah McCloughlin's kitchen table in the West Virginia cabin.

"Now don't you be tyin' yourself in knots over it, son," she said, placing a piece of pie in front of him to go with the coffee she'd already poured. "Everyone makes a mistake now and then. And the children are nearly over the scare already."

Peterson and Sanchez were playing video games with the kids in the family room, trying to get them calmed down after they'd terrified a woman and her three offspring by bursting into their home, waving weapons and ordering the shocked and innocent family to "Hit the floor, freeze!"

His stomach churned at the thought of it. Thank God they hadn't gone in firing. Thank God the man of the house wasn't home to grab the shotgun off the wall and try to fend off the invaders.

A woman and three little kids. Shit.

And all they'd found as far as high-tech equipment was an ordinary home PC. When he'd checked his messages from Kate, he found this was one of a string of blind computers, the final one that had been used to mask the real location of the sending signal.

Hadn't she warned him that something like this could happen? Yes.

Had he listened? No.

Did he dare imagine the look on her face when he slunk back to Andrews AFB with his tail between his legs, empty-handed?

Hell no.

He ate another slice of pie and kept trying to connect with Kate on her cell, but she wasn't answering.

Finally he reached her lab in the compound. One of her people told him she was following another lead. To Connecticut.

Damn! Zed was going to drag them all over the country at this rate. It was probably another dead end.

Rooker tried her phone again. It was almost light outside now, but she still wasn't answering. He wondered what was going on.

Unable to wait any longer, he ordered his team back to the chopper. They took the Black Hawk back to Andrews and traded it in for something with more range. He might make it up to Connecticut before Kate Foster got herself killed.

He nearly smiled. Sure hate to miss that.

Chapter 15

A single dim light flickered through one of the second-floor windows of the dormitory. Kate stared at it. That beacon in the predawn rosy blackness. Why did she get the feeling something was very wrong with this picture?

Zed wasn't stupid. Yet it was almost as if he were holding up a sign for their benefit: *Look here!*

Was she leading the police into an ambush? But Smith had disappeared and her two escorts were already moving her forward in short bursts of running. Off in the distance, Kate could barely make out shadowy forms in the moonlight. One crouched along the building's cement foundation. Another edged toward the main door. She imagined other men on the far side of the building.

Her heart beat harder, faster. Her mouth went parchment dry.

For a moment Kate felt as if she'd been dropped into the

middle of a true-crime TV drama. She was accustomed to long, quiet hours spent plotting trajectories, calculating positions of distant objects—satellites, moons, planets, stars—studying the lightless outer regions of known space.

She'd interned on the Hubble Space Telescope team. She'd played a vital role in saving SOHO, the Solar Heliospheric Observatory, when the satellite orbiting the sun turned unexpectedly, throwing its cameras out of alignment and making them useless. The Comm Center had exploded with cheers when, from thousands of miles away on Earth, her programming adjustments had successfully repositioned the valuable cameras.

That was her kind of excitement. Adventures of the mind! Physical danger was utterly foreign to her.

Yet the young police officers flanking her looked so calm, absolutely sure of their every move. Kate swallowed and ducked when one of her escorts pressed down on the back of her helmet to keep her low. The other man linked an arm with hers and scrambled her forward across open lawn toward the building.

Now everything was hand signals, no audible communications. She watched the amazing pantomime in the dark, able to see only shadows in the faint light of a crescent moon and the rosy glow of dawn. Figures moved soundlessly in a practiced pattern.

Dan-ger! Dan-ger! Dan-ger! Her heart pounded.

An extended hand…a raised finger…a quick jerk of a man's head, and everyone shifted positions again. They all seemed to know what to do. She could only follow along and pray she was in time. Pray that in the minutes since she'd last contacted Tommy, Zed hadn't accessed Heat Wave.

There was a moment after they'd all reached positions outside the building, as the first men slipped in, quickly, silently, when she thought her heart had simply stopped. The world held its breath. The wind ceased, and nothing moved or made a sound.

Suddenly, shouted warnings came from somewhere inside the building: "Police! This is a raid. Police! Show yourself! Put down all weapons!"

The slap, slap, slap of running feet. The nerve-shredding noise of splintering wood.

Kate's escorts reacted to something coming through their wireless earphones. One looked at her. "They've found the computer. You're on, Doc."

"What about Zed?" she gasped. "Did they get him?"

And what about Frank? Guiltily, she realized this was the first time she'd thought about her kidnapped associate in many hours. She prayed none of the police officers had been hurt, then it struck her that she'd heard no shots. Not one.

Wrong. This is wrong!

Her guardian angels in black rushed her through the door and into the building.

Inside, a wide, tile-floor vestibule led to a wooden stairway. Stopping her at the bottom, one man spoke into his mike and listened for a moment, hand cupped over his ear bud. "All clear above," he said, beckoning to her to follow him up toward the first landing.

Along the second-floor hallway doors stood open. Most appeared to have been unlocked or already open. But one, halfway down and facing the front of the building, had been torn from its hinges. A light shone from inside, throwing a brilliant stripe across the hall floor. The same light she'd seen from outside?

Smith stood in the doorway, staring with a puzzled expression at something inside the room.

Kate ran forward to join him, terrified of what she'd find. Bodies? An empty room with no computer? She stopped beside him.

"This what we're after?" he asked.

She stared at a laptop computer sitting on a student desk that had been dragged into the middle of the room as if to put it on center stage. A message in bold white letters flashed against a black background: *Hi there, friends of HW-1!*

"What on earth?" she whispered, her voice cracking.

"Is this some college kid's prank?" Smith growled.

"I don't think so." She could almost hear Zed laughing though.

As she stared at them, the words morphed into another image. Blue-and-white graphics mimicking the NASA logo. Then words appeared beneath the symbol: *Password, please.*

Kate started to step into the room. Smith's arm shot out in front of her, blocking her way. "Wait. We should call in a bomb dog first."

"There may not be time," she argued.

Reluctantly, he let her pass. Kate dashed across the room and sat in the chair in front of the screen. She entered the Heat Wave team's initiation code, praying it would work, aware of others entering the room behind her.

That'll do, the screen read. *Hi, Dr. Kate. Watch this!*

Blinding yellow-orange flames erupted across the screen. An ear-shattering explosion echoed off the walls. Everyone in the room, including Kate, cringed or ducked. For a moment, she too believed a real bomb had gone off.

"What the hell!" Smith shouted.

Boots thundered down the hallway toward them. Shouts of confusion came from all around her.

"It's a trick." Swallowing once, twice, she caught her breath at last. "To get our attention. Sound effects from the computer." At least, she hoped she was right and that was all it was.

"What for?"

"Zed wanted me to find this machine. Probably to leave me this message." But how had he known that she would personally follow the trail he'd left?

Or was this just an elaborate trap after all? She couldn't take chances with other people's lives.

"Clear the room, Lieutenant."

He scowled at her.

"National security. As few people as possible should see this message." It wasn't a very creative lie, but it would do to get him to cooperate without asking a lot of questions.

In seconds the room was cleared except for her young bodyguards, one positioned just outside the room's door, the other inside the room with her, watching out the window overlooking Long Island Sound.

Miles away, a foghorn moaned woefully, and now the morning sky began to turn a pale, airy blue. In that second, Kate wondered if this day's dawn might be the last thing she ever saw.

She hit the enter key.

The screen went blank for two seconds, then a video feed began to play.

Zed's face appeared. "We were never introduced properly. Al Ahmra Zed, at your service, Dr. Kate." He bowed his dark head in mock deference.

Icy prickles ran up her spine at the memory of facing this monster in her lab. How defenseless she'd felt, standing there while he robbed her of her life's work, terrified people she cared deeply for, killed.

"My cause," he continued solemnly, "is a worthy one, though I do not expect you to understand. What I do expect is that you will appreciate the tenuous position of your colleague, Mr. Hess. To my delight, he is still alive. And," he added with emphasis and a satisfied smile, "able with a little encouragement to help us correct your tampering with the satellite's program. Mr. Hess believes by helping us he will save himself." Zed's throaty laugh chilled her. "Such naiveté from a man of science, yes?"

"You bastard," Kate murmured.

But of course the voice continued without reaction to her comment. "I come to my point. You see now that you cannot stop us or catch us. It is only a matter of time before we have gained full control of your satellite. When we do, we will be in a position of unparalleled power, wouldn't you agree?" He glanced down for a moment, and she wondered if he was reading his statement.

"My demands are simple. You will instruct your government to deposit, within five days, ten million dollars into the account named at the end of these instructions. If they fail to do so, I will select a nice little town somewhere in this country to use as a demonstration of my sincerity." The playful twinkle left his eyes. His lips pinched at the corners like little vises. "And let me assure you, I am a very sincere man."

A blank screen replaced Zed's face. Kate held her breath. Her fingertips were trembling on the mouse pad.

A line of numbers scrolled down, followed by the words: *Banque de Belize.*

Chapter 16

Rooker hit the ground running as soon as the military transport rolled to a stop on the tarmac at Groton Municipal Airport. He left his team to handle off-loading equipment and jumped into the car waiting to take him to the nearby U.S. Navy base. It was conveniently close to the campus where Zed had last left his mark. Kate Foster had set up a temporary command center there.

What irked Rooker the most wasn't that she had been right about West Virginia being a false lead. It was her hostility and stubborn, irrational refusal to let him control the mission. Foster thought this was all about science, about outsmarting the enemy on some theoretical level way out there in the ionosphere. But he knew damn well how the minds of men like Zed worked.

Fanatics didn't give a rat's turd about science. They were obsessed with power. And power meant doing anything they damn well pleased. Arrogant, mean-spirited bullies, that's what they were. They *liked* killing people who thought differently about the world than they did. They *liked* taking things that didn't belong to them then blowing up whatever was left.

Violence was their currency. With it they claimed whatever struck their fancy. And only violence could stop them. That's what Foster didn't understand. And that's why she'd get herself and a lot of other people killed, if he didn't move her out of the picture somehow and regain control of this mission.

The car sped north along the east bank of the Thames River, past a huge chemical plant and then the General Dynamics shipyards, where the most sophisticated nuclear subs in the world were built. One of the immense vessels had been hauled into dry dock for repairs or refitting. It looked like a beached, black-iron whale.

His cell rang, and he nearly groaned out loud when he looked at the screen. "Rooker here."

"Max Archer." Homeland Security, just what he needed.

"Yes, sir."

"What happened, Mr. Rooker?" Bad news spread fast.

"We got coordinates for a computer-generated signal to the antenna. We thought we had Zed but when we arrived on target—"

"All you had was the Little House on the Prairie?" Archer's sense of humor left him cold.

"More like cabin in the mountains, actually," Rooker said grimly.

"So you got nothing for your trouble?"

"Before we left the area, we destroyed the antenna. But they can set up another in short order. Any directional high-gain antenna six to ten meters will do the trick, according to

Dr. Foster. Hell, they could drive one around on the back of a truck and keep us jumping for weeks!"

Archer was silent for one horrible moment, and Rooker wondered if he was about to be fired. ASEC and NASA were his employers, so only they could take him off the job. Technically. But the Patriot Act gave the police, FBI and even individual government officials like Archer previously unheard-of powers to act on behalf of the country's security.

Being taken off a mission this high-profile would kill his career. Everyone in government and virtually all private industry would hear about his fall from favor.

He'd do anything to make sure that didn't happen.

"You know about the demands?" Archer said at last.

"Yes, sir. Dr. Foster briefed me by phone immediately after receiving Zed's message." *She* had briefed *him!* Imagine. He swallowed his pride, hating every second of this conversation.

"We're taking this threat seriously, Mr. Rooker. I hope you are as well."

"Very seriously, sir."

"From now on, you will follow Foster's instructions—"

Rooker's blood pressure shot sky high. "Now, wait a minute, sir. With all due respect, the woman is a scientist, not a terrorism expert. My team and I need to be free to move fast and without permission from a—"

"Rooker," Archer broke in, "either you start cooperating with these scientists, or you're off the job. Got that?"

He glared out the car window at the river, sailboats gliding over gray-blue water. "But she—"

"NASA hired you. But the President can fire you. Simple as that. Got it?"

"Yes, sir." Rooker stabbed the end-message button and pressed his shoulder blades into the seat back.

The enlisted navy driver stared straight ahead at the road. No comment. A safe move, given his passenger's mood.

Damn, he hated politics.

There were so many hands in this pot, nothing good could come of it. ASEC…NASA…FBI…the police, and now the Oval Office. All fighting to cure an evil that couldn't be cured.

But if they let him, he could take out one more bad guy. And every one less in the world was good news for humanity.

Rooker found Kate Foster with Cambridge Mackenzie in a small briefing room to the rear of the building delegated as the base's visiting officers' quarters. She was working on what looked to him like an ordinary laptop computer. Knowing her, though, the thing probably was capable of launching the Space Shuttle.

She looked up from the keyboard when he walked into the room.

"Nice of you to join us, Mr. Rooker." She wasn't even close to smiling. It was still the wrong thing to say.

"Don't even start!" he barked and slammed his briefcase down on the other end of the long table. Cambridge flinched but didn't remove her crossed heels from the tabletop. "Why didn't you wait for me to get back from West Virginia before rushing off?"

"As I recall, you were the one who skipped out on me. And—" she added before he could get in a word "—you cut off communications so that I couldn't even warn you to turn around and come back."

"You took unnecessary risks coming up here alone!" He glared at her, pacing the room.

She pushed her chair away from the table and leaned back to study him. "I did what I had to do." Her voice was irritatingly cool. "We had a chance to catch Zed. I had to take it."

A good shouting match might have made him feel better, burned off some of the pent-up frustration after his conversation with Archer. Apparently she wasn't going to oblige.

"The rules have changed, Rooker."

Had Archer told her that he'd lambasted him? Rooker slanted her a look. "What rules?"

"Zed's game."

"What the hell are you talking about?" He finally grabbed a folding chair, flipped it around and straddled the seat to face her.

She looked at Cambridge. "I've been thinking. Ten million isn't a great deal of money for all the trouble Zed's going to."

"Sounds like a lot to me," the other woman murmured.

But Rooker nodded. This was a thought that had already come to him. "No. I expect this is a dry run."

"Like a test?" Cambridge asked.

"Right." Rooker turned back to Kate and, in an unguarded moment, he saw her not as a scientist but as a woman. A petite, blond-haired, jade-eyed, undeniably attractive woman. Just as the boys on his team who'd seen her had pointed out. A woman who got under his skin in more ways than he wanted to admit.

He made a concerted effort to remind himself how much she annoyed him and plunged on. "At first I thought Zed was going for one really dramatic event. Zap the Statue of Liberty. Roast the White House. If he actually was able to get the satellite to respond to his commands, he'd target a newsworthy site and any people who happened to be there, to send his political message. A one-shot deal."

"But now it's changed. Now, it's not about religion, or land, or releasing political prisoners, it's about money," Kate said, looking deep in thought.

He nodded. "Right. Just that. No message to the world, no political agenda. Which makes me think we have more of a chance to catch him. Because he'll get greedy."

"What you mean is, he won't be happy with a measly ten million. He'll come back for more."

"Exactly. If it works once, why stop there? Pick another target, a different population of victims. Demand a billion or more next time." He shrugged. "Why quit when you have a good thing going?"

"That's sadistic," Cambridge spat, crossing her arms over her chest.

"So," Kate said, "now we've learned something new about him. We know he's not really crazy, just evil. And he wants something."

"And," Rooker added, "we know more about how he works. He plants an antenna then filters his instructions to it through a string of remote computers. The owners of these linking terminals aren't even aware they're being used. A classic hacker's technique, used to cover his trail."

Kate nodded. "At the end of the Internet-connected computers is the antenna. It forwards instructions to the satellite, which generates microwave energy." She frowned, tapping a pencil on the table's edge. "What we still don't know is what he ultimately intends to do with this energy and where he intends to direct it."

"Yes," Rooker agreed. "Meanwhile, what's your status on getting a new fix on Zed?"

Kate shook her head and tossed her pencil on the table. "It's a slow process. The FBI is helping us. We could use more help from the private sector, but the government wants to limit exposure to the press. If the public were to find out how bad things could get...." She sighed.

"It's inevitable." Rooker knocked a cigarette out of a soft pack and lit up. "Reporters eat up this shit—they'll pay for information. *Terrorists capture satellite! Reign of terror!* It's only a matter of time before they track you down, Doc."

She made a face. "They were already flocking around Weston's gates before I left. Waiting to pick Jessup's bones when they couldn't get to me."

"So." Rooker looked at her over the glowing end of his cigarette. "I understand you're making all the calls now. What's next?"

She spoke with conviction. "My people back in D.C. are good. They found Zed once, and I believe we only just missed him. They'll find him again." He wished he felt as sure as she sounded. "There's one thing I haven't figured out."

He laughed. "Just one?"

Kate gave him a dirty look but otherwise didn't rise to his bait. "I keep wondering how they're going to point the microwave energy."

"What do you mean, point it?" He blew a puff of smoke in her direction.

She waved it off. "We have massive arrays of solar panels up there, as part of the configuration of the HW-1. They catch the sun's energy, it's converted to microwaves then beamed to the ground where it's converted again to electricity for everyday use. But redirecting those microwaves would be a hit-or-miss thing. The energy should be too spread out to do any real damage. Zed needs a way to focus the energy, to direct it to a specific target."

He felt a jolt of hope. "You're saying you think they're scamming us? They can't do anything with what they have?"

"It's possible," she allowed, hesitantly. Green eyes flickered around the room, as if searching for answers. "Maybe they think they can just scare Washington into putting up the money."

Cambridge looked worried. "But what if they aren't? I mean, say the President decides to call their bluff. Not pay up."

"If it's a scam, nothing happens," Kate said.

"But if they're for real—" Rooker ground out his cigarette in the tin ashtray on the table "—they roast Cincinnati?"

Kate shook her head at him. Then something lit in her eyes. "The antenna, you destroyed it?"

"Yeah. Kinsey would have been thrilled. Kaboom!" He grinned.

"Did anyone examine the thing before you killed it?"

"There wasn't time. I called Agent Winston, and we discussed options. They were going to send out an electronics expert, but then we'd chance Zed using the thing before the FBI's guy could get there. She put him on the line. I gave him a physical description, and he told me it sounded like a standard configuration. Probably military surplus, about eight meters."

"I wonder," Kate said, glancing toward Cambridge.

"What?" Rooker hated this. Worse than techno-jargon, they were beaming silent eye-messages across the room.

"Did you see any other electronic equipment near the antenna?" Kate asked slowly as if she were speaking to a small, rather dull child.

"No!" he snapped, sitting up straighter. "And Donnelly, one of my guys, is up on that kind of thing."

"Is he up enough to recognize a laser?" Cambridge asked.

Rooker stared at the woman. "What's a laser got to do with any of this?"

Kate suddenly got busy on her laptop as she explained. "They need a way to direct the energy to a specific target. Think of a laser beam as a highway, Rooker, with signs posted along the way: *This way to Vegas!* You can relate to that, I bet."

He snarled at her. "Give me a break."

She ignored his best don't-mess-with-me glare. "If they plant lasers in positions that they want to hit with high-intensity energy, they can run the microwaves down the laser beam. It would work."

Rooker stared at her. "You're serious. This is what you think they're going to do?"

"Maybe." She paused, her hands leaving the keyboard and resting in her lap as she studied information she'd called up on the screen.

"Well," he said, "if we could locate the lasers, remove or destroy them—"

She was already shaking her head.

"Why not?"

"How? They're small, could be hidden almost anywhere. But once a laser is deployed, it could be tracked."

"But not until then?"

"Right," she said with a sigh.

So, he thought, things were looking worse instead of better. Some brainstorming session this had been.

There had been another point he was tempted to bring up. It had eaten at him ever since the night of the invasion. But he had no proof. And until he had hard evidence, talking about it would only put Foster on the defensive again.

Rooker decided it was best, for the time being, to keep further speculation to himself. If he found what he needed, he'd lay his cards on the table.

But not Kate Foster's table. He'd have to go over her head. Because, in this particular case, he couldn't trust her to do the right thing.

Chapter 17

The teleconference lasted for over an hour. By the time Kate hung up, she looked over her shoulder at Cambridge and said, "I've aged ten years."

"You did what you could. Told them the truth. Let them fight it out in Washington."

The military had proposed, again, that they destroy the HW-1, but at least General Kinsey now admitted it would take them months to reconfigure a rocket powerful enough to reach the satellite.

ASEC still argued against the demolition of their multi-billion-dollar investment. Kate reiterated her warning about the danger to the population from fallout debris. And everyone else involved in the conference call had put in their two cents.

At first, Kate was reassured by the squabbling because it meant they'd do nothing, for the moment. That bought her time. Then the discussion shifted to Zed's actual ability to use the satellite, even if he succeeded in accessing the onboard computers. ASEC believed the terrorist—or extortionist, in Rooker's book—was bluffing. Kate did not.

"Don't pay," Homeland Security said. "Giving in to demands will only encourage more loonies."

Archer agreed. "The President will stand by his zero-negotiation policy for dealing with terrorists."

Rooker had sat beside the speakerphone, chin propped on his fists, his face thunder-cloud dark, brooding silently through the entire conversation. She assumed he'd been ordered to keep his opinions to himself and follow her lead.

It must be killing him, she thought, taking orders from a scientist, and a woman at that. It was almost enough to brighten her day.

Almost.

"Now what?" Cambridge asked after the call ended.

"We wait on your NASA team, right?" Rooker leaned back in his chair and crossed boot heels over the desk.

Kate nodded. She reached for the crystal paperweight she'd brought with her. It was her connection to home. To a saner world. The purple crystal of the butterfly's wings caught the light from the window. "I checked in just before the call came through. Another signal is trying to contact Heat Wave. This time the antenna's in Maryland, and the FBI is tracking it with orders not to destroy. We need it functioning. As soon as Zed realizes we're on his trail again, he'll move."

Rooker swung his long legs down and shoved himself out of his chair. "I'm out of here."

"Decided to call it quits, have you?" she taunted him.

"Nothing's happening here. I need a decent meal and a cold beer. Either of you ladies want to come along?"

Kate couldn't remember the last time she'd had a hot meal. Or a full night's sleep. Or a shower. She looked at Cambridge.

"Beats sitting on our hands and waiting for Washington to make up its mind. We all could use a break," Cam said solemnly.

Kate nodded. "All right. Everyone has my cell number. They can contact us as easily in a restaurant as they can in this room."

Her only fear was that, as soon as she put warm food in her stomach, she'd crash. Four days, with only catnaps and junk food to sustain her, had left her feeling physically depleted.

Rooker made sure his men were taken care of, then commandeered an SUV from the naval base's security office. Kate didn't ask if dining out qualified as regulation use of a government vehicle. Rooker always seemed to know how to get what he wanted whenever he wanted it—aircraft, weapons, men, information. Did he carry that ability over into his private life?

A disturbing notion, if she really thought about it. She decided not to.

They followed directions from one of the gate guards to a nearby Applebee's.

Steak! Kate thought, catching a whiff of grilling meat as soon as she opened the car door. A thick, juicy medium-rare sirloin or Delmonico with lots and lots of hot, salty French fries. Her mouth reacted with Pavlovian predictability. She was nearly drooling by the time they hit the restaurant's front door.

They sat in a booth and ordered beers, a basketball-size fried onion as an appetizer and their meals. Twenty minutes later, Kate was in heaven. She wolfed down her food and didn't even debate the wisdom of dessert. She ordered a warm brownie sundae with extra whipped cream. The combination of gooey chocolate, melting vanilla ice cream and fluffy sweetened cream was decadent and wonderful.

Thankfully, her phone waited to ring until she was spooning down the last bite of brownie, having successfully fended off Rooker's spoon attacks after he finished his own dessert.

With a contented sigh, she punched her call button.

Marissa Winston's voice came to her. "Thought you could take a break, silly woman. Did you have their half-pound cheeseburger?"

Kate smiled. "How did you know where I was?"

"It's my job. Scary, isn't it?"

"I'll say. What's up?"

"I'm in town, on my way to you right now."

"Really?" Kate pushed Rooker back into his seat. He'd been leaning over the table, trying to listen in.

"I have information about Zed that you should know. And some things Rooker might need."

"You couldn't do this without flying all the way up to Connecticut?"

"Another investigation. Long story, don't ask."

"Right." Kate closed her eyes and shook off the feeling that she was in way over her head. Oh, for the quiet solitude of her lab before all of this madness swept her away. "We're at a table in the back, to the right of the bar as you come in."

"Be there in five," Winston said.

And she was.

Rooker stared suspiciously at the FBI agent as she wove

between tables and arrived at their booth. "Have the powers that be sent you to haul me back to D.C. for flubbing the West Virginia gig?"

"No." Marissa shrugged. "The general opinion is you acted in the most logical way, as fast as you could. Trouble is, terrorists aren't always logical." She slid onto the bench beside Rooker, facing Kate and Cambridge across empty plates. "Good to see you again, ladies. I can tell you've been well fed. Had time for a good snooze yet?"

"Yeah, right," Cambridge grumbled.

Kate shook her head, feeling the carbs kick in with sedative force. She hoped she could make it to her bed in the VOQ before she keeled over.

"Well, soon maybe." Marissa folded her hands over the table, and gave the dining area a quick sweep with her eyes. Her voice dropped a few decibels. "Meanwhile, I have good news and bad news."

"Give me the bad first," Kate said, clinking the ice in her water glass with the straw.

"The *Post* reporters have dug up more details about the HW-1, its capabilities and about Zed's threat. It's all coming out in tomorrow's paper. You can expect the media here to be all over you, once they realize where you are."

"Crap," Rooker said.

For once, Kate thought, the man had it right. "We really don't need this."

"What's the good news?" Cambridge asked hopefully.

Marissa leaned forward another inch. "We now know some things about Zed's background."

Kate's heart sank. That was all? Her expression must have given away her thoughts.

"No, really," the FBI agent said, "this is important. He goes by Al Ahmra Zed but his real name is Gordon Jones. He was a small-time crook in Philadelphia—burglary, car theft, that sort of thing. Did some jail time, came out and went right back to his old routine. More jail time. Learned a trade. Came out and worked in a car lube shop for a few months before being picked up for armed robbery. Skipped bail then disappeared. No one has heard from him or seen him for months."

"Any information about his being involved with militant groups or activists?" Rooker asked.

The waitress started to come over to take the newcomer's order. Winston gave her a sharp look and raised one hand a few inches off the table. The woman about-faced and left them alone. It was like waving a magic wand.

"That's just it," she continued. "We can't find any information connecting him with known terrorist cells or even with protest groups. Usually these people have a history of fraternizing with dissidents."

"And," Rooker added, keeping his voice equally low, "even though his message to Dr. Foster refers to his *cause,* he still hasn't said what that cause is."

"Exactly," Marissa continued, looking at Kate. "Usually these wackos can't say enough about their supposedly good reasons for resorting to violence. They rationalize everything they do. Love having an audience."

Rooker looked around at the neighboring tables, as if to assure himself no one was taking an interest in their conversation. "A guy like Zed, he fantasizes about making the six o'clock news."

Winston nodded. "So although we don't know why he's doing what he's doing, we at least have a fix on who the guy is. And we're beginning to think he might not have a political agenda."

Which, Kate thought, went along with her earlier conversation with Rooker.

"What good does this really do us though?" Cambridge asked impatiently.

"Every piece of information helps us target the guy. His personal and social contacts, places he feels safe and might retreat to. You'd be surprised how many Most Wanteds run back to their home turf, even though that's the most obvious place to look for them."

Rooker nodded. "They think they have the advantage, knowing the territory."

Suddenly, Kate was having trouble focusing on the conversation. It wasn't that she lacked interest. She just kept feeling more and more distant from the group gathered in the booth.

"Kate?" It was Marissa Winston's voice, but it sounded as if it were coming to her through the wrong end of a megaphone.

It took her a moment to realize her eyes were closed. With effort, Kate opened them. "Yes?" The room swam blurrily before her. Traffic sounds from outside seemed confusingly mixed with voices all around her. "Wha—?" she mumbled.

"Come on, Rooker, help me get her into the car. Looks like it's shut-eye time."

Funny, Kate mused, they thought she needed help to walk. She smiled, cracking open one eye as she felt hands grip her upper arms and lift her out of the booth. "Are we leaving now?"

"Nighty-night," Cam crooned.

Chapter 18

Everything felt wrong.

Her mattress, usually so resilient and comforting, seemed hard and unforgiving against her bones. She liked to sleep in the silk pajamas her sister had sent as a special luxury for her birthday, but the slippery hand of the fabric against her skin was missing.

And the light. What was up with that? No golden morning sunbeams slanted through her bedroom blinds. Yet Kate felt sure she had slept through the night.

She widened her eyes. Only a thin, luminous strip seeped beneath the door that was placed too far to the right in the wall. After a moment, she made out a pair of plain chests of drawers, two industrial-design computer desks, a second narrow cot like the one she was lying on. The lumpy shape on the other one told her it was occupied.

For another breathless second Kate had no memory of where she was. Then it all came back at her in a rush.

She bolted up off the bed, tossing aside the thin wool blanket someone had thrown over her fully clothed body. Even in the low light she now was able to identify the other sleeper: Cambridge.

If both of them were unconscious, who was monitoring communications from NASA?

She stuck her feet into the plain navy blue flats beside her bed.

Swinging open the door, Kate blinked at the blinding fluorescent light in the hallway and dashed toward the room where they'd set up their temporary CC on the Navy base.

She opened the door and stepped into what appeared to be midday sunlight streaming through the windows over Daniel Rooker. His heels were hooked over the wide tabletop, her laptop computer and cell phone close beside him.

"'Mornin', lazy bones." He grinned at her.

"What the hell are you doing?" she gasped.

"Minding the store."

She raced to her laptop and hastily reviewed the screen. HW-1 was still on Safe-Hold. She checked her messages online—none—then from her cell phone. A dozen new calls had come in or gone out over her phone to NASA.

"Well, you've certainly been a busy little bee." He appeared to have been chatting with Tommy most of the night.

"That's me!" He sounded way too chipper. But his eyes, red-rimmed and watery, gave him away. A line of foam cups stained with the dregs of cold coffee suggested hours of forced wakefulness.

"How long was I out?" she asked, sitting down in the chair beside him.

"Oh, fifteen…sixteen hours. But who's counting."

Kate groaned and shook her head to dispel the final foggy traces of sleep. "I can't believe I crashed like that. I never sleep more than seven hours. Never."

"You'd been operating on fumes for days." He narrowed his eyes and looked her over. "Actually, you are a good deal more attractive with adequate sleep."

"Thanks, Rooker, like I really care." But she did, she realized. And she had to look away from his cocky smile to hide the small zing of pleasure his compliment brought. "Looks like you haven't gotten much sleep yourself."

"I'm used to it when I'm working."

"You didn't have one of your team cover communications so you could take even a short nap?"

He shrugged. "I figured you'd throw a fit if a stranger listened in on your NASA link. Top Secret, and all that rot. You already hate me, so I had nothing to lose."

She didn't argue that point. "You'd better take a turn on the cot while things are quiet."

He nodded. "No argument there." He stood up and stretched, reaching one hand behind his head to touch the opposing shoulder blade, then reversing the exercise. It looked like pure pain to her. "My guys are holed up down the hall. If you need them for anything duty-related, wake me up first. If you want something to eat, ask one of them to run to the cafeteria for you. Chow in the submarine service is reputed to be the best in the military."

She thanked him, then watched him out the door.

It was troubling, the way Rooker sometimes looked at her. She had disliked him from the beginning, of course, but he had a way of unexpectedly entering her thoughts. She wasn't afraid of the man, or even wary of him, usually. When he was in his combative mode, she could argue right back at him. But when he got quiet and drew into himself, the way he did when other people were around her, she was unsure what might be brewing in that puzzling male brain of his.

At least when he was screaming at her she knew what he was thinking.

She decided it was a waste of time, trying to fathom the unfathomable. She checked in with Tommy by phone.

"Vern is sleeping now. I took over an hour ago. They're going nuts down here, boss. Reporters jumping people outside the gates, hanging out in the neighborhood bars during happy hour to try to corner NASA employees."

"At least they can't get into the compound," she said.

"No, but someone leaked the lab's phone number, and we've gotten a bunch of calls. NASA PR is preparing a statement, hoping to satisfy the vultures." He paused. "Rooker told us about your laser theory. You could be right there."

"But the public doesn't know about the lasers yet, right?"

"Right." He hesitated. "You know, if it's really lasers they're going to use to guide the beam, we're cooked."

She nodded although he couldn't see her. "You heard about the demands?"

"Right. I don't see how we'll stop them. We've lost our ability to talk to HW-1."

Unfortunately, this was true. But there was one tool left to Kate. She could still track the satellite's telemetry. That is, she could physically observe what the spacecraft was doing. That might give them a general clue to Zed's target. Meanwhile, she hoped the FBI or local law enforcement would locate the data stick, or provide a lead that would allow Rooker to get his hands on it. Once she had the stick and the encrypted codes on it, it might still be possible for her to reclaim Heat Wave.

But that still meant finding Zed.

Cambridge woke up an hour later and stumbled into the room. "What does someone have to do around here to get coffee?" She scowled at the collection of disposable cups with muddy liquid in them. "*Hot* coffee."

"Room service is down the hall." Kate explained Rooker's solution to such urgent missions. "The boys are resting up for action, I imagine. But you'll probably get at least one volunteer if food is mentioned. I could go for three eggs over easy, hash browns, bacon and a carafe of high test."

Cam grinned. "Until last night, I didn't think you ate at all. Now you're stowing it away as if there were no tomorrow." She blinked. "Sorry. Bad choice of words."

Kate smiled at her. "After you rustle up breakfast, why don't you give Amanda a call. Maybe she can put Kristi on the phone. I'm sure your little one would like to hear your voice."

Cam nodded. "No more than her mother wants to hear hers."

The full, hot breakfast tasted like heaven. One of Rooker's young team members, Adam Grabowski, came back to pick up their trays and return them to the cafeteria. "You ladies let us know when you need anything else. We're just playing cards and watching the tube." He gave Kate a sweet smile. "You want to join us, Doc?"

"We have to take care of business," she said. "But thanks for the offer."

He turned and, giving her a parting look, left the room loaded down with empty plates.

Cambridge hummed to herself.

"What?" Kate asked.

"Boy's got the hots for someone in this room. Ain't me."

"Oh, stop it. I must be ten years older than he is. Adam's just a kid."

"He's a man. And you're an attractive woman. Or would be if you bothered brushing your hair."

"You're the second person today who's used that word on me," Kate grumbled.

"Attractive?" Cambridge twinkled at her and leaned across the conference table. "Who was the first?"

"None of your business. You watch that screen. I'm calling Tommy again."

Cambridge sighed. "If I had your sex life, I'd just put a gun to my head and end it all."

That afternoon, things started to happen again. Vernon reported that the Heat Wave team had detected a new antenna broadcasting to the satellite. No, Zed hadn't yet broken through Kate's impromptu firewall. That was the good news. The bad was that neither NASA nor the FBI had successfully traced the signal back to its sender.

Again, a string of remote computers was being used to confuse the white-hat hackers at the Bureau and Weston. Refusing to pay the ransom Zed demanded seemed to Kate like foolishly gambling with people's lives. Never mind government policies. She was convinced that the man who broke into her lab would stop at nothing to get what he wanted. It was just a matter of time before he managed to gain control of the satellite. Then he would do as he'd threatened: demonstrate the power of unleashed energy. She shuddered at the possibilities.

Rooker consulted over the phone with the police in Western Maryland, out near Deep Creek Lake, who had located the antenna. Unlike the earlier antenna, which had been owned by a satellite TV company, this one was a portable unit obviously set up by Zed or one of his people.

Rooker asked the officer in charge to post surveillance, in case anyone came back to pick it up. But, he confided to Kate, he doubted Zed would bother retrieving it. Too risky. Too easily replaced.

By four o'clock that afternoon, Tommy's tracking efforts had stalled completely. He and Vernon had hacked back through seven computers. The first in Tallahassee. The last, so far, in Boston. Zed could be anywhere.

The boys kept on working.

Rooker finally lost his patience two hours later. "I'm taking my team to Boston," he told her. "It's not that far. We'll take a chance that it's Zed."

"No," Kate argued. "We can't risk a repeat of the West Virginia fiasco. Give Tommy and Vernon a little more time. They'll find him." But would they?

Still, she felt she had to voice confidence in her own people.

"We sit tight until we're sure—then you can scramble, Mr. Rooker. And," she reminded him, "this time I'm going with you."

He tossed her a sullen look and stalked out of the room.

"That man is steamed," Cambridge said, picking at a carton of takeout Chinese with plastic chopsticks. "I can't remember. Is this chicken or pork lo mein?"

"Does it matter?" Kate asked.

"I hate chicken."

"Then don't eat it."

"But I'm hungry." She took a bite, chewed and swallowed. She stared at it. And kept on staring. Tears came to her eyes.

Kate reached out and touched her arm. "You miss your little girl."

"Yeah. Kristi, my baby."

"Maybe you should go back. You could send up one of the boys."

"No, they need to be where they are. I want to be here. It's just hard, you know?"

"Yes." Kate couldn't honestly imagine.

She'd never been married or had children. She wondered if she ever would now. At one time it had seemed an important part of her life-to-be. But somewhere along the line her career had filled up the days, the weeks, the months...until it was everything to her.

And to her surprise, she liked it that way.

Or had until the day a crazy man had taken it all away and made her science a weapon.

"Besides," Cam said with a smile, "I can't leave you alone with Rooker. He'd eat you alive."

Kate laughed. "Let him try it. He's just sulking. Sooner or later, he'll get his chance to play commando."

"If we're lucky."

If they were lucky, yes. Kate sighed and rubbed her forehead.

The door opened and Adam stepped through.

"Not another bite of food," Kate warned him. "That grinder you brought me for lunch was immense. I won't be able to eat for a week now."

The local name for a submarine sandwich or hoagie was *grinder,* for reasons no one on the base seemed able to explain. It was delicious. Overstuffed with Italian cold cuts, cheeses, tomato, lettuce, onions and hot peppers, all drenched in sweet olive oil.

Adam shrugged apologetically. Only then did she notice the long case slung over his shoulder. It looked like an assault rifle.

A jolt of fear shot through her. "Is something wrong?"

"No, I just thought you might like to try a little target practice. There's a range on the base."

She stared at him, then at the gun. "I—well, no. I don't know how to fire any kind of gun. Something as sophisticated as that thing…." She shook her head.

"C'mon, Doc. It'll do you good to get out of this room. We've got another three hours of light to the day, and it's beautiful out there."

"He's right," Cambridge agreed. "At least walk on down to the range. Your brain will atrophy, not to mention the rest of you, if you don't get some exercise."

Kate bit her bottom lip. "I don't know."

"You don't have to fire it, if you don't want to," Adam said. "But Rooker says you're supposed to go in with us this time. You ought to at least get used to hearing rounds go off."

Kate knew what *that* sounded like. Only too well. Feeling vaguely sick to her stomach but unwilling to explain her revulsion for firearms. It seemed easier just to go along with him. Get it over with. Besides, Cam was right, she did need to get out and move around a bit.

"All right," she murmured. "But my name is Kate not Doc, okay?"

He winked. "Gotcha."

Kate rolled her eyes at Cambridge as she followed the young mercenary out of the room. Cam gave her a thumbs up. The woman was hopeless.

It was still late August but some trees were already starting to turn after an early cold snap. The maples were the best, showing off deep purply-crimson leaves.

They walked past barracks, the commissary, the motor pool and several parking lots. Adam talked a solid streak the entire time, about his high school days in Ft. Worth, playing football with his brothers who went on to college at the University of Texas, and the girl he'd gone with until he shipped overseas with the Marines. He'd seen heavy action in his fourteen months in Iraq.

"Four months after my discharge Rooker looked me up," Adam said. "The pay is great, better than making bread in my dad's bakery, that's for sure. In-country, a thousand a week. Overseas, sometimes that much in a day, doing security work."

"But you're putting your life on the line. How does your family feel about that?"

"It's my life," Adam stated, a little defensively, she thought.

They arrived at the range. There were concrete dividers between shooters' positions and paper targets set at various distances, backed by mounded earth to catch bullets. She could hear a soft pop, pop, pop from down the line. It didn't sound very threatening, not like the sharp crackling fire she recalled from the day Zed broke into her lab. Or that *other* day.

She told herself to relax. She'd just watch. This would be okay.

Then Rooker stepped out from behind a barrier, and Adam gave him a nod and turned to leave. She'd been set up.

"I'm going, too," she said.

"No, you're not. This is mandatory training." Rooker removed his weapon from its canvas case. The rifle was fully assembled—a long steel barrel, composite stock, serious-looking scope, the requisite trigger—and it looked as intimidating and dangerous as she'd imagined it might.

Kate stepped back from it, fighting the urge to walk away. No, run. Her heart was operating at a gallop.

"First thing to learn is the parts of the firearm." Rooker stepped forward and held the rifle out toward her.

"Wait! No!" Kate waved both hands, backing away. "I just tagged along with Adam for the walk. And to get used to hearing rounds go off." Her pulse leaped to marathon pace.

She couldn't do this. Absolutely could not.

"Kate," he said.

"No, I'm serious. I don't want to do this. I'm going back now."

The past rushed back at her in vivid and ugly detail as she staggered away. A family torn apart. Accusations. Threats. Fear of punishment and guilt had haunted her for years and nearly destroyed her.

From that tragic day on, she'd viewed all guns as pure evil.

And she'd been reminded of that evil in more recent times. Only a few years ago she and her neighbors had lived through the sniper attacks that had paralyzed Maryland and Virginia suburbs. Like everyone else in the targeted areas, she'd taken alternate routes to work, used the next-to-last drop of gas in her car's tank before forcing herself to stop for fuel, avoided going to grocery stores and mall parking lots. And she'd held her breath whenever she turned on the radio, praying a new attack hadn't brought hell to another family.

She jerked to a stop when Rooker's hand closed around her wrist.

"It's a tool, Kate. Like any tool, you have to know how to use it safely."

"No." She shook her head. "This isn't fair. You made Adam lie to me to get me to come here. You don't understand. I can't. I just can't."

Blinking, she wished the images of the past away. A rifle in a boy's hands. A game that ended tragically.

"Kate, listen to me. It's not safe for you to be in the middle of a raid when you don't know anything about the weapons we're carrying."

She shook her head. "Rooker, believe me, it's not something I can control. I can't—"

He pulled her gently toward a bench, sat down beside her and laid the rifle diagonally across his knees, muzzle pointed away from her.

"Just listen to me for five minutes, then you can decide."

She closed her eyes and tried to breathe without shaking. "All right. Go ahead."

"What if Adam or I get hit, go down, can't use our weapons?"

She looked at him, her heart aching at the thought. "I'll be praying that won't happen," she whispered.

"But what if it does? What if the bad guys take me out and this—" he patted the rifle "—*this* is lying on the ground and one of Zed's guys dives for it. If you don't pick it up, you're giving it to him. You're giving him the power to kill you, finish me off, and hurt others in our team."

Kate squeezed her eyes shut against the image of Rooker or sweet-faced Adam lying wounded, helpless. And she was standing there, frozen. Useless as a block of wood.

"Okay!" she gasped. "I'd have to take the thing to keep it from them. I can do that."

"Sure you can." His voice was even more gentle. He pried her right hand off the edge of the bench seat and rested it across the rifle's stock. "See, it can't hurt you."

It's not *me* I'm worried about! she thought frantically.

"Now," he continued with patience, "you pick the weapon up off the ground, but the bad guy is still coming at you."

"No!" she cried out reflexively. He gave her a look of gentle reprimand. "I'm sorry. I didn't mean to scream like that. It's all right. Go on."

"Right. So you have my piece here because I've been wounded. The enemy has his own weapon. And if you don't do something, Kate, he is going to put a bullet in my head while I'm lying there."

"Oh, God!" She didn't want this. Had never asked to be put in this position. It was too much.

"You have to make a choice."

"I'm a scientist, not a mercenary," she rasped. "I do things to *help* humanity, not snuff it out."

He put an arm around her shoulders. "Yeah, but these guys aren't exactly humane, are they?"

"No," she agreed.

"So, do you want to know how to safely handle this baby?" He gave her an encouraging half smile. "You probably will never have to fire it other than here. But if it comes to protecting yourself or one of us—"

"Show me," she said quickly before she could change her mind.

Chapter 19

She told herself that looking through the scope of a rifle was like looking through her very first telescope. The one her dad had bought her for her tenth Christmas. She'd taken it out into the backyard that night and stayed outside for hours and hours, staring in rapture up at the heavens over Chicago.

Just focus on the mechanics of the thing, she told herself. Don't personalize it. It's a tool. Don't let in that other time.

She focused on Rooker's sure hands and firm voice while he demonstrated the way to hold the rifle, the heel of the stock braced firmly against the fleshy part of her right shoulder, her left hand supporting the long barrel, her right fitting around the narrow section behind the trigger guard. Index finger straight out along the side, pointing directly away from her…never on the trigger until the final moment. Never even moving into the trigger guard until she had aimed and decided to fire.

He showed her where the five-cartridge magazine slid with

a click into the belly of the weapon. Demonstrated how to slip
the shiny, gold-colored cartridges into the black plastic clip.
"You can hand-load one at a time through the breech under-
neath here if you have to. But it's better to have a couple magazines prepped."

He made her snap an empty magazine into the breech, then
out several times, until she could do it by touch. Then they
practiced finding the target through the crosshairs, and chills
crawled up her back. Her hands began to shake.

"Rook—"

"It's okay, just relax. Breathe," he encouraged her. "We're
not killing anything today. Paper targets don't feel a thing.
Imagine yourself at the county fair. You want to win that
great big purple doggy to take home and put on your bed."

Okay, she thought, I can do this. Win the stupid stuffed
animal.

"Now, hug the gun with the soft part of your cheek right
up against the stock. See the bull's-eye through the scope?
Line it up on the crosshairs."

"Got it," she said.

He brought his arm around her from behind and rested his
right hand over hers, nudged her forefinger a fraction of an
inch. "There's the safety. Feel it?"

"That little raised spot?"

"Yes. Press it."

She did.

"Now lever the bolt forward. It will snap itself back. That
puts a round in the chamber. Move your finger into the guard
and find the trigger."

"But we left the magazine out. It's not loaded," she reminded him.

"I know. You're going to dry fire until you stop shaking.

It's a tool, remember. Like a hammer. If you hit me over the head with a hammer you could kill me."

"Don't tempt me," she muttered.

Rooker laughed. "You really do hate this. Okay, now breathe and think hammer."

She did, and the shaking stopped. It helped that he had his body wrapped around her. His chest felt warm and solid against her back.

"When you like where the crosshairs are, draw a picture in your mind of what you want to hit. Take a breath in, let it halfway out, then slowly squeeze the trigger."

Kate sighted through the scope, saw Zed in the crosshairs pointing his ugly assault weapon at Rooker. Breathe in...out. Finger to trigger. Pull. Click.

It took her a moment to realize she'd done it.

"That's it?"

"Perfect. Now do it twenty more times."

She positioned herself and the rifle without Rooker's support, sighted it, safety off, bolt, breathing, trigger, click. Each time she felt a little steadier, but she reminded herself that the weapon was still empty.

"Would you like to try loading and shooting a few rounds?" he asked.

"Would you like to step into rush-hour traffic on the Washington Beltway?" she returned maliciously.

"You're still that keen on this, huh?"

"You'll never make me like it, Rooker." She sighed.

"You don't have to enjoy it. This is just to keep you and the rest of us safe, right?"

"Right." She swallowed. "Let's do it."

Now he brought out a set of earplugs for each of them and clear acrylic glasses for eye protection. While she wrestled five cartridges into a magazine the size of a baby's fist, Rooker rambled on about the rifle's specifications.

"This is a Steyr SSG, twenty-six-inch barrel, cold-hammer forged. Made in Austria, used mostly as a countersniper rifle. It's extremely reliable and accurate. Won't knock you on your ass like a shotgun when you fire it."

"A nice plus," she mumbled and snapped the magazine into the rifle's underside. She touched the safety, checking to be sure it was on. It was.

"Same routine," Rooker whispered in her ear. "Expect a little kick to your shoulder." He placed himself close behind her, as if to protect her should she lose her balance.

Kate braced herself and let motor memory take her through the steps they'd rehearsed. When she eased back on the trigger, her hands were surprisingly steady.

The recoil was less than she'd expected, and it took her a moment to realize she'd actually done it. "Did I hit the target?" she asked.

"Bloody hell," Rooker muttered.

Her heart sank. "I missed the whole thing?"

"No, you're just off dead center by an inch or so." He grinned down at her. "Okay, Annie Oakley, now let's see you get the next four rounds inside your first shot."

Kate emptied six magazines before Rooker let her stop. She never made a perfect bull's-eye, and a few shots barely made the outer circle. But not one totally missed the paper target. By then her arms were aching from supporting the weight of the Steyr. She still knew nothing about any other weapon, but this one she felt confident she could handle in an emergency.

It's a tool, she thought. A really noisy hammer.

Rooker sat down on the bench beside her to clean and put

away the rifle. "It was bad, wasn't it? The thing that scared you off guns."

"Yes," she said.

"You don't have to tell me."

"I know." She looked past the row of targets toward the horizon, washed in brilliant hues by the setting sun. This time when the past flashed back at her like a clip from a film, it didn't leave her feeling as helpless. And she wanted to tell someone.

"I stood there and watched him shoot her."

"Shoot who?" Rooker asked.

She turned toward him on the bench and opened her mouth but nothing came out. He put his arms around her and she rested her cheek against his muscular shoulder. After a moment it was easier to speak.

"I was a junior in high school, babysitting my neighbors' kids. The girl was ten years old. Her brother was eight. I had no idea their father kept a shotgun for hunting in the house."

"Damn," he breathed close to her ear. As if he knew. As if the scene repeated over and over in her nightmares had somehow become visible to him.

The dreams came less often these days. But in times of stress, they sometimes revisited her with paralyzing intensity.

"Which one got hold of the gun?" he asked.

"Danny. I was making a snack for them after school." The words spilled out. "They were playing a game—tag, I think. Meghan was it. She came back to the kitchen when I called them, but Danny was taking forever. I sent Meghan to get him."

Rooker gave her a squeeze, as if to keep the words coming when he sensed her faltering.

"Then," she said, "I heard Meghan shouting at her brother,

warning him that he was going to get in trouble if he didn't stop whatever he was doing. She tended to be bossy, and he intentionally annoyed her. Their squabbling was nothing new."

"Just being kids."

"Right. I didn't have a clue anything was really wrong. I yelled at them to knock it off and come for their snack. That's when Meghan screamed. She sounded so frightened I tore out of the kitchen and down the hall. When I came around the corner into their parents' bedroom, Danny was grinning, pointing the rifle at her."

"Christ."

"'Bang, you're dead!' he shouted. Then he pulled the trigger."

Her shoulders jerked within Rooker's embrace, at the memory of the shotgun's blast, but there were no more tears. They'd been spent a long time ago. He said nothing, just held her.

Kate finally gathered herself together and pressed away from his chest.

"Sorry," he murmured, trying to catch her gaze with his, "for upsetting you."

She shrugged.

"What happened to the little girl?" he asked. "She die?"

"No, but at the time no one expected her to make it." Kate started walking. Rooker hefted the rifle case and fell in beside her. "There I was, me with my ridiculously inadequate Red Cross childcare certification. The only thing I knew to do was call 911, put pressure on the wound, and keep Danny from running out of the house for fear of what his parents would do to him."

"So you took the gun away from him?"

"I guess I must have." She thought about that. "You know, I can't remember. But by the time the medics and police rushed in, it was sitting up on a high shelf over the stove. And I was back in the bedroom holding on to Danny with one hand while I pressed a kitchen towel over Meghan's chest."

"You saved her life."

"Did I?" She shook her head. "Her parents blamed me. Said I hadn't adequately supervised the children."

"That's a load of crap," he snapped, walking faster so that she had to speed up, too. "That gun shouldn't have been where a kid could get at it. Was it loaded?"

"I think so. Danny told the police he had no idea how the bullet got into it. Anyway, I don't think he understood the difference between pretend shooting and the real thing."

"In the movies the guy who gets blown away in Doomsday 2 shows up in Doomsday 3."

They were nearly back to the VOQ before she spoke again. "In the end I think Danny had a harder time coming back from that day than either Meghan or I. We've stayed in touch, the three of us. As an adult, he's still struggling with the guilt."

"And you're not?"

She gave him a look. "Point made."

It was strange, but as she slanted a glance toward the rifle case he carried, she didn't feel the horror of an hour earlier. She still hated all things created with the intention of killing. But, she reminded herself, the world was a violent place these days. Like it or not, she lived in it and had to survive here.

"That scenario you described—you wounded and down, Zed coming to finish you off. That's your nightmare, isn't it?"

Rooker gave a tight laugh. "We all have our own bumps in the night. Mine is some guy who comes at me when I can't fight back. But, you know, it never happens the way you expect it."

"I wouldn't want to be the one who got you or one of the others killed." She stared at the ground, walking slower. "Have you given your men orders to protect me?"

He looked away.

"Rooker?"

He shrugged. "You're the one who has to work magic with the satellite. If one of us buys it, the whole mission doesn't crash."

That was it then. If necessary, the team would put themselves between her and a bullet. And what was she supposed to do about that? Stand helplessly by without fighting back, because of a tragedy that had happened nearly two decades ago?

Kate made a decision in that moment. She'd do what she had to do when the time came.

She turned back to Rooker. "You have to promise me something."

"What?"

"The things I told you this afternoon, about the kids and the accident. You don't tell the others."

"Why?" he asked.

"I don't want to give them another reason for feeling protective of me. They'll take more risks."

He gave a short nod that she took as a yes.

Chapter 20

The intolerable waiting came to an abrupt end early the next morning. Whoops of male excitement and Rooker's gruff orders shattered Kate's pre-coffee stupor. She had gotten as far as pulling on underwear and buttoning her blouse when boots clattered down the hallway toward the tiny beige bedroom she shared with Cambridge in the VOQ.

Before Kate could snatch her jeans off her bed, the door flew back on its hinges, banging against the wall.

"We're moving out!" Rooker snapped at her. "With or without you?"

"With. And your manners are atrocious. Didn't your mother ever tell you to knock?"

Rooker winced. His voice was suddenly low. "Never knew my mother."

Kate blinked at him. "I'm sorry, I—"

"I guess my manners leave something to be desired." He

grimaced. "Some of my foster mothers tried, but they had other priorities. Like feeding and clothing us."

His blue eyes swerved to watch her step into her jeans. She quickly zipped them up over her underwear. Adam would have been a puddle at such an opportunity. Rooker? She couldn't tell if the man even noticed she was female.

But it was no wonder he was the way he was. All gruff and needing to be in charge. Being bounced from one foster home to another did that to a kid.

"Where are we headed?" Her heart pounding, Kate shoved her things into the overnight satchel that was all she'd brought from home.

He gave her a mysterious look. "I'll let Cambridge fill you in. I'm making travel arrangements now."

She frowned at his departing back. Why was he being so obtuse? It was too damn early in the morning for obtuse!

She dashed across the hall to their makeshift command center.

Cam was on the phone with Tommy. She turned, still listening to whatever he was saying, her dark eyes worried. "You're not going to believe this."

"Try me." Kate steeled herself for bad news.

"They're out of the country."

"No. Where?"

"Italy. Rome, we think, or somewhere close to it."

"Damn!" It wasn't that she was surprised Zed and his team had managed to slip out of the U.S. It just didn't make sense to her.

Why would he complicate his own plans? Why make it more difficult to plant antennae and keep track of how the government was responding to his threats by putting himself at a distance?

Unless he just felt safer in Europe. Unless that's where he knew people would be willing to hide him if things got too hot.

"Give me the boys." She held out her hand for Cambridge's phone.

"It's Kate," she said. "Has anyone verified a target guidance system?"

"We're still thinking laser. But nothing's gone active yet." There was commotion behind Tommy's voice.

"Vernon here." He was breathing hard, as if he'd just run from the far end of the installation. "Okay, this is the way it is. The FBI has been working with us. They think what we should be looking for is an array of lasers preset at possible strike sites. Could be a dozen or more, spread out over the eastern half of the country."

"Anywhere within range of HW-1," she thought out loud.

"What's up?" Rooker was suddenly at her back, nudging her with his hard knuckles.

She held up a fist in a back-off gesture. "This isn't good," she said into the phone.

"No," Vernon said. "If we track down one laser, they can deploy another, hundreds of miles away. Since a laser isn't able to be tracked until it fires up, it's guaranteed we'll lose the game."

The game. Hacker talk. Tommy was rubbing off on Vernon.

"So our only hope still is to find Zed and retrieve the programming that will allow us to recapture control of Heat Wave," she summarized.

"Right."

She turned to Rooker. "Looks like we're going to Rome."

He winked at her. "Ciao, baby."

Chapter 21

At Roma-Fiumicino airport, officers from the Carabiniere, the Italian national police, escorted Kate and the Worldwide Security team through customs. Despite the presence of Italian officials there was considerable confusion, dramatic arguments and hand gesturing over the weapons being brought into the country. A government-provided translator arrived to assist in communications.

Kate briefed the entire group, stressing the urgency of their mission while keeping details on a need-to-know basis. Her information seemed to quell some concerns but resulted in another round of questions and more red tape. Kate sensed Rooker's growing impatience.

He'd barely spoken a full sentence to her during the eight-hour night flight from New York and seemed intent on distancing himself from her. She supposed his black mood might still be due to his resentment over being forced to bring her along, then having to play second fiddle in her orchestra.

As to the Italians' reluctance to allow foreigners bearing lethal weapons free run of their city, she understood completely. Certainly such a thing would never be allowed in the States.

But in the end the Carabiniere compromised; assault rifles, machine guns, sidearms and crates of ammunition were all allowed through—with the stipulation that this operation was to be a joint effort between the Italian police and Americans. It was the best arrangement that could be worked out at the time. Rooker wasn't happy about it, but Kate was grateful they'd come to an agreement.

By the time the Americans were transported to accommodations in Rome proper, it was nearly dawn. Nevertheless, there were still more formalities to be satisfied at the Abruzzi, a hotel located on Piazza della Rotonda. The manager had been awakened and insisted on greeting them in person. Kate began to share Rooker's irritation.

Her head throbbed. Every muscle in her body ached. All she wanted to do was crawl between cool sheets and sleep. But she knew she'd first need to check in again with Washington.

The translator accompanied them to their rooms. He had glanced worriedly at Rooker as the security man's face grew redder and redder and his silence more threatening at each delay during the early morning hours.

Now, standing in the hallway as a sleepy-eyed bellboy opened the door to their suite, the man explained, "It is not customary, Signore Rooker, to rush about without properly greeting your host and satisfying local custom."

"Is it customary to drag your fucking feet while the enemy takes a bead on one of your cities?" Rooker lashed out, brushing past the man and disappearing into the suite.

Rooker's men followed him, wordlessly, inside.

"We're just very tired." Kate apologized, furious at Rooker for his rudeness. "And worried. You understand, these are very dangerous people."

The translator bowed his head briefly. "I understand the urgency of your trip. I will try to speed things along. *Gradualmente, sì?*" A little at a time, Kate translated for herself. Faster, but slowly. Only in Italy, she thought wryly.

Kate walked through the door to the suite they'd been given, closing the door behind her. The ornate decor of the central sitting area looked bizarre, crowded with young warriors popping open cases of weapons. Her worst nightmare. A zoo of guns.

But her blood was boiling by now. She stepped over gun cases, zeroing in on Rooker.

"You didn't have to go ballistic like that!" she said. "The Italian government is being amazingly cooperative, considering we've tossed a live bomb in their laps."

He continued to fuss over the Steyr, his back to her.

Kate wasn't about to let him put her off. "Unless you plan on learning Italian overnight, it might be wise to show a little courtesy."

Rooker spun on her, eyes ablaze. As if his men had already learned the signs that warned his anger had reached its limit, their usual bantering ceased.

"Listen, Doctor, I don't trust anyone except my own people in this operation, got it? We don't need to add anyone else to the mix."

She stared at him, unsure what he meant. "Don't you think that's a little paranoid? We *know* who the enemy is."

"Do we?" His features tightened, but he quickly looked away from her, as if he'd let something slip he hadn't intended.

"Yes, we do," she said. "Zed and two equally insane cohorts. Or am I wrong? *You* tell *me*, Rooker."

"Forget it."

"I won't." She circled around him to get a good look at his expression, but he refused to meet her gaze. "If you want me to be an effective part of this mission, you have to be straight with me. I've been trying to educate you on the science. How about you return the favor."

Men started disappearing into the surrounding bedrooms.

Rooker laid down his rifle and straightened up to face her. His eyes had gone from blue to a stormy gray. "It's not paranoid to think there might be a mole in the pipeline. I've suspected this from the beginning but I didn't have any evidence, until just before we left the States."

She had to tip her chin up at an uncomfortable angle to look him in the eye. "What the hell are you talking about?"

"I can vouch for every person on my team," he stated. "Can you do the same for yours?"

"My people are absolutely loyal to the mission. They are patriotic citizens, every one of them. I've worked with them for years."

"Not all of them," he said with conviction that made her blood run cold.

His meaning hit her with such impact she felt her breath being sucked away. "You've investigated my team?" She'd known the FBI was interviewing everyone connected with the project, but Marissa Winston hadn't told her she'd briefed Rooker. Apparently he'd gotten access to her reports.

"You have a Vernon Martinez. He was transferred from the Applied Physics Lab in San Diego less than a year ago."

"Vernon is a bright young man, a serious and dedicated scientist."

"Did you know he also came into the U.S. illegally?"

She gasped, surprised, then wished she hadn't been so obvious in her reaction. "No, I guess I didn't know that."

"Neither did the people who gave him a top-secret security clearance at Weston. Then there's Miss Mackenzie."

Kate felt as if the skin all over her body was being pricked by thousands of pins. "Cambridge is beyond reproach."

"You're friends with her, not just professional colleagues."

"Yes." And she was sincerely proud of their friendship. Proud, too, of Cam, whose mixed-race parentage had produced an exotically attractive woman with her father's Asian eyes and Scotch temper, and her mother's molasses-brown complexion.

"She has a child."

"She's a single mother, yes, and a damn good one. That's why I sent her back to D.C. instead of bringing her along with us. She needs to be at home with her daughter."

"The daughter she nearly gave birth to in prison?" He walked briskly into the kitchenette at the far end of the room.

Kate stared after him, stunned. It took a moment for her to get her feet moving and follow him. "You'd better tell me where you're going with this, Rooker." Prison? Cam? Impossible.

"Cambridge Mackenzie seems to have straightened out her life, but she wasn't always the model citizen." He opened cupboard doors until he found coffee, a little stovetop espresso maker, sugar packets. "When she was sixteen, she got involved with a gang in northeast D.C. Police picked her up on possession the first time. Then for theft. She and her friends were breaking into houses, stealing anything they could sell to buy drugs."

Kate's head was reeling. She said nothing.

"Daddy arranged for bail until the trial. Meanwhile, Miss Mackenzie got herself high again, as well as knocked up."

Kate eyed the back of Rooker's head coldly. She hated his tone. Hated the judgmental clip he gave each word. She didn't believe any of it, yet. But Cam had never seemed inclined to talk about her past. Was what he claimed true?

"So maybe she was a messed-up teenager," she allowed. "I understand there are a few others out there."

"Very messed up. The D.C. penal system detoxed her. She was found guilty on multiple theft charges and sent to a women's prison. But her parents appealed to the courts to shorten her term so she could have the baby in the hospital where her father was on staff, then come home to their supervision. A sympathetic judge agreed, and she was sprung."

Kate shook her head, confused. "But the woman has a degree in aerospace engineering!"

"She started taking undergrad courses while still in prison, then transferred to American University after the baby was born. From then on, she appears to have been a different person. Ideal student, perfect parent, the whole shebang."

Kate's fists clenched and unclenched in front of her body. She was shaking with rage. "So why are you even bringing up her name as a possible traitor?"

"Miss Mackenzie lied on her application to NASA, about not having a criminal record."

Kate's mind raced. "If she was incarcerated as a teenager, her record probably would have been wiped clean before she came to work for NASA."

"So, omitting the fact she's an ex-con isn't the same as a lie?"

She ached to punch him in his oh-so-smug face. "Less than a year in detention for a juvenile crime doesn't make her a hardened criminal!"

"Doesn't make her Mother Theresa either. And the fact is, that night in your lab played out like no terrorist offensive I've ever witnessed or heard of. Something stinks, Doc. Something doesn't make sense. And I think it's because someone close to you is working behind your back for the other side."

"You *are* paranoid. You really are!" she shouted and spun away from him.

Kate darted toward the end of the coffee bar, but before she could maneuver around it Rooker seized her by the arms and whipped her around to face him.

"Think about it, dammit! Use that scientific reasoning you're so proud of. There were six people working with you that night. One got blown away, one got shot up and dragged off against his will. But the rest, who saw the terrorists' faces and can identify them, were left unharmed. Doesn't that seem strange to you?"

Kate glared at him, remembering now that he'd made a similar point back at NASA. "So we count ourselves lucky," she gasped.

"No!" He released her with a halfhearted shake, but the tension in his face didn't lessen. "You were being protected. It's my guess that whoever cooperated with Zed's plan, whoever was tampering with the alarm system and cut the wire on the surveillance camera, they made it part of the deal. 'Don't hurt me or the people I work with, and I'll get you in.'"

"Oh, God," she breathed.

"Only someone *did* get hurt. Zed decided he didn't like deals, so he wasted two of your people as a warning to his pawn. 'Screw with me, and this is what you get!'"

She had been trembling with fury a moment ago. Now she quaked with fear, her stomach roiling, her body weakened by guilt and indecision. Who had she left behind in Washington that she never should have trusted?

Chapter 22

Kate stared at the ceiling above the bed, shaken. Rooker's words reverberated through her mind. Accusations. Terrible accusations that had an unfortunate ring of truth to them. And yet she was a scientist, and scientists didn't believe in unproven theories. She had to hold on to that one true thing. Rooker had no proof. He was all hot air and hunches, she told herself.

But was there at least a possibility that someone on her team had betrayed her? Since she couldn't prove otherwise, she had to admit that much. Worse than betraying her personally, though, this spy among them had compromised the entire Heat Wave project and cost the lives of at least one and, most likely, two of her associates.

Disturbing, yes, but the existence of a traitor among them held a warped kind of logic. How else had Zed known of the existence of the satellite and its capabilities? How else would he have known which of three dozen buildings was home to the Heat Wave Command Center? He'd even known that she was Chief Project Engineer, had been given her name by someone. Rooker and Winston had probably assumed this much from the beginning, but it was difficult for her to accept. A traitor.

But Cam? She simply couldn't believe the woman was capable of such deception. Cambridge Mackenzie had no motive for selling out to the Dark Side, as Tommy called all black-hat cyber warriors. Unless…no, she pushed that thought from her mind, but it came back at her again, too insistent to ignore.

Cambridge sometimes complained of the challenge of making ends meet as a single parent. The high cost of living in Washington, D.C., made it ten times worse. Next year she'd be stretching her already tight budget to afford private school for her daughter, Kristi. But then, didn't everyone struggle with household and family expenses these days? Amanda and her husband worked hard to support their three kids. This summer they'd had to cancel the annual family vacation.

But, no. Never Cam, not at any price. Unless…unless Kate didn't know the woman as well as she thought she did. After all, Cam had lied to get her job at NASA. She'd covered up a history of stealing, drugs and prison.

Deeply troubled by these facts, Kate nevertheless tried to turn suspicion in another direction. Vernon Hernandez. Solemn, nose-to-the-grindstone Vern. At thirty years old, he was a quiet, private man. He seemed mature beyond his years.

Falsifying information on a job application could result in his being fired. Maybe Vernon had more to hide than entering the country illegally. He never seemed to get too close to anyone, but he was without doubt considerate, intelligent and well-educated. An asset to the team from the first day he came on board.

But his natural reserve might mean more than shyness or fear of his deception being discovered. Wasn't that the way people often described neighbors or classmates who slipped over the edge into violent fantasies? People who sent letter bombs or opened fire on a crowd of shoppers from atop an office building?

He seemed just like anyone else. Kept to himself, never any trouble.

Then one day "he" flips out and takes out all his frustrations and disappointments on co-workers or strangers in a bloody rampage.

If Rooker was right, Zed had bought one of her people. Or maybe it was even worse than that. What if he'd collected a cult of devoted followers over the years, planting them in top-security installations around the country? Could they have been watching for years for the perfect opportunity to create mayhem?

No, that was too far-fetched. She'd stretched reality too far, surely.

Then again, these days, was any atrocity formulated by one human being to harm others beyond the pale? Years ago, terrorists crashing passenger jets into skyscrapers would have sounded outrageous, like something out of a B movie.

Kate hugged herself in bed. Who could she trust now? Anyone? If the people she had felt closest to in recent years weren't above suspicion, then maybe it was best to trust no one.

Not even Rooker, a voice whispered.

No, not even him.

* * *

After just two hours of shallow sleep, Kate reluctantly pushed herself up off the bed. She was still in her travel clothes. There was no sense in unpacking; she'd brought so little, and who was to say whether she'd be in Rome for a few hours, a couple of days or weeks?

She checked in with her people back in D.C. "I want a report every hour on the hour, day and night, from here on," she told Tommy.

"What if there's been no change?" he asked.

"I don't care. We keep communications open. We talk about anything and everything. You see a blip on your screen, or hear anything suspicious, I want to know about it. Got that?"

"You're beginning to sound like Macho Commando Rooker." He laughed.

"Oh, please," she muttered. "Just keep talking to me. If one of you doesn't check in, I'm going to assume all hell is breaking loose over there."

"Gotcha."

She hesitated. "When is Amanda due in?" It was the middle of the night in Washington, D.C.

"She's here now. She decided to come in a few hours before the kids need to get ready for school."

"Put her on," Kate said. She wasn't sure how comfortable she was with the decision she'd made. But she couldn't figure out another way to address Rooker's mole theory.

"How are you holding up, Kate?" Amanda, always mothering everyone.

"I'm hanging in there. How are the troops?" She tried to sound light-hearted, but the words came out flat and unconvincing.

"Tense. Exhausted. Biting each other's heads off." Amanda lowered her voice. "The FBI has been spending a great deal of time in here."

"Winston?"

"And two other suits. What are they doing here?"

Kate wasn't sure how much she should reveal of Agent Winston's reason for watching her team so closely. On the other hand, if one of them had turned, it might not be a bad thing for that person to know that the Feds were looking over his or her shoulder.

"Amanda, I have a favor to ask of you."

"Sure, honey, anything you want. You know that."

Kate swallowed. "You know how to reach me on my cell phone, right?"

"Tommy and Cam have the number posted in their cubicles. I'll just ask them."

"No," she said clearly, "I want you to go to my desk and look in the middle drawer. Pull out my emergency numbers. The number for the satellite cell I'm carrying is on the list. You may need to call me without anyone else knowing that you're doing it."

There was a long pause from the other end.

Then, "I don't understand, Kate."

If she had to choose one person out of the entire HW-1 team she felt she could trust absolutely, it would be Amanda. The woman would never do anything to endanger her children or result in her being taken away from them.

"I'd like you to keep your eyes and ears open for me. If you notice anyone behaving strangely or doing anything in the least bit questionable, you call me. Immediately."

Amanda sounded hesitant. "If you say so."

"I can't explain." Kate tried to keep the anxiety out of her voice. "Please. Just do this for me. I need to know if anything or anyone sets off alarm bells in your head. You're a mother. You have eyes in the back of your head when your kids are around. Pretend the team there is your kids. Okay?"

"Okay." But she still sounded doubtful.

Next Kate checked in with Homeland Security and, finally, she called Marissa Winston, but only reached her voice mail.

The FBI agent hadn't told Kate that they were now actively staking out the Heat Wave lab, and Kate resented that. She'd tell Marissa so, but she'd do it one on one, not in a recording.

She left a message, giving Marissa her hotel information so that she could be reached if her cell failed to get a signal. She carried an Iridium satellite phone, the same model DOD and the military used. It would find a signal virtually anywhere in the world, but you never knew. Something as uncontrollable as sunspots had been known to interrupt signals between towers.

When she walked out into the suite's sitting room, she found it empty except for Rooker, who appeared to have passed out, still in his working fatigues, on the couch. Apparently everyone else was sleeping in the two other bedrooms. Military types, she'd noticed before, seemed to have no trouble crashing whenever and wherever they had dead time. Until the Carabiniere, with the assistance of the Italian telephone company, hunted down the address of the sending signal, there was nothing the Americans could do.

It wasn't yet 7:00 a.m., Rome time. Kate was wound up so tight she couldn't sleep any more. It would be another hour before her people reported in. She'd go crazy just sitting here. If something happened, they could reach her just as easily in a café down the street as shut up here in the hotel.

She dashed off a quick note and stood over Rooker for a moment, observing the rise and fall of his broad chest beneath the olive-drab shirt. He'd undone the top two buttons for comfort, and he didn't wear an undershirt. His chest looked hard, muscled beneath the pattern of black hair.

It wasn't something she did every day, but standing here over him, she took the time to admire a rather pleasing example of the male physique. So what if he was a jerk sometimes? She could appreciate the anatomy.

Smiling, she placed her note on the cushion beside Rooker's head: *Gone out for something to eat. Back soon, K.*

As Kate stepped out of the hotel lobby and into early-morning Rome, she breathed in the pungent scents of the ancient city.

It was her first time in Rome, and the smells were different from those of any other city in the world. Air-dried linens, the chalky scent of marble steps heated by the sun and still giving off the odors of centuries of *passeggiatas,* the customary evening strolls. The heady, pungent aroma of warm wine, so thick in the air she could taste it when she opened her mouth and breathed in. Fish, even this early in the morning, cooking in an outdoor kitchen. Or maybe it just lingered in the air from the night before. Ripe cheeses, exotic herbs and fermenting yeast from the day's fresh-baked bread.

Everything here was sharp and real, nothing subtle. Rome came at you like a fist, refusing to be ignored even when you closed your eyes.

She gave the streets and shop fronts her full attention and tried not to think about what she'd say when it came time to speak with Cam and Vernon about what she knew and they hadn't told her. In the meantime, was she supposed to simply pretend she didn't know they'd lied to her? And what about the others? Who else among the nearly thirty scientists and techs who worked on the project had kept secrets? Who else had a clandestine agenda?

It would do no good to flog herself with suspicions now. Rooker could sleep; she would escape the tension in her own way. By being on her own for a short time, away from the constant anxiety of the search. Away from Rooker's moodiness. She'd found no time to call her own since the night of the attack on the compound. Healing solitude and this beautiful city would be her small gift to herself.

As she walked, she observed the people around her. Some, obvious couples. Married? Lovers? Strolling with their arms around each other, or hand-in-hand, stealing a final few minutes together before rushing off to their workdays. Others were alone, preoccupied with getting somewhere.

She thought about her own life, so ordered and quiet. Well, it *had* been quiet before all of this.

She couldn't remember the last time she'd had a real date. Not one of those let's-do-lunch things crammed with shoptalk but an honest-to-goodness date with a candlelit meal, white linen tablecloth, dressing up for the occasion and maybe a movie or a stage play after.

One year she'd bought herself season tickets to the National Symphony at the Kennedy Center and loved every delicious performance, even though she'd gone alone. Another year she dated a man who was involved in local theater, and he'd taken her to productions at Wolftrap and Arena Stage.

Then along came Heat Wave and suddenly there'd been no time in her life for anything else.

If the satellite were destroyed, she'd have all the free time she could possibly want for dating and concerts and doing anything she liked.

Kate didn't care. Nothing had ever excited her as much as the pure, exquisitely beautiful science that had opened up to her while she worked for NASA. When the time was right, she'd make room in her life for romance. For the right man. But at this moment, all she wanted was to get her satellite back. And keep the people and the land it hovered over safe.

She passed two cafés, already filling with people on their way to work, stopping for their morning coffee, chatting exuberantly with co-workers, friends, vendors.

Another advantage to getting out of the hotel was removing herself, if only for an hour, from Rooker's mercenaries. It wasn't that she didn't like them. With several she'd shared no more than a few passing words, while Adam continued to flirt. Soon, they all would risk their lives for their country. She needed to separate herself from them, physically now, emotionally later. If she let herself grow too close and had to watch them die, something inside of her would be lost with them.

She simply couldn't bear those dark thoughts. She shut them out, for now.

The city. Rome…Rome…Rome! She allowed herself to be swept up in the flow of pedestrians along the road. She loved people watching.

Ahead on the right, she saw a man searching for a parking space on the crowded street. He stopped his car near a space between two parked cars, no more than half the length of his vehicle. Unfazed, he drove his front wheels into the narrow opening and up over the curb. Thus positioned, the rear bumper only stuck out a little into traffic. He wedged himself out of the car and walked jauntily away.

She laughed in amazement and felt like shouting, "Bravo!" Romans made room where none existed. They drove, parked, walked, lived with gay abandon. Ignoring rules, making their own. Talking with their hands on street corners and in cafés. Angry or laughing, it didn't matter. Emotions flew in the air like pigeons scattering at a passing pedestrian. Rome was a happy place. Or so it seemed to her on this initial glimpse.

Although she'd visited London and Paris for scientific conferences, she'd never had a reason to come to Italy. And now she marveled at the blend of ancient and modern beauty in the city and wondered why she hadn't come here *for no reason at all.* Just to see it should have been enough motivation.

But there had been work, always work. As much as she loved it, her job was a greedy taskmaster. Or maybe it was her, not the job. Hadn't her superiors always needed to remind her to use vacation time? Did she use work to escape from something else?

Kate turned down a street, checked her phone to make sure no message had come through while she was walking. Nothing. She wouldn't go much further, in case she was needed back at the hotel. She still felt restless, but the darkest of her demons had retreated in the bright morning sunlight.

After looping the block and coming out in a pretty piazza, Kate settled on a tiny café with a half dozen marble-top tables arranged on the sidewalk.

A waiter approached her. *"Buon giorno, signorina."*

"Buon giorno. Un tavolo, per favore?" Kate requested, feeling awkward with her stumbling Italian. She'd studied a phrase book on the flight over, but was unable to form the luxurious mouth sounds she heard all around her from natives.

"Subito," the waiter responded. Immediately.

Good, she hadn't flubbed things too badly yet. He brought

her to a table with a good view of the piazza's fountain. The sun felt lovely. She ordered coffee and *"un cornetto,"* a croissant.

She ate slowly, savoring the delicate flakiness and rich buttery flavor of the pastry. The *caffé* was heavenly, rich and dark.

The fountain splashed and children chased a soccer ball around it. Was school in session here this time of year? She had no idea. She smiled to herself, liking the freedom of being anonymous, an uninvolved observer.

"Signorina," said a voice above her.

Kate looked up, startled when she saw it wasn't the waiter. *"Sì?"*

The man was tall and elegant and reminded her of Marcello Mastroianni in a score of old movies. Silver at the temples, a timeless smile, eyes that seduced.

"It is not right for a beautiful woman as yourself to eat alone."

Kate laughed because it was such a worn pickup line and she knew she wasn't beautiful. But it was lovely to hear the words.

They chatted for a while over more coffee—*caffé*—and then, as she got up to go, he asked to walk her back to her hotel.

She smiled and shook her head. "Thank you, no. Friends are waiting for me. I should hurry."

"Hurry on such a beautiful day?"

"I must," she insisted firmly.

A little innocent flirting had seemed safe enough in a public setting. But she wasn't sure she wanted a stranger to know where she was staying or why she'd come to Italy.

"Ciao," she said, cupping her fingers and giving her Roman admirer the backward wave she'd seen Italians do.

He started to protest, but she held up a hand and told a small fib. "Discreet. I must be discreet."

He smiled, no doubt thinking that she was married.

Rooker stood in the shadowed doorway of the *salumeria,* watching Kate. He tried to ignore his complaining stomach as the delicious aromas from the café across the piazza beckoned to him.

Back at the Abruzzi he'd felt her standing over him. What had she been thinking? He wouldn't have put it past her to give him a swift kick in retaliation for the grief he'd been giving her. But she hadn't touched him. For some reason, that was a disappointment.

As soon as he'd heard the suite's door click closed, he'd read her note and swore. No more sleep. He'd followed her to find out what she really was up to.

The first thing he noticed after she'd settled herself in front of the café was how comfortable she looked, sitting alone at the little pedestal table. She didn't wistfully ogle couples nearby, as if she needed a companion to enjoy her meal.

He remembered one of his foster sisters once saying she was never so lonely as when she had to eat alone. Carol had struggled through three disastrous marriages searching for a dining partner. Maybe Kate had the right idea.

Then, just when Rooker had decided her excursion really was innocent and was considering joining her, a man approached her and sat down. Had she arranged to meet him? Who the hell was he?

Rooker glared at them. Maybe he should make an excuse and interrupt them. Tell her that something important had come up and she was needed.

No, he'd see how this played out.

He waited to make sure she wouldn't lead the guy back toward the hotel. If she did, he would have to intercept them. The team couldn't afford to advertise their presence until they located Zed. A whisper of covert operations to the local paparazzi, and reporters would be all over them, warning Zed. For all he knew, the guy could be a reporter.

At last Rooker saw with relief that she was moving off alone. He hung back to make sure the man didn't follow her. Although the stranger cast a regretful eye at Kate's long legs as she walked away, he didn't try to go after her. Rooker tailed her back to the hotel and into the lobby.

He waited until she stepped into the elevator then quickly followed her in and pressed the button to shut the doors before anyone else could join them.

"How was your date, princess?"

She snapped her eyes across at him. "It wasn't a date." She drew her lips tight against her teeth and narrowed her eyes at him. "You were spying on me."

"The rest of the team was instructed to remain in quarters until told otherwise. I ordered breakfast for everyone to be brought up."

"I needed to get some air."

"As well as a Danish and an Italian?" He smirked. Yes, he was provoking her. No, he didn't know why. But it felt damn good.

"Just to get away." Her eyes darted to the floor numbers over her head, as if she were anxious to get off. "All the testosterone in that suite was getting to me."

"That testosterone may save your butt," he commented as the elevator wheezed to a stop on the fifth floor.

She laughed. "Oh, please." And strode off down the hallway.

"What?" He ran to catch up to her. "You think analyzing the situation to death is what will catch Zed? You think tracking him to his lair means the end of it? Someone has to take this guy out! And you'd better hope that whether it's the Carbs or my team or the fuckin' U.N., they're hyped up on adrenaline, hormones and whatever else it takes to stop this creep!"

"Stop shouting," she growled.

"I'm not shouting." Yeah, he was. So what? "I'm trying to make you realize that just because you have a sky-high IQ, that doesn't give you special privileges as far as this mission is concerned!"

She spun to face him. "Let me remind you, Mr. Rooker. I'm the one in charge of this game. *I* decide on the rules. Got that? I didn't lock your gang in the suite. If you think it's necessary to control your men, so be it. But—" she emphasized "—I'm not one of them. *You don't control me!*"

"Maybe not, but I have a right to protect the mission."

She stopped in the middle of the hallway and glared at him. "You're accusing me of jeopardizing the mission by going out for coffee?"

"I'm saying you were getting pretty cozy back there with Romeo. What did you tell him, anyway?"

She pushed past him and continued toward the suite's door. "Too bad you didn't have a wire on me. You could have heard the entire conversation." Her face flushed with anger, she whipped her entry card out of her purse and reached toward the slot in the door lock.

Rooker grabbed her wrist.

She didn't try to pull away, the first mistake women usually make when an attacker moves on a victim. He felt the muscles in her forearm contract then almost immediately relax. She let her arm drop limply to her side, still resting in his grip.

Kate glared up at him, green eyes flashing, but her voice sounded closer to bored than frightened. "Let go."

He immediately loosened his grip, not wanting to hurt her. But the stubborn little boy in him didn't let him release her entirely. "Listen, Doc, I'm not just being nosy. I have to know what you told him."

"Why?"

"Because he could be in league with Zed. We have no idea how widespread this organization might be or even what the organization is."

She closed her eyes and leaned against the metal doorjamb. "Why don't we go inside and discuss this without the strong-arm tactics."

He looked down, remembering that his fingers were still around her wrist. Slowly Rooker opened his hand and was relieved to see he hadn't left a mark. He'd been trained to act fast, on instinct, not logic. Sometimes, he realized, his responses weren't appropriate. This was clearly one of them.

Kate marched into the suite and tossed her purse on the couch, with attitude.

Adam Grabowski, Kent Donnelly, Travis Peterson and Pete Sanchez were sitting, half awake, over coffee at the table. Kip Boyt, the senior member of Rooker's team, was sitting phone duty at the desk by the window. Wade Klein was the only one not in sight, probably back in the room where the team had bunked.

Kate walked a straight course past the group, into her room. She turned in the doorway to crook a finger at Rooker. He followed her inside and she closed the door after him.

"Now, let's try having a real conversation instead of an interrogation," she said, keeping her voice low and under control even though she felt like screaming at the man.

He glared at her. "I need answers. What was the substance of your conversation with that man?"

"It's none of your business."

"It damn well is my business!" he shouted.

And suddenly, the conversation out in the other room got very quiet. She made a show of studying her watch.

"Answer me!" he roared, his face flushing.

Kate dropped all pretense of calm. "Rooker, you're a royal pain in the ass, you know that? I'm telling you—nothing was said to that man that can hurt our mission. I didn't tell him where I was staying or why I was here. Unless he followed me back to the hotel, and I'm pretty sure you made certain he didn't, I'll never see him again. Now what is your problem?"

He leaned into her face. "My problem is *you* putting *yourself* at risk!"

She blinked at him, momentarily stumped. Maybe this wasn't about her personal privacy. "What?"

"You heard me," he grumbled, turning away to trudge toward the window that overlooked the street. Taxis, buses, cars honked and squealed and roared.

"No," she said, "I don't think I did. At least I didn't hear correctly. You were worried about *me?*"

"I'm protecting the mission, that's all. Drop it."

"No, I won't drop it. You were afraid Emilio or someone else out there might attack me or kidnap me or something?"

He raked a hand up the back of his head through his hair and stared out the window with a pained expression. "All I'm concerned about is what's in your head, woman. If they get you, they have your brain...and your brain has information they need. After this is over, you can stroll through the slums of Calcutta at midnight, for all I care."

She stared at him, feeling her pulse thrum in her chest, the steady bump-bump-bump resonating inside her ears. The tips of her fingers prickled with a sensation she couldn't interpret. Why should it matter if he cared at all what happened to her? Or if he did care, what his reasons were.

"You must take me for an idiot," she murmured. "I wouldn't intentionally put myself in harm's way or jeopardize our recapturing Heat Wave."

"You might not have a choice." He turned and looked at her, hard. "Have you forgotten what happened in your lab? Could've been you they gunned down that night."

She bit down on her lip and had to concentrate on steadying her voice before daring to speak. "No, I haven't forgotten. But walking a few blocks in a civilized city in broad daylight is not the same as facing a gun-toting lunatic. You don't give me enough credit, Rooker." She drew a breath. "I'm not helpless."

He let out a huff of air, not quite a laugh. "Right. Well, I just don't want you going missing on my watch."

"Understood," she said.

"Good."

Kate didn't look around to see him leave the room but heard the door shut behind him. She let out a deep sigh, but the tension remained in her body.

Earlier, out in the hallway, she'd aborted her instinctive reaction to his grabbing her arm. If she had allowed herself to follow through, they wouldn't have needed to have this conversation.

His aggressiveness had triggered a chain of mental responses Kate had thought she'd forgotten. Apparently, she hadn't.

Back in college, she and her roommate signed up for a women's self-defense course. The techniques were inspired by the so-called gentle martial art, aikido. Based on the laws of physics and anatomy, it seemed a logical match for a scientist. She'd never needed to use her training, but it gave her the confidence to drive alone into Washington at night and park on the street when the Kennedy Center garage was full up.

Confronted by Rooker, she'd automatically recalled one of the drills: *Soften knees, relax arm, withdraw foot, turn body, palm circles up...* When performed correctly, without hesitation, the maneuver would force an attacker who had grabbed her wrist to fall off balance and release her.

Point for Kate!

But she hadn't followed through. And now she reminded herself that censoring her body's training might prove dangerous, if the risks were real.

Chapter 23

By noon the Italian authorities had launched a door-to-door search of an area in Rome along the river where they believed the phone signal was coming from. Meanwhile, Kate's people at NASA continued to check in with her. Nothing had changed. A signal was still attempting to connect with the Heat Wave's computers, but hadn't succeeded. That might change at any moment.

Time was running out. Zed's deadline was rapidly approaching.

Throughout the day, Italian military, police and government officials moved in and out of the suite as news spread of the Americans' presence. Rumors seemed to race through Rome faster than the Huns.

Soon Rooker had whipped himself into a rage. "Every goddamn crook and malcontent in Italy will know we're here! Whatever happened to 'low profile'?"

"Maybe anyone watching the hotel will just think a law enforcement convention is in town," Adam suggested, sneaking Kate a smile.

"Shit," Rooker said.

At 8:00 p.m. the tension broke when word, at last, came that the Carbs had an address. The team moved out, Kate with them.

Riding toward the suspect building, Kate kept a line open to NASA with Cambridge on the other end. "I need to know everything, no matter how insignificant it seems. I'm worried that Zed might have booby-trapped the apartment or the computer, so that a link or some kind of message to Heat Wave is triggered if anyone tampers with his system."

"Not a happy thought," Cam said.

Kate couldn't agree more. "Have you been able to make any headway in breaking the codes he used to snatch the sat from us?"

"Nothing yet. Everyone's pushing as hard as they can. It looks like a war zone here. No one's had any sleep in days. We're operating on fumes."

Kate sighed, feeling guilty for the few hours rest she'd been able to grab. But there was no way to give her people relief. They were the best, the only scientists in the world with the knowledge of Heat Wave's inner workings. If they couldn't crack Zed's codes no one could.

"Keep at it. Something's got to give soon." She was aware of the others in the car listening in on her end of the conversation. No one else was talking. She sensed the men's anticipation. The closed space began to smell of sour sweat, of fear, which surprised her. Rooker, afraid? Or just hyped up, building energy to do the job he'd been sent to do?

"Tommy wants to talk to you," Cambridge said through the phone.

"Put him on." Kate listened to the young computer scientist rattle off the steps he'd taken in the past hours to break through to Heat Wave.

She'd never before heard him sound discouraged. Every task she'd ever given him had been accepted as a challenge. No, a game. It must have suddenly hit him. This was real life. This time figuring out the puzzle counted, big time.

The penalty for losing would-be lives.

In the Heat Wave lab, they kept passing the phone around, filling her in, updating her one by one. When another idea came to her, she sent them back to try yet again. Another angle, another set of commands that had the slimmest chance of working. Whoever had engineered Zed's takeover and shut them out had known what he was doing.

The Russians, she thought. No. Maybe the Israelis or the Chinese. They all had the technology. But why would they involve themselves in something like this?

As she listened to Vernon's report, Kate let her eyes drift to the window of the unmarked white van in which she rode. Rooker sat on one side of her, Adam on the other, their hard hips pressing against hers. Marco, their translator, rode in front with the driver. All silent.

She reminded herself to breathe. *It will be all right. We'll beat him. Somehow, we'll beat him,* she told herself over and over.

They had less than one hour of daylight left. The city rushed past her: antiquity on fast-forward. The Colosseum, the crumbling ruins of the Forum, marble columns snapped off and left in mammoth chunks, lying like that for hundreds of years.

Kate prayed.

The van turned down broad and voluptuous Via del Corso

with its many monuments and glittering modern shops. As they flashed past the corner of Via della Muratte, Kate caught a breathtaking glimpse of the immense bas-relief sculptures of the Trevi Fountain. Then they turned to the right, into a maze of tiny back streets.

A few blocks farther on, the van came to a residential area cordoned off and guarded by Carabiniere officers, looking crisp and official in their tan uniforms, red stripes up their pant legs, snap-brimmed caps pulled down over foreheads and serious expressions on their faces.

"Wait here." Rooker threw himself into the street as soon as the van stopped. He quickly closed the door behind him.

Kate watched out the window and listened.

An Italian military officer approached. "Signore Rooker?"

"Yes, sir."

They conferred quietly, and Kate only heard a word now and then. "…cleared the perimeter…evacuated lower floors…no danger to civilians." The man spoke excellent English, with very little accent.

As he listened, Rooker slipped off his leather jacket, revealing the Glock beneath it. When he opened the vehicle's door to toss the jacket inside, Kate started to push her way out and past him.

"Better wait," Adam warned. "He won't take you in on the assault anyway."

"The hell he won't!" She signaled their interpreter to join her outside, just in case she needed help in getting her point across.

Looking irritated, Rooker stepped aside to let her out.

Kate ignored him and addressed the Italian officer. "Before any of your people go in," she stated, "they must understand that they can't touch or harm any electronic equipment that might be in there."

The interpreter started to repeat her words in Italian.

The officer waved him off. "I cannot assure anything of the kind, *signorina.* If the shooting starts, there will be no way to protect furniture and such." He looked annoyed at the thought of not being allowed to blow away anything he liked.

"But—" she began.

"Our orders are to apprehend or eliminate these criminals your own government seeks. We will cooperate and do the job."

She shook her head violently. "The memory stick, Rooker. Tell him how important it is!" She swung back to the officer and jabbed a finger into the air. "A satellite…up there. They must have told you about it. It's been stolen. I need this little piece of…this data stick. Without it thousands of innocent people could die!"

"She's serious, Commander." Rooker surprised her by coming to her defense. "These are dangerous people. They have access to a very powerful device that—"

"A bomb?" the Italian's eyes widened. Although a satellite thousands of miles away didn't seem to concern him, a bomb was a concept he clearly understood.

"Worse," she said. "Potentially far worse than any bomb."

He turned back to Rooker. "Your men know what they're looking for?"

"Yes, sir. We'd prefer to take the point, with your permission, of course."

Kate groaned, nearly jumping out of her skin with impatience as the two men jockeyed for position. Get on with it! she begged silently.

Finally, an arrangement was reached. The Italian officer took a contingent of men and disappeared up the street as dusk enrobed the buildings around them. Rooker's men already had piled out of the other two vehicles in their convoy and stood waiting for orders in their night camouflage.

Rooker turned to Kate. "I can't leave anyone with you. I need all of my people. You can stay here in the car until we've cleared the way. I'll get you in as soon as possible. Someone will come for you when it's safe." He signaled Adam to accompany him. The rest of his team split into pairs, apparently knowing what to do, and moved off into the dark with their weapons.

Kate opened her mouth to protest.

"Or," Rooker added, "you can go sit with the Italian comm man in the surveillance van." He pointed a block forward of them. "The blue one, up there."

"I don't need a babysitter!" she snapped.

"Didn't think so, sweetheart." One corner of his lips twitched.

She refused to rise to his teasing and busied herself checking the radio receiver clipped to the waistband of her skirt. A tiny ear bud would keep her in touch with Rooker, in case he found the stick or a reason he needed to consult with her before she could be brought into the building.

He reached out and touched the pin-size microphone clipped to her blouse, his fingers brushing her left breast through the fabric.

"It's fine," she snapped.

"Keep your radio on. Things may sound pretty frenzied in there, but don't worry—" he chuckled "—we'll all be having fun."

"Sure you will." She guessed that the bravado was an intentional cover for nerves.

Still, it infuriated her that he was refusing to listen to her, edging her out again. But if she fought him, he'd leave a man outside to guard her, then he'd be one short inside the building. She didn't want to be responsible for that.

Kate only hoped that, one way or another, by the end of the evening she'd have what she'd come for, and this nightmare would be over.

"Yo, signore, avanti." Rooker waved the translator over. "We may need you."

The man frowned, looking unhappy with the prospect. But he followed docilely along behind Rooker.

Kate paced the pavement beside the van, one ear tuned in to NASA on her cell, the other hearing Rooker's clipped orders to his people, each of his men reporting in as they closed in on the target building and took positions.

Her stomach clenched and she felt vaguely dizzy with anticipation. The street appeared totally empty of human beings now. A cat yowled from somewhere in the dark. From a distance came the motorized murmur of city traffic. Rooker's ear bud was strangely silent. She wondered if the radio was still working.

If anything was worse than violence, it was anticipating it. The next few minutes could be bad. Very bad.

It's like this, she told herself as she paced along the line of empty vans. Circumstances sometimes force you to act against your nature to protect those you care about. You can't always sit back and take whatever comes at you.

This was one of those times.

Suddenly the ear-splitting chatter of firearms burst from the tiny speaker in her left ear. Shouts of warning, orders in English and Italian, crashing sounds, thundering feet…a hundred times worse than at the college campus a few days ago. Even without her radio connection, she could hear the report of guns echoing off buildings.

Kate stood stock-still on the sidewalk. Someone was shouting in her right ear. The phone, she reminded herself. She was still hooked up to NASA.

"What's going on?" Cambridge.

"They're in. No news yet. What about there?"

"Same stuff. We're jammed out, and Zed is still trying to bring up the power systems. So far, no—hold on there."

"What?" Kate shouted into the phone. The noise from the earpiece connecting her to Rooker was so loud she had to pull it out to be able to hear Cam. "Is something happening?"

"Christ, he's connected."

Kate's heart pounded in her chest. She couldn't breathe. "Zed has established control of Heat Wave?"

"He's done it. Powering up now. Looks like a live signal from the sat. The readings are changing fast now."

"If you can't access the satellite, can you at least decipher the commands?"

"It will take time."

"We don't have time!" Kate shouted. In the background she could hear voices in the Comm Center raised, shouting out readings. They were trying to make sense of the encrypted data. "I'm sorry, Cam. It's just…do everything you can."

"I will. I'm leaving the line open now." Then it was empty air in her place.

Kate plugged in Rooker's earpiece again and immediately cringed at the scream of pain that sounded more animal than human. Someone inside the building had been hit.

Please, God, don't let it be Rooker, or Adam or…any one of our boys.

There was another cry.

"Damn."

"What?" Cambridge was back.

"I can't just stand here and not help them." Her eyes burned, and a lump closed off her throat.

"Don't you dare, girl! Only dumb movie characters take chances like that."

But Kate wasn't listening to her.

Rooker had shown her how to use his rifle. What use was learning how to fire the damn thing if she was nowhere near the action?

But if she found herself in a kill-or-be-killed position, what would she do? Could she make a decision quickly? Could she be as ruthless as Zed? Act without hesitation? Even the briefest vacillation of will would put her at a lethal disadvantage.

"Kate," Cambridge was repeating her name over the phone. "Kate, tell me you're not going in while there's shooting."

"I promised Rooker I wouldn't. But I need to get closer, to be ready when they call for me." That, at least, was her excuse for moving down the block.

She ran until she was beyond the row of military and police vehicles. Cambridge was still alternately warning, scolding and threatening her with bodily injury, but Kate had stopped listening.

Now the shouts and shots through the radio were constant and deafening. Tears brimmed in her eyes and spilled over. Rooker, Adam and all the rest, they were in that building. In hell!

Would any of them walk out whole? She'd traveled with them, joked with them, shared cold pizza and long talks to pass the time.

Who among them was dying at this very moment?

She had to find out what was going on in there, but she

didn't want to scream into her mike and distract Rooker or one of his men at a critical moment. Sweat chilled as it trickled down her back beneath her blouse.

Less than a hundred feet away was the surveillance van. The man on duty would be tracking the assault team's progress. But she, a stranger, couldn't just walk in on the Carabiniere officer at a time like this. God knew how he'd react!

Kate looked around the empty street, desperate now. It seemed so strange to see no sign of movement or life in a city like Rome that never seemed to sleep. The dark spaces between streetlights seemed less dense, the shadows clinging to storefronts easier to penetrate. Her gaze swept from the target building to the next one closer to her. It was almost directly across the street from her.

A shoulder-width space between buildings ran back to an alley that she could just make out in the dark, running parallel to the street where she stood.

Just then she caught a glimpse of a figure between buildings. Running. No, darting from shadow to shadow, his body low and compact. Moving hastily away from the besieged building.

Maybe an unfortunate civilian had been left behind in the evacuation and was running for his or her life. It couldn't be one of the assault team; he was moving in the wrong direction.

Kate froze, held her breath, stepped back into the awning-covered entrance of a closed restaurant. Had she been seen?

She watched as the clandestine figure moved slowly out from the rear alley's shelter, toward her and the main avenue. Her heart racing, she pressed herself deeper into the doorway.

The figure stepped out into the street, looking back toward

the sounds of battle. Now she could tell it was a man by his stance and broad shoulders. He wore what looked like an Italian military jacket and hat but they didn't quite match his pants. In the dark, she could make out no facial features.

After a moment, he turned and started walking casually away from the gunfire.

Kate shivered at the sinister specter. What was he doing here when the area was supposed to have been cleared?

Then he passed beneath a street lamp and, for a fraction of a second, the yellow light illuminated the lower half of his face beneath the hat brim. A thick mustache, dark skin, slightly down-turned lips.

A face she would never forget.

Zed.

Chapter 24

Kate stifled a gasp. What should she do? Without a weapon and alone, she had no chance of stopping him.

She waited until he'd moved a little farther on, out of hearing range, then she triggered the send button on her belt radio and urgently whispered into the tiny microphone clipped to her blouse. "Rooker, Zed's getting away. What do I do?"

The cacophony of battle went on uninterrupted.

"Rooker!" she rasped as loudly as she dared, keeping an eye on the departing figure.

Zed was still taking his time, still looking as if he were out for a leisurely evening stroll.

A few blocks farther on there would be the police line, a few officers left behind to make sure no one escaped the raid or wandered back into the neighborhood before it was safe. But if Zed managed to slip past them, he would disappear into the city. And with him, she had every reason to believe, would go the vital data, which she needed to recapture Heat Wave.

She tried her radio again. "Zed is walking north of Via del Tritone. I'm not sure of the street names, a lot of them are narrow and not very well lit. Rooker, do you copy?"

How Zed had escaped from the raided building, she didn't have a clue. But did it matter?

Still no response. Wasn't she operating the damn radio correctly? Maybe the noise from the battle was drowning her out. Or, worse, maybe Rooker had been hit!

Desperate, she looked toward the surveillance van. If the communications man had overheard her message he wasn't responding either. The thing to do was pound on the rear doors and shout that their man was escaping. Let him raise the alarm.

But if she took the time to do that, she'd lose sight of Zed, and precious minutes would be wasted while Rooker extricated himself from whatever action was going on inside the building.

She couldn't risk losing Zed and the memory stick.

There was nothing to do but follow him.

Kate turned toward the departing figure and started walking, just as casually as he. But his strides were much longer than hers, and the space between them gradually widened. She shifted into her exercise pace. Perhaps it would appear she was out for her evening speed walk.

She tried to look intent and athletic, although she wore a skirt-suit and panty hose. Kate ate up the stretch of smooth paving stones as the wind picked up and a light drizzle descended on the city. She looked up and down the street, into narrow alleys for any sign of the police.

Where the hell were they?

She walked faster and faster, all the while hoarsely whispering into her collar. "Rooker, Rooker, Rooker…anybody, do you hear me? It's Kate, I'm following Zed."

Nothing.

She started naming landmarks and reading street names into the microphone, when she could see any, marking her route for anyone who might be listening. "Still heading north, now passing over a narrow footbridge. Crossing a tiny piazza with a circle of statues in the middle. Looks like an abandoned fruit stand up ahead. Anybody there yet?"

What was the range of her signal? She might have already moved beyond Rooker's hearing. She kept walking, hanging as far back as she dared. If she let him get too far ahead, he might slip away. If she clung any tighter to him, he'd hear her footsteps and suspect he was being followed.

She was almost certain they should have run into the police line by now. Then she realized he'd been taking a circular route, as if he intentionally was staying within the protected area. Suddenly she noticed that these streets seemed less affluent than the previous ones. The alleys stank of urine and fetid garbage. Something darted between torn plastic bundles set out on stone stoops.

Zed was just within sight. Then he rounded another corner and disappeared up an alley so quickly her heart leaped in her chest.

She ran toward the corner, hoping he wouldn't turn again before she caught sight of him. A second later she realized how vulnerable she'd be if she stepped around that same corner and he was waiting there for her.

She stopped and stood very still, trying to think of a way to handle the situation. What would a cop tailing a suspect do? Keep on walking, she thought. Pass the corner without hesitating or looking down the side street. Move fast, as if she had no intention of turning there. Then find another route to intersect with his.

Just to be safe, she crossed the street so that she'd be on the opposite side. At least then, if Zed were lying in wait, he couldn't reach out and grab her. On the other hand, if he had a gun, she'd be out in the open as she passed the mouth of the alley.

No, she absolutely had to keep moving or lose him entirely.

Kate became aware that the commotion over the radio had settled. The shooting had stopped. She could hear harsh, stressed breathing. Rooker's? Men started calling out to each other, checking in:

"Adam here."

"You whole, boy?" Rooker's voice.

"Not a scratch. Sanchez and Donnelly are with me."

Then it was like a roll call, including the Italians and ending with Rooker's report, "I have two perps in the basement. One dead, one wounded, we need an ambulance. Anyone find Zed?"

"I have him!" Kate whispered into her mike. She'd already passed the alley and kept on moving.

"What? Who's that?" Rooker again. Confused. Everyone else silent.

Kate smiled at his shocked tone. "It's me, Kate. I'm following Zed. Where the hell is my backup?"

She could imagine Rooker trying to place her in the building. "I thought I told you—"

"I'm north of your location," she said. "Zed slipped past you. He's wearing what looks like an Italian officer's uniform jacket. Our local friends may have lost a man."

"What the hell do you think you're doing?" Rooker bellowed so loudly she had to pull the bud out of her ear for a moment or go deaf on that side.

"Pass by the vans and keep going another block then take the first left then another left." Was there one more? She couldn't remember. "I'm just past the fruit stand. He's disappeared down an alley that curves out of sight. I'm going up the next street to see if I can intercept him."

"The hell you are!" Rooker yelled. She could tell by his breathing that he was running. Toward her, she hoped.

Other voices broke in, asking what he wanted them to do.

He barked out orders to the surveillance van, to their translator for the benefit of the Italians, to his own men. "No sirens. Silent approach. Do nothing to alert him. And Foster, you stay right where you are. Don't move!"

Did he think she'd worked this hard to keep their quarry in sight only to let him disappear into the night? She kept on moving.

She began to see other people on the street. But still no sign of the police. She couldn't understand how they'd managed to leave the secured area, but obviously they had. Perhaps back at the little footbridge, which seemed to have taken her below the main street level then back up on the other side.

A few cars sped past her. She looked both ways then crossed. Three young men lounged on the next corner despite the thin rain, smoking cigarettes and laughing. They gave her a long look. One made boyish kissy sounds. The others laughed louder, whispered, elbowed each other.

When one of them tossed down his cigarette and took a step toward her, she made a sharp slicing motion with the edge of her hand and walked briskly on. To her surprise, it worked. He hesitated, looked back at his friends, then turned away.

She rushed on, wiping raindrops out of her eyes, still not seeing Zed. Had he lost her?

Through open windows she heard voices arguing, the sound of car tires squealing from a TV drama, a baby crying, a woman letting out a high-pitched wail—of agony or ecstasy, she couldn't tell.

Frantic now, Kate searched for an opening between buildings that might lead her to the other end of the alley into which Zed had disappeared but saw none. She broke into a run. No streetlights at all here. No visible street names. Darkness hugged her. Her own footsteps echoed, duplicating themselves. Or was the second set just a little faster, a little weightier? The street began to climb.

Then she saw it in the dim light from a low window. A very narrow passageway between gray stucco buildings. It was only wide enough for two people to walk through, shoulder to shoulder, and not level but formed of stone steps so ancient the passage of feet over centuries had worn a hollow in the center of each one, now puddled with rain water.

Kate stood for a moment, suddenly less sure of herself. She might have lost Zed already. She took two steps up the narrow stairs.

"Rooker, are you anywhere near?" she whispered.

"Closing on your last stated location. Stay put."

"He'll get away."

"Stay—"

An indistinct shuffling sound turned her attention to the stairs above. Footsteps were coming down the hill out of the dark at a rapid pace. She pressed back against the damp moldy wall just as a young boy darted past her. Trembling with relief, she released a held breath.

"Kate, where the hell are you? I can't see you, dammit!"

She hadn't told him about her last turn.

Leaning one shoulder against the wall to face the street,

she brought her lips down to her collar to murmur instructions. It was then that she felt the presence behind her.

A hand snaked around and clamped hard over her mouth, driving her teeth into the tender flesh inside her upper lip. She tasted the metallic saltiness of her own blood. Strong arms dragged her up steps, deeper into the narrow space between crumbling building walls.

"Dr. Kate," a voice hissed in her ear, "you are out much too late for your health."

She swallowed blood.

That voice. Zed's.

Wrestling with the man would gain her nothing. She let her body go slack, waiting for a next opportunity. A slight change in his grip. A moment when he reached for a weapon.

At least he didn't have a knife at her throat. It could have been worse. Though not much.

"You should leave the spying to the professionals," he snarled. This was a different Zed, without the thick Eastern accent. The Philly street punk was back. "Maybe I should have, too." He laughed. "But the money was too damn good."

What would he do to her?

"So are you alone?" he asked.

Her mind raced. He didn't release his hand from her mouth to get an answer. She shook her head.

"No? How many? And if you scream, you die. *Capisce?*" She could hear his pleasure in using a word he'd probably picked up from a TV mob movie. "Whisper," he said. Thick, oily fingers unrolled one at a time from her lips.

She breathed in and tasted his sweat. Was he at all worried? The suspicion that he might be capable of fear, the same way Rooker had been but refused to show it, made her braver. "Ten men…maybe more."

"Is that s-s-so-o-o." The final word lingered, a reptile's hiss in her ear. "You are a crappy liar, Dr. Kate. Two blocks. That's all it took. I knew you were on my heels. Another, I was sure you were alone."

So he'd intentionally led her away. Trapped her by circling down the alley and beating her to this deserted place when she thought she was being so clever and outfoxing him.

She blinked, feeling his left arm painfully tight around her ribs, the fingers of his right hand having shifted from her lips to her throat. A single word shouted for help, and he could easily silence her, forever.

Then her radio burped and crackled. Kate went rigid.

"Ah, yes. I thought so." He reached down and ripped the tiny mike clip off her blouse, the wire and earpiece going with it.

Even as the bud was moving away from her in his big hand, she could hear Rooker's voice reaching faintly out to her. "Kate, location. Repeat your loca—"

Zed tore the radio unit from her skirt waistband and threw it down on the pavement. He ground the little black box beneath his boot, chuckling to himself. "Not exactly the cavalry, are they?" But something caught his attention, and he shot a wary glance toward the end of the street.

A shadow passed in front of the alley's mouth, momentarily blocking the dim light from the street before moving on, distracting Zed. Her chance.

She let the muscles in her legs go limp, and fell like a rock straight down toward the pavement as she screamed, "Rooker!"

Zed must have been prepared for her to try and break away from him and run. The unexpected descent to his feet took him by surprise.

The fabric of his coat helped her slip out from between his body and arm, down to the rain-slick stones. When he bent forward to reach for her she braced her legs like springs, locked them and shot up at an angle, aiming the hard top of her head for his crotch.

Zed let out an agonized shriek that echoed down the alley walls. Clutching himself, he staggered sideways.

Kate scrambled on hands and knees down steps, over rubble, broken stone, garbage. She kept on screaming a mixture of Italian and English, hoping someone would respond, "*Assassino!* Rooker, help! *Polizia!* Rooker, here!"

The end of the alley suddenly was no longer visible, as if something had blocked it. Frantically, she struggled to her feet and tried to run. A hand clasped around her ankle, and she went down with an audible crack. Pain shot through her knees and jaw, but she managed to twist around and kick with her free foot. The heel of her shoe connected with something hard.

She heard teeth clack and grind. The fingers released.

Then, somehow, she was up on her feet again. Running down steps, two at a time. Nerves all the way up her back tingling with the premonition of Zed's big hands seizing her from behind. But they didn't, and she kept on running even as shapes flashed past her in the dark. Men running hell-to-pay in the other direction. Bursting into the street, she plowed into the side of a Carabiniere sedan.

Kate collapsed against the vehicle, gasping, seeing stars.

Hands grabbed her by the shoulders.

She fought them off, fists flying, fingernails clawing. But, at last, the words shouted at her began to make sense.

"Kate! You're all right. It's Rooker. We've got you now." He pinned her to his chest, as much for self-defense as to calm her. "You're safe. It's over."

Chapter 25

But it wasn't. Not by a long shot.

By early morning, Kate sat with a mug of hot tea cupped between her palms, Rooker's leather jacket draped over her rain-drenched blouse and chilled shoulders. Adam stood beside her as she stared through a one-way mirror into the police interrogation room where they'd brought Zed.

Three Italians, one she suspected might be the equivalent of a state prosecutor, the other two Carabiniere, pressed into the closetlike space with them. On the other side of the window Rooker and two other cops were questioning Zed with what appeared to be little success.

The data stick hadn't been found on him or anywhere in the raided building. To her dismay, NASA verified that the satellite was now fully under foreign control. The on-board computer had been moved out of Safe-Hold and was responding to signals sent by an antenna on the Adriatic coast.

Kate slanted a quick look at Adam. He looked years older than he had a few days ago. He'd come through the raid with bruises on his face and arms, and a cut that had required stitches dangerously close to one eye. All this despite his comment about not having a scratch. But Travis Peterson had taken two rounds, one in the throat, one in the thigh. He was in critical condition at the hospital. Rooker wasn't happy.

Before capturing Zed in the alley, his team and the Italian police had rounded up three more men who seemed to know nothing about the satellite or the data stick. They claimed they'd been hired by Zed for protection.

"I still don't understand what those men thought they were protecting him from," Kate said.

Adam squatted down beside her chair. "He told them he was an American entrepreneur afraid of being kidnapped."

"Really."

"Yeah. It probably made sense to them. Snatching and ransoming businessmen is considered a legitimate business in some parts of the world. It's definitely profitable."

Kate took another sip of tea and concentrated on what was going on in the interrogation room. Rooker stood facing Zed, who was shackled to a chair leg and in handcuffs. The Italians looked on grimly but they seemed to be getting nowhere.

"This could take a long time," Adam said. "You sure you don't want me to take you back to the hotel?"

"No." She studied Zed's expression. He had been on the verge of killing her. Only his delight in tormenting her briefly before he did it had given her the opportunity to escape. "He doesn't look at all worried that we've caught him."

"He thinks he's tough shit," Adam said, then blanched. "Sorry, Doc."

She smiled weakly and looked at her watch. Back in D.C. it was already morning. Zed had given them until noon to make payment. Would his threat be carried out regardless of his capture?

"If we'd only found the stick on him," Adam said.

"By now, I'm not sure it makes any difference."

He frowned at her. "Why not?"

Kate sighed. "Now that they're in, they don't need the information on the stick. And, if Zed did in fact plant a laser to direct the microwave energy, then all he needs to turn it on is a simple telephone connection. It's my guess he's looking smug right now because he's already instructed someone to do that for him."

Adam shook his head. "Then we're beat."

"Maybe not. Signaling the laser is only the first step." Still, she felt as if hope was steadily slipping away.

Rooker stepped out of the interrogation room, just as the three Italian officials left the observation cubicle. He must have heard the tail end of her conversation with Adam. His frown deepened. "You think by taking Zed we haven't stopped his plan?"

"I'm afraid so." She brought him up to speed on her thoughts about their status. "They're bouncing the signal from an antenna here in Italy over to another one in the U.S. since they can't reach Heat Wave directly from here. Probably using another satellite to make the Atlantic connection."

Rooker glowered at her. "You got any more cheerful news for me?"

"Not news…just thoughts." She stared through the one-way glass at Zed. "Look at him, Rooker."

"Yeah?"

"How would you rate that man's intelligence after talking to him for an hour?"

Rooker grinned at her. "He ain't no rocket scientist."

She made a face at him. "Exactly. Which means he probably had very little to do with the planning that went into the satellite-jacking. When he grabbed me, he said something about the money being too good."

"So, he was just a hired gun. We sorta guessed that much from his background."

"That leaves open the question of who is behind this. Remember how after nine-eleven we heard that the preparation that went into that attack must have been complex? This is no less so. It must have taken years to work out the details. It's brilliant even if it is warped."

"But you're getting a jump on them." Rooker watched her expression. "You're figuring it out, right?" He almost sounded impressed.

"I'm not seeing every move fast enough," Kate confessed. "Someone, an unfriendly country with one hell of a grudge against the U.S.—or al-Qaeda, or maybe the PLO—has supplied the brains behind this. Yeah, it's about money, but it's more than that. I just wish we knew what Zed knows."

Rooker tucked his hands into his rear pants pockets and rocked back on his heels. "Want me to beat it out of him?" he offered helpfully.

She stared at him, not at all sure he wasn't serious.

"I think the Italians would do it in a minute, if I let them." He glanced behind him through the window. One of the officers was leaning over the table, shouting in Zed's face. "They're pretty pissed off, him using their city as a staging ground for an attack."

"No doubt." She sighed and stared down into her empty mug. "Rooker, it's time we faced it. They've been two jumps ahead of us all the way. There's no reason to think, now that they've established control of HW-1, they won't use it. Whatever they intend to do, it's going to happen, with or without Zed."

He turned away from her for a moment, as if letting all the deadly consequences of her words sink in. When he looked back at her, he still appeared worried, but something had altered in his rough features.

"Sorry," he said brusquely.

She frowned. "For what?"

"I've been giving you a bad time from the start, and not nearly enough credit. We wouldn't have Zed now if you hadn't followed him." He hesitated. "Sometimes, I can be a jerk."

Adam looked away, and she guessed he was hiding a smile.

"Yes, you can," she said. "Why don't you tuck away that part of your personality for later, after we get my sat back."

"I'll try." He gave her a crooked grin that quickly washed away. "We've missed our window of opportunity, haven't we? Four more hours to their deadline, and the U.S. government isn't paying. It's official. I just got word from ASEC."

She pulled his jacket tighter around her shoulders, scared out of her mind for the innocents at the other end of Heat Wave's powerful energy. "All we can do now is wait," she murmured.

"No." He glanced over his shoulder at Zed. "I think I need to nurture a more forthcoming conversation with our prisoner."

Kate didn't ask how he intended to do this. She decided she didn't want to know.

Chapter 26

Kate and the Worldwide Security team, less one hospital-ized member, returned to the hotel, licking their wounds and demoralized.

"We haven't failed," Rooker tried to reassure them. "We did what we came to do, capture Zed. The rest of the job is just on hold. We'll get the bastards, just not today."

But Kate could hear the disappointment in his voice and feel his anxiety, a mirror of her own. In less than an hour the deadline would pass. If Zed's employers carried out their threat, hundreds, possibly thousands of people would be in-jured or killed. And she could do nothing to stop them.

She showered and changed into a warm-up suit to wait for news from the States. Her knees and chin were scraped and bruised. Her neck felt wrenched from Zed's strong grasp. But these seemed small things when she looked at the battering Rooker's men had taken. When she thought about the suffering of others to come.

More than anything Kate wanted to call her folks. But any contact with anyone outside of the mission was strictly forbidden.

She walked out into the suite's sitting room to find Rooker at the table near the kitchenette, the phone in front of him. He was staring it down, as if he expected it to leap up and attack him. She set her freshly charged cell phone on the table beside it and sat in the chair next to his.

"Wanna race?" he muttered.

She played along with his sarcasm. "My people will call before your people."

Why did humans in times of great stress fall back on humor? *And sex,* she added silently. After funerals, disasters, and a multitude of other emotionally devastating situations. Friends or even complete strangers sometimes took comfort in the intimate touch of another human being. Was it just a distraction from the pain?

Something raw and needy tugged from within her. She glanced at Rooker, then quickly away. A sensation of warmth spread up from her bottom. She squirmed a bit on the chair to make it go away.

Rooker stared at her. "Something wrong?"

"Umm…no." She grimaced, embarrassed. Such thoughts! What had gotten into her?

When she met his eyes again, they were a deep, disturbingly perceptive blue. She looked away quickly.

"Well, well," he said.

She slowly drew a breath. "Well, well, what, Rooker?"

"Your pheromones are glowing, Doc."

"Where'd you learn a big word like that?" she snapped back but couldn't look him in the eye.

He didn't respond. What was the man thinking? She couldn't let it go. "And yours?"

"What do you think?" An invitation to check him out.

Kate bit cautiously down on her bottom lip, still raw from her confrontation with Zed. Slowly she turned to face Rooker.

He lounged in the wooden chair, long, blue-jeaned legs straight out in front of him beneath the table. Boots crossed at the ankles. The image of a man at ease.

But she could feel heat radiating off him. And an underlying tension in the muscles of his body telegraphed lust.

Her gaze drifted to his lap for an instant then away. "Oh."

"All your fault."

Okay, she thought. The right thing to do now is get to your feet, pick up your phone and walk calmly out of the room.

But then she'd feel she'd surrendered something to Rooker by avoiding the issue—their shared arousal. She forced herself to meet his gaze.

"Do you get this way after every battle?" she asked conversationally.

"Most of them." A whisper of a smile. "There isn't always an appealing partner to help out with the release mechanism."

She opened her mouth. Closed it. Tried again to come up with something witty. Nothing.

"What about you, Doc? After discovering a new star or launching a probe to Saturn, you feel sexy? Jump some physicist's bones?"

"Rooker—"

"Took it too far? Huh." He shrugged but didn't look at all remorseful. "Well, any time you feel the urge to celebrate, you know where to find me."

"Sure." She laughed, hoping he'd think she was taking it all as a joke.

But when she glanced back at him, he wasn't smiling. He reached out and touched his finger to her lips, once, lightly. "You won't forget."

"No," she whispered. "No, I won't forget."

The call they'd all dreaded came at twenty minutes after noon, Rome time—6:20 a.m. on the U.S. East Coast.

Kate's satellite cell rang, and Rooker turned immediately to her before looking down at the phone on the table.

"It's NASA," she said when her lab's number came up on the screen. She picked it up, pressed the speaker button so that others in the room could hear. "Foster here."

"It's happened." Cambridge, sounding out of breath.

Rooker swore.

Kate closed her eyes. "God help us." She couldn't breathe, her chest felt so tight. "Rooker's here with me. What's going on?"

"The target wasn't a specific town or city as we'd expected."

"What then?" Rooker barked.

Kate pressed a hand to his shoulder, urging patience she knew neither of them had.

"Microwave surges disrupted then shut down the major power grid serving the eastern U.S. So far it looks as though at least ten states and all major cities, including New York City, Boston, Philly, D.C. and Atlanta, are without power. It happened about half an hour ago."

Kate thought, the Department of Energy must be freaking out.

Rooker looked puzzled. "So it's not that bad, right?" Behind him, his team gathered to listen in. "I mean, people can live without their lights for a while. Happens all the time after a bad storm."

Kate shook her head solemnly. He didn't get it. "We're not just talking about doing without the AC or TV for a few days. If the energy from Heat Wave was sufficient to knock out the grid, it's also interfering with every vital electrical system."

Cambridge continued. "Homeland Security has started to hear from hospitals and metro transit systems. Air traffic control at Kennedy and Dulles are down."

"Operating rooms and life support in critical care units can switch to their generators for a limited time." Kate was thinking out loud now, focusing on the phone, her lifeline to the people at home who needed her.

She'd failed them. Dammit! Why hadn't she seen this coming?

Kate stared at Rooker. Her voice cracked but she forced an explanation. "Anything electrical is affected by high-level microwave emissions. Pacemakers, medicine released through implanted dosing mechanisms. People are dying over there!"

Cambridge broke in. "We're coming up with coordinates on the laser. Homeland Security has ordered its destruction."

"Good. That will effectively remove Heat Wave's tracking capability. Without the beam to follow, it won't be able to target the energy to the ground."

"Until they deploy another laser?" Rooker said.

"Right. But we'll at least have bought some time."

Rooker's expression was lethal. This was a man the wise person wouldn't push too far. Zed had already crossed that line.

Kate pressed aside thoughts of what he'd do to the people behind this nightmare if he ever laid hands on them.

"Is Special Agent Winston there?" she asked.

"Yeah, how'd you know?"

"I had a feeling she'd stay close to the action. Put her on."

Marissa Winston's voice sounded grim and half an octave lower than the last time Kate had spoken to her. "How are you holding up, Kate?"

"A little battered, but okay, I guess."

"I heard you went in for a little hand-to-hand combat last night?"

Kate laughed wearily. "Not my choice." It wasn't a topic she wanted to dwell on. Besides, now there were more important issues. "Are there fatalities yet?"

"Too soon to say. I've just checked with Johns Hopkins and Washington Adventist hospitals. They're beginning to get some E.R. admissions but haven't had enough time to evaluate the causes. We expect serious radiation burns to anyone in the immediate area struck by the microwave emissions. That's the Hudson Power Station, upstate New York. The Red Cross has been alerted."

Kate nodded and pressed a hand over her eyes. The elderly, infants and, possibly, fetuses in the womb would be most vulnerable. But direct exposure to high-intensity microwave energy could kill anyone.

Winston continued speaking, but all Kate could focus on was the misery she might have prevented.

"Kate, you still there?"

Rooker cleared his throat. "The doctor has been through hell, Agent. I think she needs to be relieved of her position as—"

"No!" Kate objected, although she was even now fighting back tears. "This is *my* responsibility."

Marissa's voice came across low, solemn and controlled.

"Kate, you didn't do this. Creeps with no respect for human life did it."

"You don't understand. If I'd ever once thought that I might be creating a weapon, I'd never have supported this project. I believed I was doing only good." She gasped, holding on, so close to the edge.

Kate sensed Rooker waving the men away from them. They silently retreated to the other end of the room. His hand rested on her back, reassuring, but unable to make things better.

"It's not your fault," Winston repeated. "Rooker, you there still?"

He leaned toward the phone. "Yeah, here."

"Get that woman into bed. See that she gets some rest. We're going to need her."

"The first part I can do. Whether or not she'll get any sleep is—"

"Not funny, Rooker!" Winston growled.

"Yes, ma'am. Are we to stay in Rome or ready up to move out again?"

"As soon as I know anything more, I'll let you know. Meanwhile, sit tight."

Kate slid out from beneath Rooker's hand. "Marissa, I should come home and be with the team in Heat Wave lab. It might make a difference."

The agent seemed to consider this for a moment. "No. They're on top of things here. You're most valuable sticking with the search team. When Rooker nails down whoever is behind this, you still need to be there to handle the technical stuff. You know the satellite better than anyone."

"Yes," she agreed, heartsick and feeling helpless, regardless of the compliment. "Yes, I do."

"We can't let them win, Kate."

"I know." But it was hard. So very hard. Because, when all was said and done, sometimes the dark side did win.

Three hours later they had a preliminary casualty count. Directly related to radiation sickness: four hundred hospitalized, twenty-six DOA. Police, fire and rescue workers were evacuating the area bombarded by microwave rays as quickly as possible. Other injuries and accidental deaths attributed to the strike on the power grid numbered in the thousands, all up and down the East Coast of the U.S. The entire country had panicked. Congress demanded to know the facts behind the attack. The President was being criticized by the press for not acting, and his political opponents were already talking impeachment.

Kate stayed with Rooker and his men in the suite, refusing to rest, turning down everything but a cup of hot tea while they waited out the hours. Finally, the laser was located and destroyed. But, as Kate had pointed out, that would only buy them limited time.

As she stared out the window at the streets of Rome, a city that had survived invasions throughout all of civilized time, her determination to prevent further suffering doubled.

She would find a way to take back what was hers or destroy it. Or die trying.

Chapter 27

Rooker didn't wait for Washington to provide new intelligence and tell him where to deploy his team next. As far as he was concerned, the government had blown it with its ridiculous noncompliance stance. Not that he thought extortionists should be rewarded for their efforts. Far from it.

To his way of thinking, you didn't play fair with the Hitlers and al-Qaedas of the world, you played them. Told them, "Yeah, sure, you'll get your money. Yup, we're so scared, we'll hand over a country or two."

Promise them the world. Match lies for lies, deceit for deceit. That was the only way to outfox the devil.

Rooker had lured, trapped, captured or killed a dozen Zeds, and worse. When it came down to the moment of truth, some chose not to be taken alive, others possessed egos so immense they believed they could outfight anyone. He pulled the trigger, and lost no sleep over it.

You didn't go after maniacs and killers half-assed. You went at them as hard as you could. Because if you didn't, they sure as hell would keep on bringing misery to the world and loving it.

Yes, he'd known from the beginning that calling Zed's bluff by refusing to pay the ransom was a mistake. As it turned out, the cost in human lives and loss to the American economy was far greater than the ten million he'd asked.

Worse than that, Rooker was certain that this was only the beginning. There would be higher demands made by whoever had taken over for Zed in the organization, and other strikes. Maybe far more destructive.

Meanwhile, it would take weeks to fully restore the damaged electrical grid. Any unfriendly country observing this weakness might see it as an opportunity. Take advantage of the temporary paralysis of the American government and economy. A country without communications or reliable transportation was a veritable sitting duck.

His country was a sitting duck!

That was why he'd contacted a man as dangerous as Antonio Ricci.

Rooker had first met Ricci in Naples, nearly ten years earlier. After leaving Iraq and cutting his ties with the CIA, he'd done some freelance work for Ricci, before starting his own business. On the surface, Ricci ran a legitimate Rome-based private investigation and security service that provided protection for Italian industrialists, bankers, politicians and visiting celebrities. Fortunes were being made, these days, in security. Italy was no exception.

But Ricci played the game with a twist. People who chose to hire bodyguards from competing services sometimes ended up being kidnapped anyway, their families running in desperation to Ricci for help in recovering their loved one. Curiously, Ricci had an extremely high success rate of working out deals with kidnappers and bringing home victims. Usually in one piece or, at least, with nothing more vital missing than a finger or two.

Rooker suspected that a good chunk of the ransom money often ended up in Ricci's pocket, along with the substantial finder's fee.

However, the Italian could be useful because he knew how to find virtually anyone in Italy, and so Rooker contacted him. When he was invited to drive out to meet with Ricci in his villa in the Sabine Hills, he rented a car and drove the thirty kilometers to Tivoli, passing beyond the industrial areas immediately outside of Rome and through travertine quarries and then the gray-green olive groves that climbed the ancient hills where the wealthiest of Romans, two thousand years ago and more, had built their homes to get away from the pressures of city life. When he reached Ricci's estate, he was amused to find it patterned after the Emperor Hadrian's villa, which happened to be not far away.

"Diabolico!" Ricci exclaimed, looking properly disgusted by the actions of Zed and his gang when Rooker had enlightened him. He sighed. "But these *criminali* you seek, they may have left the country by now."

They sat beside one of three outdoor pools surrounding the villa, sipping Camparis in the sunshine. Several nubile young women decorated the patio. Reaching for an almond biscotti, Rooker wondered if the man considered all of them his mistresses. An interesting fantasy—worth dwelling on another time.

"It would be the logical thing, to keep moving," he agreed.

Ricci peeled a blood orange. The patio around him was littered with the red-flecked skins. He ate them constantly.

"A pity. I'd like to be in on this." No doubt the entrepreneur saw a good possibility of profit. "I resent outsiders. Besides, I've had good customers among Americans. I wouldn't like to see my clients toasted." His gaze fell placidly over the pool, observing one of the young women diving into the clear blue water as he ate the juicy fruit.

"I was hoping you might circulate word of our problem through your associates. They might listen for anything helpful from the streets," Rooker said. "Bragging is half the fun of pulling off something this big. Someone involved will want others to know."

"An indiscreet word in a bar?"

"Or in bed." Rooker knocked back the rest of his Campari. He was a vodka martini man, but the stuff had a bitter kick to it that wasn't half bad. "This isn't the kind of effort that could be mounted without involving more people than just Zed and the two thugs he brought with him into the NASA installation."

"*Sì,*" Ricci murmured, turning back thoughtfully to his guest. "Those four men you took in the raid in Roma. They were of a local *banda*. No brain, just muscle. This Zed, I do not know."

"He's definitely an American. And not the brains behind this either. Whoever is ultimately responsible for the satellite-jacking won't be the one to talk. The henchmen might."

Ricci nodded. "I will let you know."

"It has to be soon," Rooker reminded him.

"Of course." Ricci smiled and tossed a crimson skin over his shoulder. "I will do this for you, my friend, as a personal favor."

Rooker winced. Being indebted to Ricci wasn't a comfortable position to be in. Unfortunately, he had no choice.

Chapter 28

Kate looked up from her folded arms. She'd fallen asleep on the couch. Someone had thrown a spare blanket over her.

Adam was cleaning his weapon, sitting in the armchair nearest to her. The suite was quiet.

"Where is everyone?" she asked, pushing herself up and stretching. Her gaze automatically slid to her cell phone. No messages. But no news, in this case, wasn't necessarily good news.

"Rooker gave them shore leave."

She smiled. "Watch out, women of Rome!"

Adam grinned. "Yeah. The boys are a little wound up."

"Why aren't you out with them?"

He shrugged. "I had stuff to do." He nodded at his Glock and the Steyr.

She didn't point out that he had plenty of time to tend to firearms. He'd been looking out for her.

"And where's Rooker?"

"He said he had a meeting."

A meeting of the same sort as his men? she wondered.

"I think I'll take a walk to wake myself up. Or has your boss ordered you to keep me here?"

Adam looked unsure whether he should answer or not. "You might want to be sure you take your phone."

"Will do," she said and went off to find her athletic shoes.

As it happened, she ran into Rooker on her way out, in the lobby. "We need to talk," he said, taking her arm as she stepped off the elevator.

"I was going to get some exercise. Can we do that while talking?"

"No problem."

By the end of the first block Kate had revved up to a long, loping stride, her arms pumping at her sides. By the middle of the second she'd hit her normal workout pace and Rooker had to break into a jog to keep up with her.

"So, what do we need to talk about?" she asked.

"I have to know what will happen if we can't run to ground these perps and General Kinsley gets his way after all."

"You mean, if it comes down to destroying the Heat Wave?"

"Right."

She assumed since Rooker wasn't off chasing down new leads with the Carabiniere, they'd gotten nothing useful out of Zed—such as who had enlisted him or who the others were in his organization.

"I don't believe the White House will let him," she said. "But if Homeland Security gave the nod, and the President went along with it, their best bet would be to put a missile in a trajectory that matches Heat Wave's." She hated to even think of this option, but it was something they all had to consider.

"So he can get close enough to blow it up?"

She shook her head. "In movies people blow up stuff like meteors and invading spaceships. You can't really do it that way when there's no atmosphere. Explosives don't work the same way they do here on Earth."

"So how does a missile take out a satellite?"

"Probably they're working on a collision plan. Ram the satellite with something bigger, destroy it that way."

He thought about this. They wove around slower-moving pedestrians, Kate murmuring an occasional *"Mi scusi!"*

"And I gather from what you've said before, the little pieces left over don't just flutter to Earth like harmless snowflakes."

"They don't do anything, actually. As long as they're in orbit, the wreckage keeps circling in the same path. Besides, there are all sorts of international implications we haven't even begun to think about."

"Like who owns what orbital paths?"

She glanced at him, surprised. "Impressive, Rooker."

"I do use something other than a gun to think with sometimes."

"I'm sure you do," she said, dropping her eyes down his body meaningfully.

He grinned. "That, too."

She shook her head at him, keeping her stride fast and hard. "I'm sure."

"So what international problems?" he asked.

"The missile might accidentally strike another country's satellite. That could be interpreted as an act of war."

"Right. But if it was done right, if it did demolish Heat Wave, you could just abandon the remains up there. That would avoid the danger you mentioned back in D.C.—the possibility of wreckage falling on populated areas."

She shook her head. "Orbital space is too valuable. We already have more than eight hundred satellites circling Earth, launched by dozens of governments and private companies. It's too dangerous to leave junk floating around."

They crossed another street. He was breathing easily, keeping up with her now with no noticeable effort. "So how do you clean house up there?"

"Do you remember the satellite the U.S. intentionally brought down that made the news a few years back?"

"The one that crashed into the Utah desert?"

"Right. It had collected immensely valuable material. We'd hoped to learn a great deal from it when we retrieved it. We still had full control of the computers, so we altered the trajectory and brought it back within our atmosphere. Parachutes were supposed to slow its return to the ground."

He nodded. "They even had a crew of Hollywood stunt guys who were supposed to snag the thing from a plane as it descended, to keep it from getting busted up."

"Right. But the 'chutes never deployed, and it hit full force. Nearly disintegrated on impact and left one heck of a crater."

"You could do that with the HW-1, couldn't you?"

"Yes, but we first have to regain computer control. And it would be a very tricky job. The HW-1, with all its gear attached, is half the size of a football field. Can you imagine what would happen if it survived reentry? What if the calculations were off and it came down in Brooklyn?"

"Or in China or the Middle East somewhere. Talk about causing an international incident! Dangerous toys, these," he mumbled.

"Exactly." She was starting to breathe harder now, and it felt good. Moving, doing something instead of sitting in the room, energized her mind as well as her body. "I think our only real hope still is to find whoever is controlling Heat Wave."

"What if in the process of catching up with them, we end up killing the only person who knows how to access your sat?"

She shook her head. "That would not be good."

Chapter 29

Kate tucked the cell phone between her shoulder and ear while she pried off her athletic shoes. Jessup, chief of operations at NASA-Weston, hadn't been easy to reach, but she wanted to clarify her position. "Just because the FBI wants me to stay in Italy doesn't mean I have to, does it?" Kate asked.

"It wasn't their decision." Jessup's voice sounded unusually stressed. She didn't doubt that he was taking a lot of flak for what had happened, from everywhere including the Oval Office and the Pentagon. "Homeland Security is making all the calls. And now that you've tracked these terrorists outside of the country, NSA has been brought in."

"Good grief." She tossed her shoes in the general direction of her luggage and gently rubbed her knees, still sore and bruised. "Don't we have enough cooks in the kitchen without the National Security Agency?"

"Bringing in fresh brainpower can't hurt."

Maybe, she thought.

"What's happening with that man Rooker's team nabbed?"

"Zed? The U.S. State Department and Italian government are haggling over legal jurisdiction."

Zed had been on Italian soil when he committed an act of terrorism, but the signal that had ultimately caused the satellite to strike the power grid came from an antenna located on U.S. soil. She could see a whole new can of worms in international law opening up and, honestly, she wanted nothing to do with it.

Kate finished talking with Jessup, checked in with her people at NASA again, then decided to take a shower.

She still felt the places where Zed had grabbed her, leaving deep, purply-green bruises at her throat and across her ribs. Aside from soothing sore places and washing away the sweat she'd worked up exercising with Rooker, some of her best ideas came to her beneath a steaming spray of water.

However, the first step to inspiration was always wiping the slate clean. She firmly put the problem of Heat Wave out of her mind. Turning off the conscious part of her brain was essential. Then she gave her subconscious permission to take over while overworked ganglia recuperated.

Kate was down to bra and panties when a voice called out from the other side of her door.

"You in there?"

"Yes, Rooker, I'm here." She sighed. All she wanted was a few minutes of peace. Alone.

The door flew open, then closed behind Rooker's back. Kate aborted bra removal and glared at him. "I said I was here, not that I was entertaining company."

His gaze took in her naked parts, then skipped back to her face. He grinned. "Best view in the city!"

"Give me a break. You don't even like me."

"I never said that," Rooker protested.

"It's obvious. And to tell the truth, I'm sick of bickering with you. Sick of this whole business. I just want to catch these monsters and go home."

"We all want to catch them." He stuffed his hands into his pockets and studied her body openly. He seemed to be enjoying himself, until his gaze settled on her bruised ribs. His expression hardened. "I didn't know he'd hurt you that bad."

"It's nothing. I'm fine. Now get out of here so I can take my shower."

"Is that what you want?" His smile came back, but his voice sounded different.

She blinked, remembering their banter at the table, how turned on she'd felt. And how annoyed she'd been at feeling that way.

"Out," she said.

"Funny—" he strolled toward her "—you're trying to look pissed off at me. But I have a different impression of your mood."

She refused to look at him but could imagine his eyes—dark, dangerous, interesting…seductive. "I didn't ask for your opinion on the subject."

"I think you're horny as hell."

"Screw you, Rooker!"

If she'd had something to throw at him she would have. Instead she turned her back on him and headed for the bathroom. "Just because I admitted, in a very weak moment," she tossed over her shoulder, "that I had a few trauma-induced sexual fantasies, that doesn't mean I'm lusting after you in particular!"

He moved quickly, putting himself between her and the bathroom door. His arms closed around her gently, avoiding her bruises.

Kate braced her palms against his chest and pushed him. "What the hell do you think you're doing?"

"I'm taking the edge off, for both of us."

"The hell you are!" She jerked her knee up with purpose between his thighs, but he shifted his hips and she came up in empty air.

"Now, now," he scolded. "That wasn't very nice."

"Let me go or I'll scream. Your men will find their chief in a dishonorable position."

"They're still out carousing."

"Adam then."

"I chased him out. We're alone."

"Damn." But she didn't put a lot of conviction in her cussing.

"Kate, I'm not going to hurt you. I just want you to think about something."

"What?" She closed her eyes and rested her forehead on his chest. Leaning into him was just easier than fighting his strength, she told herself. But the truth was he felt good. Really good. All of him up against her this way—solid and hard in all the right places.

Of course, she wasn't about to share that with him. He'd never let her forget it.

"I just wanted to tell you, you scared the hell out of me when I couldn't find you and you were chasing down Zed."

She laughed. "Thought you were going to lose him, huh?"

"Thought I was going to lose *you.*"

Her eyes flashed open. A sudden warmth seeped into her, and she thought how unexpected these tender words were, coming from Rooker, of all people. Who would have thought?

"Things can only get worse," he whispered. "This situation, I mean. I don't want you in the middle of it."

"I've been ordered to stay in Italy," she reminded him.

"You can refuse. It's not as if you're in the military. You're a private citizen. You said you want to go home. Do it. Let us take care of things here."

How tempting that was. "You know that's impossible, Rooker. I might have to disarm Heat Wave. We've gone over this a dozen times."

She could feel his body tense. "Kate—"

"Yes?"

"Aw, hell, we've probably both got warrior's itch. That's all."

Kate turned her face into his shirtfront and breathed in his musky male scent. Nice. Yes, this could be just about sex. Or not.

But there was one thing she couldn't let go of. He cared. The arrogant, overbearing bastard cared about her. "I have a suggestion," she whispered.

"What?" He sounded prepped for rejection.

"Kiss me."

Rooker went still for a moment, then levered her a few inches away from him and lowered his mouth over hers.

She went liquid inside. Darn if he wasn't right. She wanted him…or *it*…or something!

Her body felt as if it had launched itself on a new trajectory. Out of Safe-Hold, rocketing into hyperdrive. Suddenly sexually aware. For how long had she been without these kinds of feelings?

She hadn't been in a relationship since the second year of the Heat Wave Project. Hadn't wanted one. Didn't miss male companionship. Her science had consumed the days and nights. Her staff had been both family and friends.

But now…now she felt this man's erection through his clothing, and her own body was responding. Compelling her to get even closer to him, although that was physically impossible without…well, actually, yes, without letting him inside her.

And of course that was such a preposterous thought. She'd never *just have sex* with a man. Sex, like everything else in Kate's world, was the result of a series of logical events. She'd even written them into a formula:

$[(M + F) R] L = S$

But as Rooker's hands started to wander, she found it difficult to recall what all of that meant.

Rooker flicked two fingers behind her back, and she felt her bra snap open. She gasped at the intimacy of his hand on her flesh between her shoulder blades.

Concentrate. The equation. Yes, that was it. *M for male. F for female. Factor into the relationship R for respect, then Love and the result was S—Sexual gratification.*

Respect Rooker? Love? Hah!

"Oh, my!" She was having considerable trouble breathing. "That feels so…won-der-ful." She looked down at the top of his head. Where had her bra gone? His mouth was over her breast. His tongue moved. She quivered.

To hell with equations!

Kate hooked one leg up and around the back of his thighs, clamping him against her, and let out a gasp of pleasure.

"Doc? You okay in there?" Adam. Back in the suite. Outside the door. And now she could hear other voices and the door to the main corridor closing.

Rooker swore under his breath.

"Fine, Adam," she managed to answer. But her voice sounded too breathy to her own ears.

There was a moment's hesitation from beyond the door. She could imagine the men exchanging looks. A wink. Adam's pout: the infatuated boy-man.

"God, what are we doing?" she whispered.

"Don't know, but it sure is fun." Rooker raised a dark brow in supplication. "Do we need to stop?"

She couldn't face those men out there if they thought she and their boss were—

"Rooker, I told you!" she shouted. "Whether you like it or not, I'm staying right here until this crisis is settled!"

"Oh, that'll fool 'em," he whispered in her ear.

"Shut up," she hissed.

Kate took a step back from him and covered her breasts as best she could with folded arms.

Rooker made an agonized face, punched the air with both fists—one, two—scuffed at the carpet and finally paced away from her while making low, growly sounds of frustration.

"Oh come now." Bad choice of words. But she didn't dare laugh at his temper tantrum because she was paying too.

Hormones revved, she'd been just as ready as he. And now her body was trying to deal with a barrage of potent chemicals that had nowhere to go. She knew the biology, just wasn't sure what to do about it.

Kate ducked into the bathroom and came out wrapped in a towel. "I can't do this. Not with a cheering section."

Rooker stopped shadow boxing and turned to her, looking hopeful. "Plenty of other hotels in Rome."

But she had regained a thread of sanity. "We have work to do." She ignored his eye roll. "And I have to figure out what just happened here."

The hard edges of his face softened, but only a little. "You think too much, Doc…Kate."

"Probably," she admitted.

Chapter 30

Kate plugged into the NASA database. Although a massive effort was being made at home to drive a wedge through the hijackers' control of HW-1 and reclaim the satellite, the white-hat hackers kept hitting cyberwalls. She couldn't simply sit and wait for the next strike.

Kate propped herself up in bed with her laptop, blocking out the chatter and male energy beyond the bedroom door. She had a carafe of hot, black coffee on the bedside table. She focused on her screen and drank cup after cup until her head buzzed and the figures streaming before her eyes seemed to vibrate.

No matter what combinations she tried, nothing worked. Maybe, after all, they had lost the game. She felt sick at the thought.

There was a knock on her door and she looked at the clock—2:38 a.m. If it was Rooker, she didn't have the strength to either jump him or fend him off. She pulled her robe around her.

"Yes?"

"Saw the light under your door. You decent, Doc?" Adam cautiously poked his head around the edge. "I made some herb tea. Noticed you sometimes liked it. Maybe time for a change from the high-test?"

"Sounds good." She smiled and couldn't help thinking how much he reminded her of her younger brother. It didn't matter how good-looking he was. She'd never be able to react to him the way she had to Rooker. "Thanks, Adam."

He set the steaming mug on the nightstand but didn't leave. After an awkward moment he said, "The guys and I...we all wanted to say we're glad Zed didn't hurt you bad."

Peterson was still in the hospital, but it looked as if he'd be able to fly home within a few days. He'd asked Rooker to let him rejoin the team to finish the mission, but Rooker had refused. He could have called up another man to replace him, but decided the team would work just as well with a tightly coordinated six.

People must be insane to voluntarily go into this line of work, she thought.

"Thank you. That's very kind of you," she murmured. "All of you."

Adam nodded. "Better get some rest, Doc. They lock down on another signal and we'll be off again."

She must have fallen asleep without realizing it. Kate woke up with a start at the sound of her computer screeching at her. She sat up on the bed, pulled the laptop over to her, shut off the e-mail alarm and checked the screen.

Cambridge had been trying to reach her for the past two hours. Messages with little red exclamation marks crowded the screen. She grabbed her cell phone from the night table. "Damn!" How could she have forgotten to charge it? The thing flashed an angry "low-battery" symbol at her.

But why hadn't NASA contacted Rooker if something critical had happened?

Quickly Kate scanned the urgent messages, plugged in her phone and connected with the lab.

Cambridge picked up before the first ring died. "Where the hell have you been?"

"Right here. Passed out cold."

"I hope the party was worth it."

"No party. What's up?"

"A lot of things." She hesitated. "Bad news all around, I'm afraid."

Kate's heart sank. "Hit me with it."

"They've found Frank."

It took her a moment to equate finding her chief physicist with bad news.

"He's dead?" she whispered.

"I'm sorry, Kate. His body was in a stolen car out on some country road. He was…" She choked up. "They said it was made to look like he'd crashed it into a tree. The thing was totally burned out with Frank in it."

"They're sure it was him?" She didn't want to believe it. Until now, she'd held out a slim measure of hope.

"Not much left of the body, but his NASA ID and key cards were melted into him."

"Oh, God."

"Are you all right?"

Kate pressed her fingertips into her eyes and rubbed away the burning. There was more. Cam had said there was more. She had to hold on.

"Yeah. What else?"

"While I was trying to reach you, a new demand was made by the hijackers."

"Yes?"

"The *Chicago Tribune* received an anonymous call about an hour ago."

Kate winced at the name of the city where she'd grown up.

"At first they didn't know if it was legit or a hoax," Cambridge continued, "but the paper contacted Homeland Security immediately. The FBI ran the recording and believe it's from the terrorists. Archer got word to us."

"Where in Chicago?" Kate asked.

"No specifics. It could be another major power grid or something else entirely."

Kate imagined the awful possibilities: a sports stadium filled with thousands of people, the downtown Loop area of office buildings jammed with workers. But mostly she thought about her parents in the house on Lake Shore Drive that had been her grandparents' home. The house of her childhood.

"How much time do we have?" she asked.

"Forty-eight hours. They want ten billion this time."

So Rooker was right. They'd shown their strength. Now they were going for the big money. And maybe a worse catastrophe? Why not. They were having fun.

Kate's thoughts whirled. She tried to reach out and pluck something coherent out of the maelstrom. "Forty-eight hours," she breathed. Time…a little more time. But how to best use it?

"Don't your mom and dad live somewhere around there?" Cambridge asked.

"Yes, my brother and his family, too."

She couldn't wrap her mind around the idea that she might lose them in one immense burst of energy.

"Oh, Kate," Cambridge said. "I'm so sorry."

She forced thoughts of radiation sickness from her mind. "Do we know yet where the command signal is coming from?"

"NSA says it's still originating from somewhere over near you. In the Veneto Province. The Italian government and utilities are trying to get a fix on the actual phone."

Kate shoved herself off the bed and dashed across the room. She pulled a map of Italy from her traveling case and shook it open. "The Veneto includes Venice and a wide area around it to the north."

"Yes."

"How long do they estimate it will take to find the sender?"

"Maybe days. They don't know." Cambridge sounded less than confident.

Kate closed her eyes and focused on nothing. Let the ideas come to her.

Cambridge spoke softly. "Kate, are you all right? Tell me what you're thinking."

She didn't know what she was thinking!

It was all so overwhelming. She only knew that everything they'd done so far had been wrong, gone nowhere, just delayed worse disasters and fed the enemy's ego by allowing him to taste success. Whoever the enemy was, Zed appeared now to be just a pawn. Rooker seemed to think there was a major power behind the plot. A sophisticated terrorist cell or possibly even a country bent on destroying the U.S.

"Did Archer say whether or not the government will pay the ransom this time?"

"He expects they will, but the White House hasn't officially given the go-ahead."

Kate nodded. "Good. Call Archer and suggest that if the President is seriously considering paying them, he can help us by stalling as long as possible. Assure the terrorists they'll get their money, but it will take the full forty-eight hours to produce it. Government red tape, Congress needs to pass an emergency bill, he can make up anything he likes."

"Stall them?" Cambridge sounded doubtful. "Why?"

"I can't explain now. Just do it. Please."

Kate broke the connection. *Because,* she silently answered. *It's personal now.*

Maybe Rooker was right when he'd accused her of taking Heat Wave's theft to heart. *My satellite.* That's how she'd always thought of it. So if that were true, if she had made the project her own, might someone else identify her with it? Thinking back, there had been the taunting message left on the computer screen in Connecticut. It was meant for her, no one else. And now Chicago was a target. A coincidence that she'd grown up there and still had family in the city?

What if Rooker was wrong? What if the entity behind this plot was doing this for money more than for political reasons, as she and Rooker had discussed earlier? The hijackers had hit on an ingenious and ruthless form of extortion.

But might there be another underlying motive? Was there a reason why she felt the prick of a knife blade with every move these people made?

And didn't it make sense that for something to be personal, it had to involve someone who knew her? Someone from her past, maybe, or someone who even now was working against her. It was a troubling thought. Without realizing it, she might have unconsciously instigated this nightmare. The possibility set her head spinning, her gut wrenching.

Forty-eight hours.

But it was enough time to fly back home and stand face-to-face with the only people she could think of who might have betrayed her and their country.

Rooker glared down at her. Never had a woman so thoroughly annoyed him. No, this was worse than annoyance. Kate Foster seemed to always choose to take the most illogical path, which happened to be the one that crossed his.

"I thought you'd finally decided to be sensible," he grumbled.

She'd told him she was flying home, then immediately instructed him to hold off any plans for a raid in the Veneto until she returned to Italy.

Now she was throwing clothing into her overnight bag. "I need to eliminate a black hole, Rooker. A gaping, super-destructive black hole in our system."

"Don't start spouting that techno jargon again!" he growled, pacing away from her to stare out the window. Rome suddenly felt hot and oppressive. He wanted out, wanted to move on the latest intelligence. Giving her the lead on this mission had been a mistake. "Honestly, what's this all about, Kate?"

She didn't respond.

He tried a gentler approach. "Are you worried about your folks? Tell them to get the hell out of Chicago."

"I can't explain yet. If I did you wouldn't…" She shook her head.

"You think I'm too dim to understand your fancy science? Put it in English."

She rolled her eyes at him. "It's not that. I just have to be sure I'm right before I accuse anyone."

He moved away from the window, feeling his gut tighten with suspicion. "You know who's behind this?"

"I can't be sure of anything until I talk to a few people."

He was used to getting answers. "You owe me an explanation!" he shouted but she didn't look intimidated. "You're hanging us out to dry here. Tying our hands while you go off to—"

"Shut up, Rooker. We've been playing your game more than mine from the beginning. Now it's time to get to the root of this insanity." She turned away, shutting him out.

"Dammit, talk to me. Please, Kate!" He reached for her, but she ducked away, back to her suitcase. How could she fit so much in such a little space?

"I'm going. You know how to reach me." Kate chucked her makeup pouch in with the clothes and snapped shut the case. "If everything works out in D.C., we'll have the answer to who is behind this. If it doesn't, I'll meet you in Venice in two days. Archer has assured me he can keep negotiations open that long."

Rooker shook his head. This was bad. Real bad. But they'd tied his hands. Except for Ricci. He still had the Italian's network looking for Heat Wave's captors.

"Okay, the team will set up in Venice and wait for word from you," he agreed. "But what if we locate an address tonight? Or tomorrow?" He stepped between her and the door, blocking her, his fists tight at his sides because if he lifted one of them it would end up through the wall. "You think I'm just going to sit on my goddamn ass and not go after them because you're jetting all over the goddamn globe?"

Kate gave him a severe look. "You're waiting, because I'm in charge and I say so. Got that, mister?" She stepped around him.

"I don't know why I ever wanted to screw you!" he shouted at her back.

She reached for the doorknob without hesitation. "I don't know why I'd ever let you."

Chapter 31

Agent Marissa Winston was waiting for her at Dulles when Kate stepped through the gate and into the glass-and-steel terminal. Whereas normal people weren't allowed through airport security without tickets, apparently FBI agents had no trouble accessing the passenger gates.

Marissa looked at Kate's overnight bag and broke into a brisk jog-walk that Kate easily matched. "You check any luggage?"

"No."

"Good. I have a car waiting. We'll go straight to NASA-Weston, right?"

"No. We're to meet the others at La Hacienda."

"The Tex-Mex restaurant near the compound?"

"I don't want this to come off like the Spanish Inquisition," Kate said firmly. "We're here to uncover the truth, not place blame." Kate didn't like Winston's silence. "You have to promise me not to do anything rash. Listen to them. These are good people."

"Good people who may have already killed hundreds."

Kate turned to study Winston's expression. A blank wall, eyes straight ahead.

"We don't know anything yet. I'm just operating on a feeling that someone close to me might be somehow involved in what's happening."

"You'll do what you have to do. I'll do what I need to do," the FBI agent stated. "There's too much at stake to tiptoe around each other."

Kate blinked. Right. She might be torn by loyalties, but there was a good possibility she'd have to turn in a friend.

They speed-walked out through electric sliding doors and straight up to a black sedan, its motor idling. The driver hit the gas without a word from Marissa. The car sped through the city. In twenty minutes they were out of D.C. and over the Maryland state line into a mixed commercial-residential area with the unglamorous name of Beltsville. Marissa gave the driver directions to the restaurant.

"Has anything been done to prepare Chicago if we can't stop this strike?" Kate asked.

"O'Hare is already on orange alert. They'll shut down the entire airport—no incoming or outgoing flights—starting twelve hours from now."

"In case the power grid there is hit and they lose their guidance systems?"

"Right. After what happened on the East Coast, we won't take any chances." A glitch in the guidance system could mean multiple midair or ground collisions.

Kate looked out the car's tinted side window. After Italy, the late-summer landscape of Maryland appeared parched and bland. But her surroundings faded from conscious thought as she focused on the job she had to do now. A job she loathed.

"What about evacuation of the city?" she asked.

"Mayor Reston claims it's impossible to evacuate a city the size of Chicago in two days." Marissa shook her head. "Anyway, where do you put nearly three million people?"

Kate sighed, thinking of her parents. They'd stay, even if she called and begged them to leave. Just as people will ride out a hurricane, her father would stand by his family's home. She knew others would too, concerned about looting or vandalism, thinking they could somehow physically protect what was theirs against natural forces.

And who or what was she trying to protect by coming here, now?

Kate looked across the seat at the FBI agent. "You ordered everyone on the Heat Wave team to be investigated."

"Yes." Marissa squared her shoulders as if she was prepared for Kate's anger.

"But you didn't arrest anyone—not even Cambridge or Vernon, who you discovered had lied about their backgrounds."

"No, I didn't."

"Why?"

"Because as hard as I tried, I could find no evidence of their collusion with Zed or anyone else involved in this operation. Nothing at all." If she'd been wearing makeup earlier in the day, it had worn off, leaving her looking exhausted and under immense strain. "Hauling the two of them in would have done no good. We were better off watching them."

"To see if they slipped up or led you to someone involved in the plot?"

"Right."

"So you…what? Tapped their phones? Tailed them?"

"Both," she admitted without hesitation. "Didn't do any good. Maybe you can shake something loose today."

"I hope so," Kate said. Because they didn't have much time left. She felt physically ill at the thought of the price to be paid for her failure.

The car pulled into La Hacienda's parking lot. It was a popular hangout for employees of nearby high-tech companies and government branches. She looked around for familiar cars and was glad to see they'd arrived first.

Inside, Kate asked the hostess for a table near the back of the dining room, where they would have privacy.

Her guests arrived all in one group, as if they'd ridden together in a single car or met up outside by prior arrangement. She'd called together the surviving team members who had been with her the night of the assault on the compound. Amanda, Tommy, Vernon, Cambridge—each one gave Marissa a quick, surprised look, glanced at Kate and then away.

Guilt? Or just nerves? Kate wondered.

When they were all seated, Cambridge voiced what they all must have been thinking. "We've got a deadline. Why the hell are we sitting around in a restaurant?" She looked as tired as Kate felt, but over the fatigue a cloud of anger hovered.

"Because," Kate began, "we need to talk. This time without holding anything back."

Amanda stared at her in confusion. Tommy and Cambridge shifted in their seats.

Vernon shot to his feet. "If you're going to accuse me of having anything to do with—"

"No one's accusing anyone," Kate said firmly. "Sit down, Vern."

He didn't. "So what's the freakin' Bureau doing here?"

"Agent Winston has agreed to come as a witness to this discussion, off the record if necessary." The second part was definitely stretching the truth.

"The hell she has," Cambridge muttered.

Marissa leaned across the table, looking the other woman in the eye. "Tell me fairy tales if you like, Ms. Mackenzie. I'll listen. But if anyone at this table has inadvertently done anything to aid the enemy, we're prepared to offer immunity in exchange for whatever you might know that can help us stop these people."

Vernon finally dropped back into his seat but didn't look any happier.

"Listen," Tommy whispered, his voice quavering, "you can save the rest of them the grilling. I'm the one you think is behind this, right?" His eyes filled up, wide and terrified.

Kate touched his arm. "We haven't singled anyone out. We just need the truth. There's no more time. People are going to die. A lot of people."

The waitress came and placed water glasses around the table in front of people, but when she took out her order pad Marissa gave her a look that sent her scurrying meekly back behind the bar.

Tommy inhaled deeply then wiped at his eyes with the back of one hand. "Everyone knows my background. Once a hacker always a hacker—that's what you're thinking."

"We recognize the addictive behavior of Internet hacking," Marissa said, her voice gentle. But her eyes never lifted from his, and Kate could feel their intensity from where she sat. "The challenge. The thrill you feel is powerful. Seductive. At least, that's what the hackers we've caught have told us."

Kate watched helplessly as Tommy nodded. "You break

into a system, and it's a power rush like you can't imagine. Secrets unfold before your eyes."

"And money," Kate said.

"That, too," he admitted. "There isn't anything you can't buy 'cause you can put your hand in anyone's pocket. Bank accounts, credit cards…but I stopped all that a long time ago."

"Except for one last adventure," Winston said, and everyone at the table stared at her.

Tommy's face went pure white. "I…yeah."

A chill crept up Kate's spine. She'd trusted this young man.

The FBI agent said, "You busted the Pentagon again."

Kate closed her eyes and heard Cambridge moan. Amanda let out a whimper of distress.

Tommy was sobbing now. "But that's all I did. I broke in and ducked out again. I didn't think they'd even detected me. It was just to prove I could still do it, you know?"

"Yes, I know." Marissa's voice sounded oddly sympathetic.

Kate stared at her, then at Tommy. "Then he didn't have anything to do with hijacking Heat Wave?"

Marissa shook her head. "Right, Tommy?"

"No, I didn't. I swear I didn't." He was still crying but looked suddenly relieved. "God, I've been so scared. Afraid you'd come after me thinking the Pentagon hack had something to do with Heat Wave."

"So, except for that one relapse, you did break the habit. How?" Kate asked.

"I found another drug. Space." Tommy's face took on a little more color. He swiped at his eyes with his shirtsleeve. "Using the computer to reach out there and talk to satellites and discover stuff. It was like owning the universe. A new kind of high."

A high, an addiction. Yes, Kate thought, that was part of what she felt, too.

Marissa didn't let the relieved silence last long. "Fine. One down, three to go."

"You can't be serious. You think that one of us helped Zed steal the satellite?" Amanda cried.

Kate intercepted before Marissa could answer. "It occurred to me that, without realizing it, any one of us might have inadvertently aided the person who planned this operation." She put her hand over the older woman's trembling, ice-cold fingers. "Please, Amanda, just cooperate. We have to consider every possibility, no matter how far-fetched it might seem. The aim is to trace unconscious remarks or events you may have forgotten. I don't need to tell you how desperately we need your help."

Even as she said those words, Kate wondered how honest she was being. Marissa had never completely eliminated the possibility there was an active conspiracy that might include one of her staff.

"Well, I didn't leak information to anybody," Cambridge stated flatly. "I never discussed mission-critical data with anyone on the outside. And if I had, I wouldn't try to cover for myself or lie about it."

Kate stared at her coldly. This was the moment she'd most dreaded. "Maybe your lies weren't directly linked to the mission, but they were critical to my ever trusting you again."

Cam's black eyes flashed. "I don't know what you're talking about." The conviction in the woman's voice almost had Kate believing her.

The noise from the bar continued, but not a sound came from anyone at their table in this dim end of the room.

"We'll come back to you in a moment. You'd better think hard about what you keep to yourself." Marissa turned to Vernon. "Let's hear from you now, sir. You came into this country illegally."

He gave the FBI agent a surprised look that segued to defiance. "Yes."

"You were how old?"

"Six."

"Tell us about it."

He released a long breath and shook his head. "My father brought us over the Mexican border and we lived in a crappy apartment in Los Angeles with three other families, all of us terrified of being sent back to Colombia."

"And you grew up running with gangs," Winston said.

Kate sat back and watched Vern's face work itself through a range of emotions. "Yes," he admitted at last. "Until I was sixteen, then the cops picked me up for the fourth or fifth time. Instead of sending me to jail, the court put me in a program for kids like me. I was still locked up, but they gave me a new friend."

"Who was that?" Kate asked softly. The way he said it, she expected it had something to do with religion.

"A computer hooked up to the Internet." Vernon shrugged at her surprised expression. "I didn't know shit. I thought the world was the streets, then I saw what was out there and I couldn't believe it. I didn't want to run scared all my life, live in a rat-trap with a bunch of losers and illegals."

Kate smiled. "So you somehow educated yourself."

Vernon nodded. "I picked up some inner-city scholarship money and worked for the rest of it. Got an internship with the Applied Physics Lab, worked my way up, then this job came along." He looked pleadingly at Kate. "I wouldn't risk losing everything I have. I've come too far."

She nodded and looked at Marissa who seemed satisfied. But then, you never knew with her.

Cambridge shifted forward on her chair. "All right. If he can do it." She shot Vernon a small smile. "I falsified my job application with NASA. I wanted to work here more than anything in the world, but I didn't think they'd take me if they knew about my past."

"You had a rough childhood too," Kate said, wanting to move things along. She was aware of precious minutes leaking away.

"Yeah, but not like Vern. My parents were both educated professionals. I had every advantage in the world, and I blew it from the day I hit fourteen. I started running with a rough crowd and got myself tossed into juvie for doing drugs, then a real jail for a robbery that went sour. Someone was hurt. Bad. So they threw the book at us. Trouble was, by that time I was pregnant."

"With your daughter."

She nodded. "My parents pleaded with the courts and got me out early so I could have the baby at home. It nearly killed them, what I did to them." Her head dropped to her hands but she kept on talking into the tabletop. "God. I couldn't explain all that on a job application! How could I?"

Kate sighed. "You could have come to me."

"And put you in a tight spot because you knew I'd lied? Ex-cons don't get Top-Secret security clearances these days."

Kate sighed. That was certainly true. She turned to the woman beside Cam. "Amanda? Do you have anything to tell us?"

Her project tech drew herself up with dignity. "Money

gets short sometimes with a houseful of kids. But I've never stolen in my life."

Marissa cleared her throat. "So," the FBI agent said, "everyone's 'fessed up, but no one can think of a word they might have let slip to anyone. Nothing that can be connected to what happened in the Heat Wave lab that night or in the days that followed." She took in the entire table with one sweeping glance.

For a moment nobody said a word. Then—

"Frank and David." Cambridge tucked in her lips thoughtfully, then slowly let her gaze drift toward Kate. "They're the only members of the team who were there that night and haven't cleared themselves."

"Christ! What are you saying?" Tommy yelped. "Frank or David helped Zed steal the HW-1? They're freakin' dead!"

"That's plain crazy talk." Vernon snorted. "Even if they weren't dead."

"You can't ask us to pick on those poor men when they aren't here to defend themselves!" Amanda wailed, tears rolling down her cheeks.

"David Proctor and Frank Hess are all we have left," Marissa agreed, her voice tight. She looked around the table. "Just because they were killed by Zed's people doesn't mean they weren't somehow involved at the beginning."

"She's right," Kate said softly. Something was coming to her, a scrap of memory she couldn't quite shape in her mind. "Go ahead, Agent."

"Conversations with Hess and Proctor," Marissa continued, "think back. Forget about how bizarre it might seem. Did either of them ever express political or personal dissatisfaction with NASA or with the U.S. government? Any motives at all for taking advantage of their specialized knowledge?"

After several minutes' silence, Kate spoke. "Maybe I've known something all along, but I didn't think it mattered."

"Yes?" Marissa said.

"This goes back years." Kate swallowed, still unsure of connections between the past and now. "I wanted this job, Chief Project Engineer, above all else. It was what I hungered for—the extraordinary level of science being done at NASA, the chance to challenge myself and grow. I went after the position as aggressively as I knew how."

"So?" Tommy said. "No one can blame you for that."

"Others wanted it, too." Kate looked down at her hands and consciously untangled her knotted fingers. "Frank wanted it."

Tommy's soft blue eyes skipped from the FBI agent to Kate, to Vernon. "Well, yeah, lots of us compete for jobs, but that doesn't mean the guy—"

"Wait," Kate said. "There's more. He was really angry at first. You remember his temper." Nods around the table. "Then he went from obviously angry to just sort of sullen."

"He used to argue with you over decisions you made," Cambridge remembered.

"That doesn't prove a thing. I give you grief, too," Tommy pointed out.

"No, it was different. It was almost as if he were trying to rattle me, make me less sure of myself so that I'd make a mistake. But I hung in there. After a couple of months he calmed down. Things went smoothly between us for the most part."

"Do you think someone approached him during that time?" Marissa asked. "Someone made him an offer: 'Help us capture this satellite and you can get back at the woman who took your job.'"

Kate shook her head. "I really don't know. It just never occurred to me that Frank Hess would ever be anything but loyal to the project, if not to me."

"But Frank wasn't a computer expert," Amanda argued. "He was a physicist, and besides, they *shot him* right in front of us!" Amanda wept into her napkin.

"The shooting could have been faked," Vernon said, and everyone looked at him. "Right, Agent Winston? Like in a movie."

"Yeah," Tommy chimed in. "They put a squib, a little plastic bag filled with red liquid in his clothing, shoot a blank at him. He punctures it with something sharp and it looks like he's bleeding."

"But David was really killed," Amanda objected.

Kate thought about that night. "Yes, but he was shot by the woman. Zed shot Frank. So only his gun might have had blanks."

Marissa nodded. "We ran a test on the stains on the carpet where Hess fell. It's real human blood and matches his type, but he could have drawn some before the invasion and prepared a squib."

Vernon turned to Kate. "Frank knew I lived in L.A. We used to talk about Hollywood, how stuff didn't seem real out there sometimes. I think I told him about being on a set once, seeing how they faked gunshot wounds."

Cambridge swore.

"I might have said stuff to him, too." Tommy looked worried. "You know, without realizing he was going to—"

"What?" Kate asked.

"Frank was *the man* as far as astrophysics, you know?" Tommy drum-rolled his fingertips on the wooden tabletop. "I mean, like a genius, right? But he was a little behind the times with the computer stuff at first. I helped him out. Gave him some tips and suggested a few books that might bring him up to speed."

"And?"

Tommy's face flushed. "The man was a sponge. Amazing."

Amanda's eyes looked wild with horror. "I can't believe...I can't think that Frank... He wouldn't have let them kill David! He wouldn't!"

"Maybe," Kate said gently, "things got out of hand." She remembered what Rooker had told her about it being odd that the terrorists had left the rest of them alive. "It's possible he made a deal with them not to harm us, but once it all started to go down he lost control of the situation." She recalled, too, the look of shock that crossed Frank's face when they gunned down his fellow scientist.

Marissa turned back to Tommy. "Do you believe Hess had the necessary knowledge to mastermind this hijacking?"

Tommy shrugged, trying to reclaim his casual self. He still looked visibly shaken. "Maybe?"

A few minutes later, Kate and Marissa were back in the sedan outside the restaurant.

"So," the FBI agent said, "it's possible that Frank Hess dug his own grave by conspiring with Zed and his friends."

Kate nodded, unable to answer. She stared at the traffic jamming the ramp onto the Washington Beltway, still in shock at what they'd just learned.

Kate's phone buzzed against her hip. She'd set it on silent page. When she unclipped it from her belt and checked the LCD display it was Archer's office.

Homeland Security was text messaging her:

Laser deployed from Chicago. Shut down before tracking attempt complete.

"God," she murmured, "they're testing the laser. *My family! My home!*"

"We're getting you on the next plane back to Italy." Marissa tapped her driver on the shoulder. "Dulles, fast." She started punching numbers into her phone.

Marissa would wave her magic FBI wand to get Kate a seat on a flight that was probably already booked solid. Kate wanted to fly in the opposite direction. She'd gather up her loved ones and rush them as far away from Chicago as she could! But what about the rest of the innocent people there?

Kate slid back into the leather seat as the car took off. No, it was up to her to stop this madness. She just hoped Archer would be able to stall long enough for her to reach Venice and Rooker before the bastards deployed Heat Wave again.

Chapter 32

Rooker wasted no time moving his men. Within two hours after Kate's departure from Rome, the U.S. Air Force brought a chopper down from the NATO base at Vicenza then transported the team and their gear to Chioggia just south of Venice.

Had he wanted to, they could have set down in the middle of St. Mark's Square to a welcoming flurry of pigeons and paparazzi, but Rooker wanted to keep their arrival as quiet as possible. That hadn't worked in Rome, but maybe here it would.

From the lower tip of the Laguna Veneta the WWS team took a vaporetti into the city proper. The high-speed power launches were to the Venetians what taxis were to New Yorkers.

Once again Rooker requested the help of the police in locating civilian accommodations and staying low-profile. Happily, the only attention they attracted was from the desk clerk, who raised a questioning brow when he saw the long ship-ping cases containing the rifles. He didn't ask.

Although the Dolceaqua was a very old hotel, rarely no-ticed by tourists, with a nondescript exterior, it wasn't at all grim or run-down inside as Rooker had expected it might be. The lobby looked as if it had once been the great hall of a sixteenth-century palazzo. The guest rooms were enormous and, although there were no closets, a huge wooden armoire with ornate carvings graced each one.

The place smelled of aged oak, candle wax, wine and cit-rus oils. The floors throughout every part of the structure were of rose-and-green marble with glittering black flecks, polished to an icy sheen, so that it looked to Rooker as if he were walk-ing on a thin layer of water flowing over flower petals and ferns.

The walls had probably once been white but were grace-fully yellowing. The top layer of paint appeared to cover so many others that you'd have to take a chisel to them to get down to plaster. Real oil paintings, not cheap prints, their can-vases thickened and cracked with old varnish and pigments, hung everywhere. Over Rooker's bed, in the bathroom, down every corridor he walked along. The place was a museum.

Gorgeous.

Rooker thought how silly it seemed, mercenaries biv-ouacked in such luxury. Then he envisioned Kate's eyes pop-ping at everything she touched and saw. He wished she were here with him, but immediately wished her away.

In his bones, he felt the enemy close by. Felt the threat, the nearness of his prey, the way other men sensed a good fish-ing spot or heard a warning knock in their car's engine. It was tempting fate to think they would both survive the next twenty-four hours.

* * *

An hour later, Rooker left his men to meet with Ricci again. This time right in Venice. The man got around.

As he walked toward the café where they'd arranged to exchange information, his phone rang. *Kate.* He sat on the stone wall surrounding a Bernini-style fountain in the middle of the cozy piazza.

"I'm on my way back." She sounded burnt out. "Alitalia. Flight 8011. The plane takes off in twenty minutes."

"A wasted trip, huh?" He couldn't help feeling a little smug that he'd been right.

"Not exactly," she said slowly.

"What's that supposed to mean?"

"I think you were right about the mole. We believe Frank Hess was in on the plot."

"Damn. Tell me more."

"There's no time to talk now. I'll be in Rome in less than eight hours. A charter will bring me to the civilian airfield outside Venice. Have you located Zed's buddies?"

"Yes and no. The phone company is still narrowing down the area. It's a slow process. But I have another source."

"What's that?"

"You don't want to know."

"Rooker…" In the background he could hear an amplified voice announcing a final boarding warning. "I have to go."

The signal cut off. Rooker stared at the phone. Hess? Damn. Like everyone else, he'd assumed Hess was a hostage.

Ricci was waiting for him at the Caffé Lavena in the Piazza San Marco. It was a good enough hangout for Wagner and his father-in-law, Franz Liszt, and it was good enough for Ricci. Besides there was more sun on this side of the piazza, or so Ricci claimed. He was like a big cat, loved the sun.

Rooker pushed suspicions and theories from his mind and focused all of his attention on the man seated across the table from him. "So, my friend, what have you found? A rat or two in the canals of Venice?"

Ricci blew smoke from his cigarette and kicked back an espresso, as black and thick as molasses. The little cup looked like a child's toy between his huge fingers as he set it down.

"Three foreigners, Americans, have rented space in a warehouse, connected to a local factory. One of them, a man, has been hiring local *criminali* as guards. He tells them he is worried about industrial espionage."

"Could be our guys." Three, he thought, so…Zed's two sidekicks and a wild card.

"They claim to be chemists, working for an American glass-making firm."

Rooker ordered a plate of little veal meatballs with potatoes and radicchio at Ricci's suggestion. When the waiter left he asked, "You believe there's a chance they may be legitimate?"

Ricci shrugged. "It would be wise to make sure you don't attack innocent industrialists."

"Where are these innocents?"

"In Murano. Are you familiar with this place?"

"One of the islands across the lagoon." Farther north than Chioggia.

"*Sì.* In the sixteenth century the glass artisans moved their factories and studios to Murano, to prevent the furnaces from burning down the city. It is a short trip by vaporetti."

"What makes you think these are the people we're after?" Rooker asked, sipping a *caffé corretto* while he waited for his order of meatballs. The shot of Sambuca woke up his taste buds and put a nice edge on his mind.

"One of the bodyguards they solicited is cousin to one of the men. He wished he'd asked for more money before agreeing to take the job."

"Why?"

"Because it is a very dangerous job, and he says there will likely be shooting."

"That doesn't tell us much."

"Also—" Ricci held up a finger "—because the woman in charge of the operation will soon have billions of dollars at her disposal."

"Definitely sounds like our—" Rooker stared at the Italian. "Did you say *woman* in charge?"

"*Sì.*" Ricci slipped a hand inside his jacket pocket and pulled out an envelope. "I thought a few photographs might be helpful."

"If I were a religious man you'd be in my prayers every night." Rooker tore open the envelope and took out a half dozen glossy digital prints.

"If you are going after these people, you had better say your prayers, religious or not." Ricci pointed to several shots of thick-necked thugs standing on a corner and smoking in front of what looked like a medieval-era storehouse. "I assume you have the support of the Carabiniere when you go after them?"

Rooker nodded. "Where exactly were these taken?"

"Murano. Outside the glass studio."

Rooker flipped to the next photo. "Holy shit."

Ricci looked over his shoulder. "She's a tough one, isn't she?"

The tall, pale woman with white-blond hair shaved close to her head was looking nearly straight into the camera. She was a dead ringer for the woman Kate and her team had described after the invasion of the lab. Beside her stood a man with a predominant scar who could easily be the other member of Zed's team.

Chapter 33

Approaching Venice by plane was surreal. An iridescent cloud of pigeons rose up out of Piazza San Marco as the small commuter aircraft dove down out of the clouds and circled the city. The S-shaped Grand Canal wound between closely packed stucco and stone buildings. Even from a thousand feet in the air Kate could recognize and name some of the bridges she'd studied years before in her college art-appreciation class—the Rialto, the Bridge of Sighs, the Scalzi, the Accademia. Hundreds of years old, their designs eternal and exquisite.

Before she'd settled on a major, she'd fantasized about becoming an architect. But scholarships had been available for women interested in pursuing the sciences. She'd decided that taking a few courses in physics and astronomy might help pay her tuition. By the end of the second semester, she was hooked.

Architects were Earth-bound. As an aerospace engineer

she could build bridges to the stars. Space had virtually no creative limits.

But now was not the time for dreaming of worlds and universes yet undiscovered. By tonight Rooker and his team would need to make their move on this planet.

He had left a message on her cell phone, which she retrieved on landing in Rome. A man named Ricci, who sounded like a northern Italian version of a Sicilian godfather, claimed to have located the terrorists on one of the islands close to Venice proper. She prayed their intelligence was on target.

By nine-fifteen darkness had thickened around the city and Rooker moved his team to the Fondemente Nuove wharf area on the northernmost edge of the city. From there they would take police power launches across the lagoon to the island of Murano, but once there they'd need a less obvious mode of transport.

As in Venice, the collection of islands that formed Murano were connected by a series of narrow canals. Gondolas were regularly used by merchants and tourists to reach many locations, including the glass studios. Now they would be closed, only a few watchmen drowsily keeping an eye on the precious crystal created by the artisans and the ever-burning fires.

Kate gazed across the Laguna Veneta, as smooth as a mirror that night. A moon hung low over the city, huge and orange and angry looking behind the spires of the city. Patches of stars appeared between clouds, then were swept away again.

Kate stepped out of the police launch and onto a wharf on the island. Here the night air seemed steamier, and the sun's heat lingered in the stone of the buildings and the wood of the piers. Rooker's party exchanged the noisy power launch for traditional black lacquered gondolas—the next best thing to being invisible because they were everywhere.

Kate sat on one side of the garish red-velvet-upholstered passenger seat, Rooker on the other. His right hand rested on his Steyr SSG—the same antisniper rifle he had shown her at the range. She remembered how heavy it had felt to her, how terrifying it had been at first, looking through the cross-hairs of the scope.

But now she was glad Rooker had it and she knew how to use it.

She didn't exactly feel safe because of it or the men who'd be carrying it. But being surrounded by enough weapons to fight a small war did have a strange calming effect on her knotted stomach. She looked around her.

Carabiniere, dressed in gondoliers' costumes, poled the boats along a Murano canal. Ancient buildings on either side of the prong-bowed hulls looked to Kate like a set from a Shakespearean play. A lantern burned in each bow, lighting their way, casting eerie orange shadows over passing walls and wharfs.

Adam Grabowski and Travis Peterson hid beneath a tarp in the bottom of Kate's boat. Each carried a 9 mm Glock in a shoulder holster, a smaller pistol strapped beneath a pant leg as backup. Adam hugged his Steyr. Travis was one of two machine-gun men. She could see its bulky shape beneath the olive green canvas. Before boarding the boats she'd seen other weapons clipped to belts, some of them hand grenades.

Three other gondolas were visible now, each with two obvious passengers, two more hidden in the bottom, and a gaily attired pole man. All were heading languidly along the canal. At a branch, two of the boats split off to approach the warehouse from a different side of the building.

"Let's go over the plan one more time," she whispered. "What happens first when we get there?"

"I should tell you to wait in the boat, but a lot of good that's done in the past," Rooker grumbled.

She laid a hand on his knee. "Please, let's not fight now. I don't want…" She tried to ignore the raw nerves tugging at her insides. "If this doesn't work…if something goes wrong, I don't want our last words to have been angry ones."

"Fine. I like your classy outfit." He glowered into the dark. He'd been in a mood since they left the hotel, when he'd begged her one final time to stay behind.

Kate looked down at the plain black uniform, the smallest of the SWAT team style in Rooker's supplies. She still had to roll up the pant cuffs and the sleeves and cinch in the waist. Why was it that in the movies women warriors and superheroines always found convenient, sleek catsuits to pour themselves into before the big fight scene?

"*Signore.*" The gondolier spoke.

"Yeah?" Rooker looked up at him.

"You are two supposed *innamorati, sì?*"

"I guess." Rooker glowered suspiciously at the cop.

"You do not look like lovers, sitting so far apart. You will bring suspicion, don't you think?"

"Oh, Christ," Rooker grumbled.

"He's right," Kate said, "we don't look terribly affectionate."

"Sit close to her," the Italian suggested. "*Sì*, now put your arm around her."

"Anything else?" Rooker complied but didn't look happy about it.

"It would look far more convincing," he added with a straight face, "if you kissed the *signorina*. Passionately. That is, if she did not object to so disagreeable a man."

Kate smiled back at the cop who seemed to enjoy annoying Rooker.

"It's all right," she said. "I've kissed worse." But she felt a little ping of anticipation as she remembered the one time they'd kissed before.

"Good grief, let's get it over with!" Rooker's hand came up behind her neck and pulled her toward him. His kiss was long and deep. A very convincing piece of acting, she thought, then was distracted by the puddles of warmth spreading through her.

When he at last released her, it took Kate a moment to catch her breath and settle herself back down on the velvet cushion.

Rooker looked around restlessly and positioned one arm across his lap.

He's turned on! she thought, pleased.

"For the cause, right?" He wouldn't meet her eyes.

"Right," she said, not a hint of a smile.

"Just don't go taking that seriously," he warned her. "Because it felt like you were putting a lot of, you know, heart into that kiss."

"Dreamer," she muttered. The good feelings were washing away, her irritation with him returning. "Do you honestly think I could ever fall for a man like you, Rooker?"

"Why not? Plenty of women have."

"Give me a break," she groaned. "When I fall in love, it will be with a man I can spend the rest of my life with. A companion. A soul mate."

He got very still, looked away across the water. "Like such a thing exists." He laughed. "He'd have to be Einstein to please you."

"Obviously, you don't have a clue about such things. Just as well. You'd make horrible husband material."

"You got that right."

"I just…" Where were the words that kept tickling at the back of her throat, wanting out? "I just wanted to say, before we go into that building, that…" She drew a breath and plunged on, knowing he'd laugh at her and telling herself it didn't matter. "That I respect what you've been trying to do, what you're risking tonight, too. And—" she swallowed once, then forced out the words all in one breath "—youdon'ttotallyturnmeoff."

Rooker went stone quiet. She couldn't tell if he was still breathing.

Adam scowled up at them from beneath the tarp.

"Head down!" Rooker ordered.

For a moment there was only the whoosh, whoosh of the water against the boat hull. Kate wasn't looking for anything in response from him, she told herself. All she'd wanted to do was let him know how she felt.

At last he turned back to her. "You're staying with me, this time. The B team will clear the way. Your only job is to mess with the electronics once we've secured the area and taken prisoners."

"I know my job," she snapped. "Do you know yours?"

"Keeping your ass alive until your goddamn satellite is powered down."

She nodded. "Sounds simple enough."

"A cinch." But the dark places deep within his eyes told her he didn't believe a word of it either.

One by one the gondolas drew up to a dock alongside the Mencina Glass factory. Stealthily, figures in black moved up from the bobbing hulls, onto the pier then the narrow walkways between the dark water and crumbling rock walls. There seemed to be no one at all around the commercial area. Not even a single stumbling drunk or a stray dog.

Kate wished for a sound, any normal sound—a TV, a slamming car door, a cat's yowl—anything to break the unbearable tension.

Maybe Rooker's intelligence was inaccurate and they'd walk into an empty factory, surprising only a sleeping guard.

We should have considered other options, she thought frantically as she tossed aside the bright shawl that had covered her night camouflage. A bomb. Do away with the bad guys without endangering the Italian police or Rooker's men!

But then—a selfish thought—there was the chance she'd never recover the HW-1 prototype, setting back alternative energy research by many years. Just as importantly, even a contained explosion would shatter precious treasures in glass and destroy centuries of history—glass molds and records of artisans' techniques stretching back hundreds of years. A history of beauty would go up in flames. And they couldn't risk spreading fire over the entire island.

"Come on," Rooker whispered urgently to her.

He wore night-vision goggles and an armored vest, as did all his men. The goggles were bulky, difficult to use and required training. Kate had decided against trying to use them but she did wear chest protection.

Besides, her job began when theirs ended. First they must find the computer that might, even now, be sending an encrypted message to Heat Wave, telling it to bombard a target in Chicago. Once the team had secured the area, she would use the electric torch clipped to her belt to help her work on reversing the program. But until the assault was complete and the infrared units no longer necessary, she'd have to keep her light off or risk blinding anyone wearing night goggles.

She ran in a crouch down the alley alongside the low wall, keeping up with Rooker's bursts of motion. Silently moving from shadow to shadow. She lost track of the others. They melted into the darkness. Only a soft scurrying sound now and then, which might have been a small animal frightened by the sounds of their steps. Only a flash of a gloved hand in the moonlight, signaling: *Go right, go left...hold up!*

Rooker stopped suddenly and turned to her, pointing at two tall wooden doors that looked as if they'd been designed to run wagons and teams of horses through. "Ready?"

"Yes." No. Blood pumped double-time through her entire body. She felt blazing hot, then chilled and dizzy.

Kate stood with her back pressed to the cool stone while Rooker waved two men inside who'd suddenly appeared from nowhere. They were instantly swallowed up by the immense black mouth of the open doors.

She held her breath and strained to hear anything at all that would tell her they'd made their way through safely. Had one of them been Adam? She was almost certain it was, although in their soot-blackened faces they looked so much alike.

"Now!" Rooker barked into his microphone, and the sudden loudness of his voice close to her ear startled her.

Kate ran after Rooker through the door and into a dirt-floored storage area. There were no lights, and little moonlight filtered through the dusty skylight and windows high above. She might have stumbled over the rough ground, but Rooker gripped her by the arm, pulling her along with him.

She stepped where he stepped, trusting that he could see where he was going.

After a minute or two, her eyes began to adjust and she at least could make out dark outlines of tall plank shelves and the dimly glowing shapes of glass pitchers, bowls, goblets and vases stacked to amazing heights. All were backlit by the gold-and-orange flames behind furnace grates.

The dull roar of flames was punctuated by the shuffle of running feet. In the next second, she could hear neither above the chatter of gunfire from the floor above them.

Rooker slammed into her from the side, knocking her back into an alcove that smelled like a tomb. Hundreds of years of silicon sand, soot, and chemicals used to color the glass filled her nostrils, and she started to choke.

"You all right?" Rooker asked. He'd hit her hard and must have thought he hurt her.

"Yes," she croaked.

Now the gunfire sounded closer. Rooker held a hand over his ear, shielding the headset's earpiece. Listening. "They've made it to the second floor. There's a locked room up there. They think that's where the communications are set up. They're going to blow it."

"Let's go," she said.

"No, someone came up behind them and is guarding the staircase. My guys will clear it first and—"

A deafening explosion drowned out even the gunfire. Rooker's face froze.

She gripped his arm. "What?"

He looked at her, his expression mirroring her fears.

"Was Adam in the team clearing the st—?"

"Report in! Repeat, report in all units," Rooker hissed into his headset.

Kate waited, prayed, breathed, prayed again.

"Carry on," he said at last, in response to whatever he'd heard. He glanced quickly at her. "The staircase was booby-trapped."

"The boys, they're—?"

"We can still make it up to the second floor." He wasn't even trying to reassure her about the men. "There's a freight elevator up the back side of the building. Come on."

As they ran past the rubble that had once been a long flight of open-back wooden stairs, Kate stared up at the remains. Although the explosion had ripped away most of the outer treads, a tongue of wood stuck out from the stone wall where each step had been. She quickly estimated the remaining size and stability. Most looked wide enough for someone with a small foot to climb, although the handrail was completely gone. Besides, finding an alternate route to the top would take valuable time.

She grabbed a handful of Rooker's shirt, hauling him to a stop. "Wait! You go around the long way, without me. And make lots of noise."

"What?"

"Let whoever is up there know that you're coming. And radio your guys not to shoot me."

Rooker stared at her in exasperation. "Why would they shoot you?"

"Because I'm going up what's left of those stairs. It's the most direct route."

"Aw, shit." He seized her by the arm and started dragging her across the hard-packed dirt floor.

"Rooker," she protested, "I'm serious. It's the safest way now that they think they've made the steps unusable."

He released her, rolled his eyes toward the jutting planks, groaned. "Okay, I don't have time to argue. But take this." He shoved the Glock at her. "Safety off, you've got a magazine with ten rounds in it."

"No." She stepped back from the gun. "I can't."

"Take it or I don't let you go."

She took it.

"And don't put your finger on that trigger unless you mean it. Two-hand it, arms straight out in front, point and squeeze. Fastest lesson you'll ever get."

Chapter 34

"Damn you, Rooker," she muttered, trying to find a way to stick the Glock in her belt. Then again, she'd probably shoot off her foot.

Kate held it in her left hand and pointed it away from her body while she used her right to steady herself as she started up the remains of the stairs. One cautious step at a time, hugging the wall.

Kate forced herself to breathe evenly, slowly. Although she could hear firing from another part of the building, it sounded as if the battle had moved away from the area of the stairwell.

She looked up. Hanging over the edge of the second floor was a hand and wrist, the fingers hanging limp. The uniform cuff was tan-colored, not black. One of the brave Carabiniere. Her heart sank.

She swallowed. The computer running Heat Wave was somewhere just above her. There was a chance that it had been left unguarded. She had to get to it. Lives were being risked and lost to give her that chance. Many more would be sacrificed if she failed.

Step by step, Kate edged upward. Placing a foot cautiously on one riser, testing it with her weight, slowly ascending until she was more than halfway to the top. Now she could see a section of hallway above her, smoky and smelling of burnt powder from fired ammunition—a sharp metallic bite in the air. She took another step up.

From a distance came shouts, the crashing of glass and tat-tat-tat of machine guns. Whose? Theirs or ours? A solid wave of dizziness and desperation struck her at the thought. Blood trickled down the stair treads from the floor above. She swallowed back a bubble of bile.

Not now, she told herself. This was not the time for a panic attack. *Act! Move! Go!*

As Kate leaped up the last few steps she heard a familiar gravelly shout and what sounded like a herd of elephants crashing through walls on the other side of the building. She nearly smiled. Rooker. Doing his job. The man was damn good at making noise.

At last on the second-floor landing she looked down to see men burst across the lower room, dodging between shelves of glassware, firing at each other across the vast work area between furnaces. Glass shattered as bullets flew, sending jeweled shards into the smoky air.

Kate ducked, scampering low toward the unmoving Carabiniere officer she'd seen from below. She felt for a pulse at his throat, but could find none. A single bullet hole marked his temple just below the band of his cap. The blood had stopped flowing now.

Her heart racing, Kate turned down the hall and ran past

a row of open, dark rooms. A sallow light filtered from beneath a door farther along the hall. Was this where the computer was? But Rooker had said his guys were going to blow the door open. Why was it still closed?

Kate reached it, looked up and down the hallway. No one in sight. The sounds of battle all coming from below.

She tried the knob. Locked. She threw herself against the heavy oak panel, crusty with age. Didn't even budge. With a sigh, Kate looked down at the Glock in her hand. Well, she thought, it's a tool, right? So use it.

She took a step back, flicked off the safety, held the gun in an overlapping grip, lined up the two pin sights with the door lock and fired. Wood splinters flew. The door shivered, she kicked it open with one foot and stepped through the doorway at the same moment a white-hot sensation stung her left shoulder. Stumbling forward, her first thought, after the excitement of actually having shot a door open, was that she'd run into the sharp corner of a shelf in the dim light. Or something had bitten her. A spider? A bat?

Kate leaned against the heavy worktable in the center of the room and reached up to touch her upper arm. Immediately, the sting transformed into a fierce burn that set her gasping. She brought her hand away, fingers bloody.

"It's too late, Doctor," a voice said.

Kate spun around, but with the motion of her body, the room swirled, too. A woman with spiked white hair stood in the doorway, smiling at her. She held what Rooker had told Kate was probably a Kalashnikov rifle, like the ones the intruders had carried when they'd broken into the compound. Belatedly, it occurred to her that the reason her arm hurt was she'd been shot.

"You—" Suddenly short of breath, Kate tried to lift the

Glock. But it felt immensely heavy in her hand. She couldn't seem to heft it higher than hip level.

The woman smiled. "Put it down. You look silly, carrying that thing around like it was a snake about to bite you."

Kate hesitated, not because she meant to be defiant. It was just that it was so difficult to convert a thought to action. And her coordination felt off-kilter.

The scientist in her understood what was happening. Loss of blood. Her body had gone into shock. Try as she would, she was unable to override her body's natural reactions and force herself to move.

"All right. Hold on to it then, and I'll put a bullet in your other arm." The vest protected her vital organs, but left her limbs open to injury.

Kate awkwardly dropped the handgun on the table. "Listen," she said as she slowly straightened up, gripping the edge of the tabletop for support, "if you help me now, I'll make sure they don't hurt you."

The woman laughed. "Hurt *me?* It's you who's hurt, bitch. And I'm not going anywhere until I get my money."

Kate frowned, leaning harder against the table to keep from falling down. "*Your* money?" Had Rooker said something about this to her? About the woman in the trio possibly being in charge? She couldn't remember.

"You think that wimp of a scientist Hess was the brains behind this? Don't be ridiculous." She smiled, her silvery eyes slipping out of focus for a moment as she assessed the clamor from below. They snapped back to Kate. Apparently, whatever was happening didn't concern her.

"Funny how men always underestimate women, isn't it? Bet you had a tough time convincing the good old boys at NASA you were the right 'man' for the job. Frank certainly didn't think you deserved it." As the woman spoke she moved toward a wall of shelves. She hit the end of one with the butt of the rifle, and a panel slid open revealing a stone passage-way. "Medieval Venetians were ingenious. A convenient war-time escape route. Now move!"

She shoved Kate into the opening then followed. The wall slid closed behind them.

Kate shook her head. "I don't understand. Frank agreed to help you steal Heat Wave because I got the job?" It wasn't enough.

"Frank and I were lovers," the woman behind her with the gun explained. "You do things for a lover you never think you would. But he really was very bitter about losing the job he wanted to you."

Kate's vision blurred. She felt herself slipping away even as she staggered along the low-ceilinged passage. Rooker would never find her now. Not down here in a tunnel he didn't even know existed.

The barrel of the rifle jabbed Kate from behind, forcing her to keep stumbling forward.

The woman was rattling on, as if for her own amusement. "He needed direction, poor dear. I gave him a way to get back at you, and at NASA for not appreciating his talent. At first he thought it was too much. Stealing a satellite, even for just a few days, to make his point." She chuckled. "But I convinced him that you might lose your job as a result. And who would be the big hero?" She improvised a newspaper head-line: "Kidnap Victim Eludes Captors! Returns Stolen Satel-lite to a Grateful U.S. Government."

"But you never intended to let him surrender control to NASA."

"Of course not. Are you mad? Not once I realized what he

was capable of making it do! I could name my ransom. No amount would be too high."

Kate blinked down at her feet. A steady dribble of blood fell from her fingertips to the rough stones with each step. She glanced back over her shoulder, and there seemed to be two white-haired women. Then three. She blinked. Pain radiated from her shoulder down her arm and up into her chest. She coughed.

"Feeling a bit woozy, are we?"

"You shot David Proctor that night, for no other reason than to show Frank who was boss."

"Did you see his reaction? He probably wondered if I'd do him next." She laughed. "Until then I don't think he'd even considered that I'd eventually kill him, too."

Gulping down air, Kate faltered to a stop. "I don't think I can go on." She planted both feet, unsure how long her legs would hold her. The pain was nearly unbearable.

"I'd put you out of your misery now, but someone wants to see you." White hair shrugged. "Now move!"

When they emerged a minute later from the tunnel and into an ordinary-looking room, the only other person there was a man, sitting at a computer with his back to them. Even before he turned around Kate knew who it was.

"You're not dead!"

Frank Hess turned and smiled weakly at Kate. His expression wavered when his gaze fell on her blood-soaked arm.

"Good God! What have you done to her, Mona?"

"I warned you that she probably wouldn't cooperate," the woman said. "What do you need her for anyway? I thought you had everything under control."

"I do…I do," he said quickly. "But I just need to check one equation before we power up the laser." He gave Kate a quick, unreadable glance. "Are you all right?" he asked softly.

"Do I look all right?" Her voice shook, and she felt sure she was about to vomit. Dropping into a chair beside her chief scientist Kate stared in disbelief at him. "The body in the car wasn't you. Your ID was planted."

"Well?" Mona snapped, ignoring her now. "They haven't paid up yet and they've sent their goons after us. Are you going to do it?"

"They have nearly an hour yet," Hess said wearily. "You want your money, don't you?"

She glared at him. "Fine. We give them fifteen minutes, but that's it. We can still get away through the lagoon. And next time they'll know they can't play games with me."

"You'd better get the boat ready then," he said. "Just in case your brother and his men can't stop them."

Mona shot the bolt on the Kalashnikov, and Kate felt the sharp metallic clack through every nerve in her body. She closed her eyes and leaned back in the chair, desperate to conserve what little strength she had left.

When she heard the woman's steps retreat down the secret passageway, she whispered, "Was it worth it, Frank?"

He moaned. "I never intended it to go this far! You have to believe me."

"Does it matter?"

"I'm sorry. I just thought if I...I don't know now what I thought. I believed her when she said I could make them notice me. I'd be a hero, you know? She made me feel like a hero. Important. I thought she loved me."

Kate pressed the bullet wound with her hand, trying to slow the flow of blood. She calculated she'd already lost at least a pint, probably closer to two. She didn't have long before she'd pass out. Minutes after that she'd bleed to death.

"You must have realized after you left the compound with the three of them, after she shot David, that it was about something more than making you famous."

He dropped his head into his hands. "I did. I knew, but then they talked about all this money. Enormous sums. And I thought, well, make the best of things. Who needs a job when you have billions sitting in a vault?"

Kate drew a shaky breath. "She's already ditched Zed. What do you think she'll do to you when she no longer needs you?"

"I know…I know…" He banged the heel of one hand against his forehead. His eyes looked sunken and watery when he looked up. His hair, what little he had of it, seemed thinner than she remembered, unwashed. "But I don't know how I can change things now. You've seen what she's capable of doing."

"You can stop it here and now," she said.

"Too late…too late," he moaned, rocking on his chair.

"She's going to kill both of us, Frank, and anyone else in her way. You have to refuse to make the connection."

"No."

"I won't help you. Whatever it is you need from me, I won't give it to you."

"There is nothing," he murmured. "I lied to her. She would have killed you otherwise."

Kate felt the room begin to fade out of focus. An inner voice whispered: Too much blood. *Not much time. Have to do something.*

She looked at the computer. "It's there, isn't it? The altered FARM. You have the link set up."

"Yes," he said miserably.

She nodded, listening for the thud, thud, thud of the

woman's boots coming back toward them in the passageway. Mona, back with her Kalashnikov. Back to make sure Frank finished the job. Then she'd finish Kate, at least, and probably him as well, as soon as he assured her the money had been deposited in Belize.

"You can make it up to your country," Kate whispered hoarsely. "Go to the door and listen for her. I'm going to shift the HW-1 back to NASA control."

"No!" he yelped. "She'll kill us." His eyes flew wide with terror, his mouth working soundlessly. "She...she's ruthless!"

"Let me do it, Frank." There was ice in her voice although her body was on fire. "Go over to that door now. Tell me if you hear her coming."

He didn't move.

"She's going to kill you anyway. Archer has the money and is just holding payment until the last possible moment. She'll have her money in half an hour or less. She doesn't need you any more."

He was whimpering, tears flowing down his unshaven face, but he got up out of the chair and shuffled toward the door. "It's no good! She'll come back and—"

"Shut up, Frank." She had to concentrate. Had to make her mind work even though her body was past functioning.

Already her peripheral vision was graying out, leaving her only tunnel vision. The three cellular phones. They were backups to reach the laser. Nothing to do about that now. Anyway, the laser beam was just a guidance system for the microwave energy from satellite to ground. Whether the laser was deployed or not made little difference if she could recapture the satellite.

Big if.

Tremendous if.

She focused on the computer monitor. Just as he'd said, Hess had already made the connection with Heat Wave. But now she had to reprogram the FARM so that NASA would again be able to access its onboard computer. The scripts necessary to do that were complex. Any other time she wouldn't have trusted her memory, she'd have Tommy or Cam double check her input with their logs.

There was no time for caution. No time for checking.

She typed in the encrypted codes. Punched Enter. Counted the seconds.

Nothing was happening. No response.

"She's coming!" Frank screeched from the doorway. "Oh, God."

Kate didn't move from the screen. "Come on…come on…" she whispered, pounding her right fist on the table, her left arm resting useless across her lap.

The drip, drip, drip of her blood hitting the floor. Head spinning.

"Come on. Please!" Even as she heard the heavy boot treads approaching the room.

All of a sudden, the screen blipped and lines of figures scrolled down the screen. The most beautiful sight she'd ever seen.

"We did it," she whispered.

"No!" a voice bellowed from behind her. "What did you do, bitch?"

Kate turned to see Mona standing in the doorway, her eyes afire, jaw clenched. The rifle in her hands, she leaped forward and was nearly halfway across the room before Frank Hess tackled her from behind, nearly missing her ankles. But the effort was good enough to send her crashing to the floor.

"Grab the gun from her, Frank!" Kate found the strength

to shout. With a final set of keystrokes, she signed off and shut down the computer.

Now it was up to NASA. They were monitoring the sat and would see the command changes. They'd know what to do.

Frank and Mona were wrestling on the floor. The rifle slid out from between them and skittered across the tile away from them. Kate tried to stand up but couldn't. Going down on her knees she crawled toward the weapon, the scene before her wavering like a reflection on water. The most she could do was to fall on the Kalashnikov, pin it down with the weight of her body.

Hess was sobbing hysterically.

Her body felt heavy against the floor, as if she were sinking into it. Then someone was tugging the rifle out from beneath her, and she hadn't the strength to hold it.

A single deafening crack brought sudden silence to Hess's wails.

It's over, Kate thought. *At least it's over.*

HW-1 was home. Chicago and her parents and brother's family and many, many more were safe.

Her eyes were open but she could see nothing except the few inches of dusty floor in front of where her cheek rested. She watched her blood spreading across the tiles like a morphing Rorschach blot.

Rooker, where are you?

Then even those few blessed inches of reality dimmed, as she drifted into a vacuum as vast and black as the deepest space.

Chapter 35

The room was dark because Rooker wanted it that way. Sunlight, the cheerful chatter of the nurses as they made their rounds to patients, he wanted none of it. He'd just come back from the morgue. Arrangements had been made by the U.S. Embassy. All he'd needed to do was sign off on the paperwork.

The body would be shipped home, military transport. Draped in an American flag, in preparation for a hero's burial. That's the way the government wanted it handled.

He thought about Kate Foster. Who would have guessed that little Einstein could have put up such a fight. She'd hung on till the end. Somehow, in those final nightmare moments before he'd reached the subterranean room, tracking her by the trail of blood, Kate had worked her techno-magic and returned control of the satellite to her people at NASA.

How she'd done it, as severely wounded as she'd been,

he'd never know. He'd seen heroism in his lifetime, but never anything like this.

Never anything that hit him this hard.

He slumped in the chair by the window's closed blinds and dropped his head back to stare, wet-eyed, at the ceiling. "God, Kate."

"Yes?" A faint voice came from the bed in the hospital room.

Rooker squeezed his eyes closed, opened them but couldn't look at her yet. He'd stood over her bed for hours, praying for this moment, fearing it too. She'd hate him for what he'd put her through.

He hadn't been there for her when she most needed him. If it had taken him another three seconds, Mona Lescroat would have finished Kate off. Instead, when she heard Rooker and his men approaching, she'd chosen to run.

"Rooker, don't pretend you're not there. The room may be dark, but I can see you."

He had to cough and clear his throat before he could trust his voice. "Course I'm here. One of my guys gets messed up, I come by to say 'hey.'"

She saw the water glass on the bed tray and started to reach for it, but he jumped to his feet. He held the glass to her lips while she sipped. She let her head fall back on the pillow and frowned up at him. "I'm one of the guys?"

"Officially." He shrugged. "They voted you in. Said you proved yourself. Wasn't my decision."

"I see."

"So you don't consider me a *guy?*"

He smiled. How could he not? "Not by a long shot."

She nodded. "What do you consider me?"

Daniel Rooker stuck his hands in his pockets and tried to

find something safe in the room to focus on. "Listen, I just thought if you woke up I should be here to brief you."

"I missed a few things," she murmured.

"Yeah." He laughed because it was something to do other than sobbing with relief. "You fell asleep on the job. Been out close to thirty-six hours. I had Cambridge call your folks, tell them you're okay."

"Thanks." Lifting her right hand out from beneath the sheet covering her, she beckoned to him. "Come closer."

He took her hand and squeezed it. It felt warm, and that was damn good. Back in Murano her skin had gone cold as death. He had thought he'd lost her.

"After I passed out, what happened? Did you get Mona?"

He shook his head. "She escaped, unfortunately. Those old buildings are like rabbit warrens. The Italian police are pretty sure she's left the country. A woman matching her description was seen at the Austrian border. Interpol has been alerted."

"And Frank?"

He shook his head. "They're shipping his body back home tonight."

He decided the rest could wait. How Homeland Security and NASA wanted Frank Hess to be seen by the public as a patriot. Kidnapped, forced to aid his captors, he valiantly tried to disarm the terrorist who held him and another scientist, Kate, at gunpoint. Rooker couldn't quite figure out why they wanted to whitewash Frank Hess, but supposed it had something to do with preserving the appearance of solidarity on the home front.

"Poor Frank." She blinked, took a too-deep breath, winced.

"Shoulder hurt?"

"Like hell. Painkillers must be starting to wear off."

"I'll grab a nurse." He started to move away but she latched her fingers tighter around his.

"No, wait. I have to say something, and I don't want you to think it's the drugs talking."

He moved back to her side and looked down into her soft green eyes. Eyes he'd thought might never open again to him or anything else. "Yeah?"

"What I said about not being able to imagine why I'd ever let you…you know."

"Sleep with you?" He intentionally used a more refined choice of words than during their previous exchange.

"Make love to me," she amended. "I just want you to know that, in the right circumstances, if you had a mind to…I might not totally object."

"Dr. Foster, are you trying to seduce me?"

She laughed, then groaned as her face went white. "Damn, that hurts."

"Bullets will do that to you." He leaned down and kissed her on the forehead. "I think a little recuperative time is in order before we venture into hay rolling."

"Okay." She smiled up at him, breaking his heart and warming his soul all at once. "In that case, bring on the drugs."

Kate soaked up the view from the balcony of the house in Treviso. The classic town to the northwest of Venice had its own canals then rose to meet low hills. In the near distance, majestic, snow-tipped Alps sparkled in the sunshine.

Treviso attracted few tourists in comparison to Rome or Venice. It was a busy, friendly town, both modern and ageless, with amazing restaurants and singing every day in *osterie* until late in the night.

They'd been here for over a week, and she was finally regaining her strength. She loved strolling through the town, using Rooker's arm less for support now than for the feeling of companionship. Her Waterford butterfly rested on the antique dresser. A huge bouquet of flowers had arrived from her parents, along with many cards from her siblings, wishing her a speedy recovery.

Now she gazed out over the Piazza dei Signori, wrapping the light cotton robe around her body. Laughing to herself she watched a woman shoo the family's goats out through the kitchen door, to be led by her children to graze. She marveled at planks of bread dough being taken to communal ovens, for not everyone had one in their own home. The air smelled of olive oil, grapes, yeast and wood smoke from the ovens.

Since they'd been here she'd eaten as much and as often as she liked, and it was all delicious. They often visited the *Caffé ai Soffioni,* just across the fountained square from the house. She knew she'd never again be satisfied with frozen pizza when she went home. Which wouldn't be for another three weeks.

Jessup had called from NASA while she was still in the hospital in Venice. She suspected that Rooker had already spoken with him, perhaps exaggerating her condition. "I don't want to see you back in the compound in less than thirty days," he told her firmly. "You need to rest after what you've been through."

"What will I do?" she asked him. "I'll go crazy hanging around the house for a month, and I can't stay here in the hospital when they need the bed for other patients."

"Stay in Europe. Tour the continent."

"I could," she said. Or she could just find a pretty place in which to nest…perhaps in Naples, on the French Riviera, or in London. She loved London.

Rooker had made the choice easy. "Remember my friend

Ricci? He has a cousin whose mother owns a house in Treviso. She rents out rooms to visiting businessmen."

"Perfect," she agreed.

But a house in Italy is never really just a house. This was
a cross between an in-town villa and a palazzo. It had once
belonged to a duke and was modernized only as far as the
plumbing and electricity. All else was as it would have been
centuries before. Kate loved every inch of it.

She ran her hands along the wrought-iron balcony rail, then
over the crimson petals of geraniums growing in pots hooked
over it.

"What are you doing?"

Kate turned back toward the bed where Rooker lay, the
sheet tossed away from him, revealing plenty of man. "Touching things."

"Touching things." He puckered his whole face. "I thought
we'd taken your mind off of analyzing stuff."

"You have." She smiled, her body still tingling from their
last encounter in those sheets, less than two hours ago. "I just
want to remember all of this. It's so beautiful. Like being in
another world."

He laughed. "Like that's unusual for you?"

She went to sit on the edge of the bed and reached for him.
He went still.

"That's different," she explained. "Space is endless, exquisite in so many ways, but we can't touch it. Not yet anyway."

"You like touching things, I see." He looked down.

"I like touching things." She moved her hand again.

"Damn, you're good."

She stood up and slipped off her robe. "I know."

"I'm starving," Kate murmured, stretching lazily. "Feed me."

"Do I have to get out of bed to do that?" he asked.

"I expect so. Signora Pasquino doesn't offer room service."

"Damn." He made a show of flinging himself off the bed and stepped naked across the marble floor. "What do you feel like eating?"

"It's still morning, isn't it?" she asked.

He looked at his watch as he buckled it around his wrist. "Just barely."

"Breakfast then."

"How about a *cornetto*, fruit and coffee. We can go out for a big lunch later."

"Perfect." The buttery Italian versions of croissants were her favorite way to start the day. She stretched out between the sheets. "I'll take another nap while you're gone."

When Rooker had finished dressing and left, she closed her eyes and let her mind drift pleasantly to thoughts of his body lying alongside hers, entering her, filling her, tenderly bringing her to climax. Too soon, these slipped away, replaced by the stark realization of how close she'd come to death.

It would take a very long time for her to forget that. Perhaps she never would.

Get up and move around, her subconscious told her. Keeping busy she'd be less likely to dwell on the terror. That's how you made nightmares go away.

Forget Venice. Forget Mona and Zed and the men who gave their lives to stop them. It was over.

Done.

Instead of reaching for her robe, she pulled one of Rooker's T-shirts over her head. It fell nearly to her knees and felt cozy. Something of him in her, something of him on her. Good stuff.

She wandered to the window and looked down into the piazza, gently rolling her left shoulder to encourage circulation in the healing muscle. It felt better every day, although it still throbbed when the Tylenol wore off.

The fountain spouted crystal water from nymphs' mouths. A carved stone Diana, holding her bow, rose from the froth. Directly below the balcony, Kate could see Rooker—Daniel, she corrected herself—striding out into the piazza.

She smiled as she watched his strong back and shoulders in retreat. His dark hair was still mussed. Her fingers had clenched and tugged at it moments earlier. She wished she could see his face. She would wait here until he came back toward her with their breakfast. Maybe he would look up, sensing she was there without her calling out to him. That would be a good omen.

Did she love him?

It was too soon to say. She'd never before felt so intrigued by a man, so in tune with him in the most unconventional ways. Whereas he was all about physical strength, she was all about using her head. But he was good at using his mind in tight situations, and she had discovered a strength in her body that she hadn't known she possessed.

She'd always been thrilled by her discoveries out there, in space. Now, miraculously, she was discovering herself.

Rooker continued away from her. In another few moments he'd disappear into the caffé.

A movement caught her eye. For some reason it seemed unconnected to the usual flurry of activity: zipping Fiats, chasing children, grandmothers knitting in their doorways. Kate looked straight down toward the curb beneath her and saw the driver's door of a black VW slowly open. A figure stepped out.

Her heart stopped.

A tall, slender woman with a scarf tied over her head stood very still between the driver's door and the open side of the vehicle, watching Rooker. Arms slowly rose and braced themselves on top of the car door, a silver-gray pistol sandwiched between gloved hands.

Mona! Not in Austria. Here.

You've seen what she's capable of doing! Frank's prophetic words.

She'd hunted them down, for vengeance.

Instinctively, Kate knew that if she called out a warning to Rooker, it would be too late. He wasn't armed. The Italian police had insisted that all firearms be packed for shipping back to the States as soon as the mission was over. Ammunition too, in separate parcels. The airline's rules.

Rooker was about to pass behind the fountain. Mona would have to wait until he reappeared on the other side of Diana to make her shot. Kate had twenty seconds…no more.

Frantic, she rushed back inside the room, dragged the long rifle crate out from beneath the bed. She pried off wooden strips, clawed away tape and wrappings inside.

Rooker's Steyr, the one he had forced her to practice fire. Ammunition?

Stacked beside the French doors were the remaining boxes to be shipped. There would be magazines, with any luck loaded. Snap one into the gun's breech and she'd be ready. But there were no magazines in the first package, none in the second one. Seconds ticked past.

Kate leaped up and peered down over the edge of the balcony. Any moment and Rooker would step out from the other side of the fountain. She dropped to the floor, shredded another package. Only boxes of loose shells!

She remembered Rooker saying something about loading

individual shells, but then she'd only have one round in the chamber. And once that shot was spent the delay of loading another one would give Mona a chance to open fire on Rooker.

One shot was better than nothing. Kate rushed to the balcony.

Supporting the rifle against her knee to aid her weak left arm, she slipped the single brass-colored cartridge up into the breech, slid the bolt, ticked off the safety with the tip of her thumb and aimed over the rail. The crosshairs lined up with the red kerchief over Mona's head.

Finger to trigger.

One shot. One shot!

Mona reached a hand up to tug off the scarf and show herself. So that the man she hunted would see her and know that she'd won. "Rooker!" she shouted.

Kate didn't look to see if he turned.

Breathe in, let it halfway out. Target image. Pull.

The rifle kicked hard against her good shoulder. She staggered backward under the impact.

Please, God. Please, oh please! she thought, as she listened for other shots following hers. But none came.

Kate lunged for the balcony rail and stared down at the scene below. People were running toward Mona Lescroat, lying on the pavement. She wasn't moving.

Kate slowly lowered the rifle to her side. It had happened so fast. She had reached for her nemesis, a weapon she'd hated all of her life. She had killed a living thing.

An evil thing.

She didn't regret it.

Looking up at her with a stunned smile, Rooker shook his head in amazement. His words were lost in the noise of cars screeching to a halt, shocked screams and, already, a police siren.

But Kate read his lips: *I owe you one.*

Damn right, she thought. And she'd have a few interesting suggestions for him come payback time.

* * * * *

There's more Silhouette Bombshell coming your way!
Every month we've got four fresh, unique and
satisfying reads that will make your day....
Turn the page for an exclusive excerpt from
one of next month's releases

RARE BREED
by Connie Hall

On sale August 2005
at your favorite retail outlet.

Moonlight cast a long sparkling shadow down the center of the Zambezi River as Wynne crept along its bank. The water current and bellows of hippos drowned out her footsteps. An occasional splash warned of a croc looking for an evening snack. A rich brew of animal musk, vegetation, and the dank scent of fresh water clung to the air.

Tonight there was enough moonlight to see across the river to Zimbabwe's shore. The Zambezi River acted as a natural boundary between the two countries. It also gave poachers a quick escape route into Zimbabwe. It was September, the end of the dry season, and the river had shrunk to a fourth its size, making it easier for poachers to cross. Poaching was rampant in Zimbabwe. Endangered species were all but wiped out. The country was too impoverished to control it and animals had fled into Zambia for protection.

It made sense the bushmeat poachers would transport the

meat along the river into Zimbabwe. And she wasn't surprised she hadn't come across these men in her nightly patrols of the river. The rangers never made a move unless they checked in with base camp and the LZCG. Whoever was on duty would know she regularly watched the Zambezi at night. It was common knowledge among the rangers. She never failed to catch small-time local poachers, but never these new bushmeat poachers.

Wynne paused as she spotted five female elephants with a three-year-old calf and an infant. They seemed frightened and unsure of approaching the river, raising their tusks and scenting the air, keeping their young at their sides. Years of poaching and the slaughter of thousands of elephants had made them fear man and they would rarely take chances in drinking in the open along rivers and streambeds during the day. But since the park had cracked down on poaching, the elephants had been overcoming their fear. At seeing this herd disoriented and afraid, Wynne felt a stab of anger in the pit of her gut at the memory of the elephants poached today.

She waited as they eased forward and drank, then plodded back into the forest, following Broken Tusk and her infant. Wynne vowed to see them unafraid and drinking out in the open again.

She spotted the place where the poacher had said he was supposed to hand over the goods. Sausage Tree Camp was nothing but a bush lodge, named for the huge sausage tree that marked its location. The tree grew along the river's edge, centuries old, its boughs as thick as the tires of her Rover. Phallic-shaped fruit hung from its branches. Some native healers used the fruit to treat skin problems and cancer. The fruit was also used for a secret ritual that supposedly predicted the size of an infant's penis when he reached adulthood.

Wynne cracked a smile at the thought, then shifted her gaze to the lodge. It could sleep nine, but it was hardly more than a massive tent with a cement floor, though its lavish description on a safari tourist pamphlet made it sound much more inviting.

Tonight it looked empty. No trucks, or tethered horses—they were often used on bird-watching safaris. Bolts of mosquito netting stretched across the open tent windows. Zambia was a malaria zone, a fact reserved for the pamphlet's fine print.

Wynne was attuned to the sounds in the bush: the shrill chatter of monkeys; the trumpeting of an elephant; the cough of a hunting leopard. The sounds were always present, a gauging of normalcy, comforting in a way. She heard none of them now, only her own breathing and a dead eerie silence. Had the poachers gotten here before her?

She scanned the area behind the lodge. The trees. Along the road. She was about to take off her slingshot and follow the herd when someone touched her shoulder.

Wynne screamed in surprise and wheeled around. She kicked her attacker in the side, but the large man grabbed her leg and tossed her to the ground. As he came at her again, she jabbed his legs with her knee and knocked him off balance.

He staggered back and hit a tree trunk.

Wynne leaped to her feet, ready for the next strike.

He used an aikido side arm thrust this time. She deflected the blow and got in a lucky kick to his ribs.

He flinched a little, but stood his ground, solid as a mountain.

They circled each other, hands up, on the defensive. His face was in shadow and she couldn't see his eyes. It was important to see an opponent's eyes; they gave away every intended movement. She felt blind fighting him.

For a broad-shouldered man his movements were decisive and quick and hard to anticipate. He was a head taller than her five-foot-eleven-inch frame. She looked most men in the eye, but not this guy.

"We could do this two-step all night." His voice was deep, honey-coated by a Texas drawl.

"You're American?" It took her aback for a moment, but she didn't drop her guard or stop circling him.

"Last I checked." Amusement laced his voice. He paused and looked too at ease, hardly out of breath.

He'd been sparring with her, not using his full strength. What would have happened had he really felt threatened? "Who the hell are you?" Wynne paused because he paused. They stood three feet from each other. She kept her gaze on his hands.

"I was going to introduce myself when I tapped you on the shoulder—that is, before you attacked me like a cat with its tail caught under a rocker."

"I didn't hear you behind me. It was knee-jerk reaction."

"Guess I should have cleared my throat." He sounded genuinely contrite. "My mistake. Bygones?" He shoved a hand at her.

Wynne leaped back as if avoiding a mamba attack.

"Whoa, there. Touchy thing, ain't you?"

"Keep your hands where I can see them." She narrowed her eyes at his dark form. It seemed massive against the backdrop of the moon. She wished she could see his eyes.

"Anything you say." He slowly raised his hands.

"You didn't answer my question," she said, certain he was enjoying toying with her. He had this pleasant harmless act honed to perfection. She felt her patience slipping. "Tell me your name."

"I could ask you the same, darlin'."

"I'm a ranger, and *so* not your darlin'. Your turn."

"Jack McKay—nice moves you got. You study under a *sifu?*

"Fifteen years." She wasn't about to tell him his form was as good as hers—a different discipline than the karate kick-boxing she had studied, but impressive. His eyes were hidden in the dark, but she could feel him eyeing her up and down. "And you?" she asked.

"Ex SEAL."

A good-ol'-boy and a SEAL, a lethal combination. That explained why she didn't hear him sneak up on her. "Okay, Lone Star, what are you doing in this area? The park closes at night."

"Most people call me Jack. And I was just walking. Any law against that?"

"The park's dangerous at night. Big cats and crocs hunt at night along this river, and so do hyenas and wild dogs. Stick to walking in daylight when the park is open. And don't ever sneak up on someone again. Now, I'm going to have to frisk you."

"Help yourself, darlin'." He turned and assumed the position with his hands outstretched and feet apart all too willingly. "I'll warn you, I'm packing," he said.

She stood behind him to be on the safe side and patted his ribs none too gently and she enjoyed it when he winced. "Guns are not allowed in the park."

"It's a man's God-given right to protect himself."

"This isn't Texas, or the Alamo." She felt the shoulder holster, then found the gun. A massive thing, a .44 Magnum. Dirty Harry had nothing on this guy.

"Careful now. It's loaded. Wouldn't want a lady hurting herself."

He had just pushed the wrong buttons. She hurled the gun as far as she could. It plunked into the river with a loud splash.

"Hey, that was the first gun I ever bought. I'm attached to that gun." The sugarcoating left his voice, a steely edge in its place.

Was that the true MacKay surfacing, a hint of dark center behind the Texas butter cream icing? "No guns in the park." She finished patting him down.

"Y'all really know how to show a guy a good time around here."

"Jeez, I'm sorry our social director is off. You got stuck with me." Wynne finished patting down his legs and decided not to search his crotch. He might like it too much. "You're clean."

"Do I get to search you now?"

"You can, if you want to be staked over a termite mound." Wynne listened to him laugh loudly, an exaggerated roar from deep within his chest. She rested her fists on her hips and said, "Now, I suggest you go back to where you came from."

"Can't. My jeep broke down." He gestured to the dirt road that led into camp.

"You said you were out walking?"

"I was. I knew the camp was here, so I walked here to find out if there was a phone."

"A phone?" Out in a bush camp. Malarkey. And he'd snuck up on her in a perpendicular direction to the road. What was he up to? Was he the contact the poacher had spoken about?

"What were you doing driving here to begin with?"

"You're mighty nosy."

"Technically you're trespassing on a Zambian national park and a managed game area. I could bust you for having a gun. So answer my question."

"All right, no need to get your hackles up. But I kinda think you like gettin' 'em up."

She heard the smile in his voice and said, "Just answer the question."

"I heard of the bush camp and wanted to check it out and see if I might want to spend a week or two along the river."

"Why?"

"Let's just say I'm the outdoorsy type. Isn't that what lures most people to Africa?"

She suspected there was a lot more to his motives than he was admitting. "Where are you staying?"

"Why, you wanna join me for a drink?"

She wanted to toss him in the river, too, and said, "Just answer the question."

"At Hellstrom's Tours. Signed up for a safari."

Wynne's gut clenched. Hellstrom. There was his name again. Was cowboy Jack just a tourist? Or sent here to throw her off, or perhaps alert the poachers? The way to the truth stood before her, one hundred and ninety pound of Texas machismo packed nice and tight in a pair of jeans and a flannel shirt. For some reason the sausage tree fruit ritual popped into her head.

She quickly squelched that line of insane thinking. He was the enemy. She said curtly. "I'll take you back to Hellstrom's."

"I'm fishing Jefferson Davis out of the river first."

"Jefferson Davis?"

"My gun."

"Help yourself. I'll keep watch for the baboons."

"Baboons?"

"They like to tease the crocs, so it's like a natural alarm. But there's no warning for hippos."

"I don't care how many crocs or hippos I got to fight to

get my gun. I'm gettin' it." His voice held an Alamo, Davy Crockett, do-or-die tone.

Something told her it was going to be a long night.

If you enjoyed what you just read,
then we've got an offer you can't resist!

Take 2 bestselling
love stories FREE!
Plus get a FREE surprise gift!

Clip this page and mail it to Silhouette Reader Service®

IN U.S.A.
3010 Walden Ave.
P.O. Box 1867
Buffalo, N.Y. 14240-1867

IN CANADA
P.O. Box 609
Fort Erie, Ontario
L2A 5X3

YES! Please send me 2 free Silhouette Bombshell™ novels and my free surprise gift. After receiving them, if I don't wish to receive any more, I can return the shipping statement marked cancel. If I don't cancel, I will receive 4 brand-new novels every month, before they're available in stores! In the U.S.A., bill me at the bargain price of $4.69 plus 25¢ shipping & handling per book and applicable sales tax, if any*. In Canada, bill me at the bargain price of $5.24 plus 25¢ shipping & handling per book and applicable taxes**. That's the complete price and a savings of 10% off the cover prices—what a great deal! I understand that accepting the 2 free books and gift places me under no obligation ever to buy any books. I can always return a shipment and cancel at any time. Even if I never buy another book from Silhouettte, the 2 free books and gift are mine to keep forever.

200 HDN D34H
300 HDN D34J

Name	(PLEASE PRINT)	
Address	Apt.#	
City	State/Prov.	Zip/Postal Code

Not valid to current Silhouette Bombshell™ subscribers.

Want to try another series?
Call 1-800-873-8635 or visit www.morefreebooks.com.

* Terms and prices subject to change without notice. Sales tax applicable in N.Y.
** Canadian residents will be charged applicable provincial taxes and GST.
  All orders subject to approval. Offer limited to one per household.
  ® and ™ are registered trademarks owned and used by the trademark owner and
  or its licensee.

BOMB04   ©2004 Harlequin Enterprises Limited

Silhouette BOMBSHELL™

ARE YOU READY FOR PINK?

Her deadliest weapons are a calculator and a fast comeback....

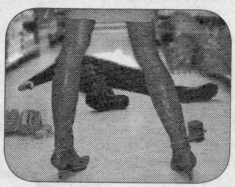

Meet Whitney "Pink" Pearl, forensic accountant extraordinaire. Her smart mouth gets her into as much trouble as her knack for investigating shady financial deals, but embezzlers, boyfriends and threats of bodily harm won't stop her from following the money....

SHE'S ON THE MONEY

by Stephanie Feagan

August 2005

Available at your favorite retail outlet.

www.SilhouetteBombshell.com

SBSOTM

COMING NEXT MONTH

#53 DEVIL'S BARGAIN by Rachel Caine
Red Letter Days

Desperate to clear her partner of a murder conviction, former police detective Jazz Chandler made a deal to start her own P.I. agency. The agreement included a loose-cannon new partner and one all-too-sexy lawyer—and making any case that arrived via red envelope top priority. The seemingly innocuous cases soon threw her into a shadowy world of clandestine societies and hidden agendas where Jazz would have to choose between two evils to save them all.

#54 RARE BREED by Connie Hall

Young, idealistic Wynne Sperling put her life on the line every day working as a park ranger in Africa. Protecting the endangered animals she loved was certainly better than pushing paper in Washington. But when Wynne's attempts to thwart a deadly poaching ring got her into hot water, would her trusty slingshot and help from a mysterious smart-mouthed Texan be enough to prevent *her* from becoming extinct?

#55 SHE'S ON THE MONEY by Stephanie Feagan

She should have known better than to take on a client called Banty. But Whitney "Pink" Pearl couldn't say no to billable hours—and now the fearless CPA was knee-deep in trouble and sinking fast. Seems the oil-well scam she was uncovering led to secrets someone would kill to keep. And with death threats, tangled paper trails and two amorous suitors to juggle, it would take some bold moves to keep Pink out of the red.

#56 THE PROFILER by Lori A. May

A serial killer was on the loose in New York City, and FBI agent Angie Davis was on the scene. But this case was straining even Angie's highly developed profiling abilities...not to mention trying her patience. It was bad enough that she had to work with maverick NYPD detective Carson Severo, but as the body count rose, an unsettling pattern emerged—the victims all shared a connection to Angie. Was she next on the depraved killer's hit list?